**Fabrice Humbert** was born in Saint-Cloud in 1967. He teaches literature in a French-German lycée near Paris. His previous novel, *The Origin of Violence*, was published by Serpent's Tail in 2011 and won the first ever French Prix Orange and the Prix Renaudot for best paperback. *Sila's Fortune* was the Winner of the Prix Jean-Jacques Rousseau 2010.

## Praise for Fabrice Humbert

'Highly intelligent and moving . . . a novel of rare scope, substance and strength' *Scotsman*

'Convincing and poignant' *Jewish Quarterly*

'Beautifully written' *Herald*

D0110349

# Sila's Fortune

## FABRICE HUMBERT

Translated from the French by Frank Wynne

Culture

This project has been funded with support from the European Commission. This publication reflects the views only of the author, and the Commission cannot be held responsible for any use which may be made of the information contained therein.

A complete catalogue record for this book can be obtained from the British Library on request

First published as *La Fortune de Sila* in 2010 by Le Passage Paris-New York Editions

First published in 2013 by Serpent's Tail, an imprint of Profile Books Ltd
3A Exmouth House
Pine Street
London EC1R 0JH
website: www.serpentstail.com

ISBN 978 1 84668 824 9
eISBN 978 1 84765 848 7

Designed and typeset by Crow Books
Printed and bound in in Italy by L.E.G.O. S.p.A

10 9 8 7 6 5 4 3 2 1

Sila's Fortune

# Prologue

The man ate. The courses kept coming, graced by precious names carefully articulated by waiters: murex, tuna tataki with obsiblue prawns, lacquered pork belly, Sicilian snakes, Buddha's hand, *merinda* with rare herbs, goujons of sole in a cornflour veil, white summer truffles . . . Precious poetry. And the flavours, mingling delicate ingredients into a coherent multiplicity, melted on the tongue in explosions of flavour, constantly conjuring new subtleties.

But the man, who was about thirty, heavy-set and broad-shouldered, was as insensitive to words as to taste. He consumed this culinary bliss with complete indifference. From time to time he exchanged a few words with his partner, a young woman with a careworn expression, or glanced over at his son, a boy of six or seven wearing a baseball cap who was finding it difficult to sit still.

There were some twenty tables in the hotel restaurant. The decor was simple, the whole aesthetic was focused on the food and perhaps also on the ballet of the waiters, making room on the tables for new courses.

The clientele was entirely in keeping with this stately

3

solemnity. An international clientele of refined tastes, some of them guests at the hotel, others discovering one of the finest restaurants in the world. Several couples, a few families, at one table two elegant young men, one olive-skinned, the other blond and pale. Some distance away was a group of four men, obviously a business dinner. At another table sat a stern-faced man of forty or forty-five with a very pretty dark-haired woman. The *maître d'hotel* spoke to them in Russian.

The one false note in this serene atmosphere: a boy in a baseball cap. Bored to death, he had decided to get down from his seat and get in the way of the waiters, who, not knowing what to do in such a confined space would stop, stare, then step around him. They glared at his father who carried on eating. Perhaps he did not realise his son was blocking their path or perhaps he thought it unimportant. Whatever the case, he made no attempt to call his son back to the table. A waiter carrying a tray almost tripped and fell.

'Would you please go back and sit at your table?' he said to the child.

The boy stared at him, astonished. The father turned to look at the waiter, who repeated himself, this time in English. The boy looked at him obstinately, arms folded, body rigid, refusing to budge. So the waiter, a young black man, took him by the arm and led him back to the table. The father got to his feet, face black as thunder, took a step forwards and punched the waiter in the face.

*'Don't touch my son!'* he roared.

The waiter stifled a howl. The tray flew from his grasp and crashed to the ground as he buried his face in his hands, trying to stem the blood gushing from his broken nose.

A stunned silence descended. Everyone had stopped eating to watch. The father, hunkered in his violence, had returned to his seat and persuaded his son to do likewise.

A distant, contemptuous, slightly disgusted expression could be seen on the face of the Russian. The young dark-skinned man looked about to intervene, as did the Russian's wife, but a sort of nervous reticence held him back; meanwhile his friend surveyed the conclusion to this display of force, fascinated, lips trembling. The young man made to get up, but seeing no one was prepared to join him and that the black waiter was stumbling away, a handkerchief pressed to his nose, as one of his colleagues frantically tried to pick up the broken plates, he sat down again.

Around the restaurant there were soft murmurs, then slowly conversations resumed. The father had gone back to his meal. Back turned, indifferent, he ate.

Part One

# I

Sila balanced precariously on the lip of a stone wall, left foot slightly higher than his right. There, in the sunshine, a big smile playing on his lips, he stood pissing. Back then, no one could have dreamed that one day, halfway across the world, he would be a waiter standing in a kitchen, his nose broken, waiting to be taken to hospital.

He laughed as the piss splashed over the photo of a man in a discarded newspaper. The black ink ran and faded, a pale stain eating into the cheek making the large face seem more harsh.

Sila jumped down from the high wall. Out of curiosity, he gingerly picked up the object of his target practice with two fingers. A white man of about fifty, fat, with grey hair. Sila was about to toss the paper away again when a number caught his eye: two billion dollars. Running a finger under the words, he deciphered the article. From what he could make out the number referred to how much this man earned in a year. But he was not sure he had read the piece correctly. He had been an able student once; then school had stopped.

Stuffing the article into his pocket with the steel blade, the sharp-edged stone and a length of wire collected during his peregrinations, he went on his way, sometimes walking, sometimes running, skipping about aimlessly.

At times he seemed to hesitate, to become more cautious in those areas of the city where landmines from the latest war lay buried and forgotten. Once, during a football game, one of his friends had stepped on one of them. He kept his eye on the ground, on the footprints, moving cautiously. Then, either because the danger zone was past, or because he was buoyed by the immortality of youth, he once again began to run and leap like a gazelle.

He crossed the ruined neighbourhoods, the ochre of ravaged sands, the gutted buildings, stopping only to play for a moment with a grey-whiskered donkey with a filthy coat. He patted the animal's muzzle, talked to it, then climbed onto its back. The donkey trotted away, braying. Swaying dangerously, Sila clung to the animal's mane, half fell, hung on by one leg, then let himself crash to the ground beneath the doubtful gaze of a stray dog. And then all three – the dog, the donkey and the boy – remained motionless.

An hour later, he went down to the beach to join his cousin Falba. A skinny man of about thirty, with protruding ribs, wearing nothing but a *pagne* tied round his hips, Falba was mending his fishing nets. Sila watched him thoughtfully for a while then, without saying a word, he too set to work with the same air of patient indifference. All around them other fishermen did likewise.

When they had finished their task, they got to their feet. The man barely came up to Sila's chest. His bronzed body, with its enormous knees and stick-thin legs seemed deformed. There was a thick scar across his belly, the mark of a bullet that had perforated his intestines, requiring a complicated operation at a humanitarian camp. Sila buried his hands in the pockets of his jeans. His fingertips brushed against the newspaper clipping.

'You know how to read, can you explain this to me?' he said, holding out the printed page.

Falba looked at the article warily.

'Why don't you ask the Uncle? I don't know much about this stuff.'

Sila nodded. The Uncle. Of course. The Uncle knew everything.

The Uncle was at home, cooking up a gruel of cornmeal and fish, turning the long ladle in his white-gloved hands. He seemed irritated by Sila's request, but he picked up a pair of broken glasses with only one cracked lens remaining and carefully read the article.

'Where did you find this?'

'In town, it was lying on the ground.'

'And you thought it was interesting?'

'A little. I picked it up.'

'Because of the man's face?'

'No. Because of the number.'

'Two billion dollars?' said the Uncle.

'Yes.'

'That's the amount of money this man, an American banker, earned last year.'

'That's what I thought,' Sila said with a hint of pride.

'And why did you find that so interesting?'

'Because that amount of money . . .'

'It's happening far away. In the United States. It's not our world.'

'But people obviously talk about him here. In this . . .' Sila gestured towards the city. The city of a thousand privations. The city of shanty towns, the city without a city, since it had no centre, no suburbs, nothing but an amorphous sprawl.

The Uncle shrugged.

'It's not important,' he said.

And with a solemn concentration, he returned to his task.

Sila left the kitchen, which doubled as a dining room, a living room and sometimes as a bedroom, not for want of space, since the whole building – or what was left of it – was deserted, but simply because there was no way to distinguish one room from another since all were vast, ruined, eaten away by the sand that rose like the tide. There was sand everywhere, pouring through every gap, through the crevices and the cracks. A vast sea of sand was smothering the city and would some day make it one with the desert, like a dream of the past, like a city abandoned by its mirages. As Sila set off again, walking easily, almost dreamily, the Uncle's words came back to him: 'It's not important'. But for the first time the Uncle's words did not ring true. There was no logical flaw and he could not quite put into words the troubling, slightly awkward feeling that had come over him, but Sila felt ill at ease. Money had never been important in his life – simply getting food every day had been much more crucial – but this fabulous, enormous sum of money unsettled him. It seemed vulgar. He remembered how his mother used to scold him as a child when he was rude. Yes, this American was very rude. All the men in the country, including those up North who drove cars, had probably not earned such a sum in the year. Who knows? Perhaps all of them together would barely earn such a sum in the course of a lifetime. And they were a vast multitude, while the American was just one man. Two billion dollars. How could anyone earn so much? Had he caught millions of fish? Had he stitched piles of clothes that reached all the way to the moon? Had he built buildings, working day and night, brick upon brick, for thousands of years?

Sila sat down on the ground, hugging his knees. He waited for nightfall. And on the sand he fell asleep like an abandoned child, an adolescent too quickly grown, torn between childhood and manhood.

He woke, shivering, in the darkness. He had no difficulty finding his way. The Uncle said he could see in the dark like an animal. And it was true that his step, lithe, nimble, unvarying in its rhythm, was like that of an animal. An hour later, having wolfed down some of the Uncle's gruel, Sila rolled himself in a blanket and continued his night.

It was brief. His cousin Falba woke him before dawn with an affectionate prod. Sila groaned, but a few seconds later he was up and rekindling the fire. They gulped down their gruel, then, without a word, they headed for the ocean. They padded across the sandy beach. They pushed the boat out. All along the water's edge others were pushing, other bodies stretching and shoving. The first boats were already passing the wall of waves, the white wall of breakers that marked the end of the shallows. Beyond was freedom, the open sea.

Sila's belly quivered at the contact with the cold water. Then he leapt into the boat and began to row, as Falba was already doing, paddling with surprising power and pace given his slight frame. The waves propelled the boat back towards the beach;

to make headway they had to make the most of the ebbtide.

'Now!' shouted Falba.

This was the signal. Sila heaved on the oar with all his strength. The dark skiff plunged into the streaming white foam, faltered for a moment, seemed to slip back, until, with a powerful stroke of the oars, the boat reached the peak, quivered for a moment on the crest of the huge wave, then tumbled back onto the glassy expanse of ocean. They headed out towards the open sea, paying out the nets, heading for those places where fish were plentiful. Falba constantly bemoaned the fact that there were fewer fish now than when he was young. When he was a boy, he would say, there were so many fish they would leap into the boat. Now the shoals had thinned, and catches were smaller. Falba believed that, scared away by the war, the fish had sought refuge in some secret kingdom in the heart of the ocean.

'It's the noise of the bombs that scares them away,' he would say.

The Uncle always looked pained when Falba said such things.

'Fish are deaf. They don't have ears, they have gills.'

'In that case how do you explain the fact that they've disappeared?' Falba would say, his hands on his hips. 'You remember what the catches used to be like . . .'

But today, the catch was good. Swimming along the seabed like a broadnose shark, merging with the rocks and the algae, Sila managed to gather three big lobsters, which he brandished triumphantly as he broke the surface.

They got an excellent price for them at market. A slim young girl approached. She was holding out her hand to take the lobsters when, honking its horn, the ramshackle Mercedes belonging to the Commander made its habitual entrance, driving at great speed and ploughing into the sand in order to stop since it had no brakes. The Commander, in full uniform, climbed out and, with military bearing, strode over. Every week, he bought their finest fish and he paid handsomely, never haggling too much.

'Would you like some lobsters, Commander?' Falba called to him.

The young woman turned towards the Commander without a word.

'I'll take them all,' said the Commander, 'I adore lobster.'

'They're already taken,' Sila whispered to his cousin. 'This girl was here . . .'

'The Commander comes first,' snapped Falba.

Sila got to his feet.

'We'd love to sell you all of them, Commander, but this young woman was here before you. You'll have to share.'

The Commander shuddered. Sila handed him two lobsters, keeping one back for the girl. His honour was safe: two lobsters, that might be enough. Nonetheless, to make clear his displeasure, the Commander tossed the coins on the ground, stalked off without a word, climbed into the car and roared off, the horn blaring.

'Thank you,' said the young woman.

Sila nodded.

'Are you out of your mind,' Falba fumed as soon as she had left, 'refusing to sell the Commander the lobsters?'

'I didn't refuse, the girl was here first. Anyway, he got his two lobsters.'

'He wanted all of them. He's our best customer and he's a commander.'

'The war's over. There's nothing for him to command any more.'

'But he won't come back. Besides, once a commander, always a commander.'

At the end of the morning, as Sila looked at the coins and banknotes in his hand, the proceeds of the whole day's catch, he realised it would take hundreds of thousands of years of catches as good as today's for them to earn as much as the American. And once again he was overcome by a disagreeable feeling, a feeling he could not put a name to, which was neither envy nor hatred but a sort of vague disapproval.

They went home and gave the money to the Uncle. Then Sila went back to his wandering around the city. He was kept busy playing football for a while. He ran, defended, scored two goals, shouted. The bundle of paper and plastic which the players tried as best they could to fashion into a football finally burst and the match had to be abandoned. The boys gradually drifted off in groups, commenting on their exploits, and by the time he came to the outskirts of the city Sila found himself alone. The wind was blowing. Ruins rose up against the desert, abandoned strongholds. Vestiges of the destruction. In a few years more the sand would cover them, swallowing a little more of the ghostly city. The Uncle often said they were all on borrowed time. That they were not living but surviving, like the nomads of the sands, and that even their survival was the product of memory: they existed so they might remember the war. And as that memory slipped into oblivion, they too slipped slowly into the shifting African sands.

A city of old men and children. A city whose women had disappeared, been raped, kidnapped, murdered; whose men had been tortured, slaughtered, imprisoned. The children had grown, become adolescents, their lives would pass as in a dream. A breath of wind shifting the sands.

A hundred metres farther on, Sila thought he saw the looming form of a giraffe lumbering slowly behind the houses, moving with the curious, easy indifference of wild animals. And then the vision disappeared. The City of Dreams. The City of Nowhere. A white world choked with sand and forgetfulness in which men moved as in a slow, repetitive dream, where forms gradually faded.

As he neared home, Falba, who was waiting for him in the next street, grabbed his arm.

'You can't go home,' he said. 'The Commander's men are looking for you. They're going to kill you. They say you humiliated him. You have to leave.'

In the City of Nowhere, life had no meaning. Bodies moved like deep underwater algae carried by ocean currents.

The alga that was Sila broke free. He stowed away on a cargo ship – one of those improbable hulks of rusted steel powered only by a miracle – without knowing where it was headed. There were one or two like this every week. No one really knew what cargo they carried. What was there for them to find in the City of Nowhere? Yet they existed, their sirens blared as they arrived and again as they weighed anchor. One more piece of cargo, Sila stowed away in the hold for a whole night and a whole day, but at the end of his first day he was discovered by a sailor. He was brought up on deck. The captain told him he would be thrown overboard. Sila knew the rules. Stowaways were shark food. Everyone knew the rules. He did not protest.

The cook intervened. He needed a ship's boy and the lad was too young to die. His childhood had already been a living hell, surely now he had a chance to escape, they could hardly toss him into the deep.

'If we let a stowaway live, it sends the wrong message to the others,' said the captain.

'There aren't any others. He's alone. I'll take care of him.'

The cook's name was Fos. Before now, he had been neither good nor evil. This was the day he earned his stripes as a good man. He probably did need a ship's boy, he was probably tired of working alone in the galley, but the fact remains he saved Sila's life, and to show his gratitude the boy worked as hard as he could. Never had the galley been so clean, never had the meals been served with such care. Remembering his Uncle, Sila wore white gloves to serve the captain – though it took a little imagination to think them really white. One evening, the captain admitted: 'We did well to spare your life.'

Sila supplemented their everyday fare by fishing. Sometimes, he wanted to dive into the shimmering water. He longed for the light. To dive into the light. Into the sun reflected in the ocean. But the cargo ship was moving too quickly, the deck was too high, he would never catch it up.

Fos was a chatterbox. He talked endlessly to Sila, asked him about his life. Sila was reluctant to answer. He came from the City of Nowhere, from the city engulfed by sand. Perhaps it no longer existed now, perhaps it had vanished as the ship pulled away, breaking the spell.

'Of course it doesn't exist any more,' said Fos during one of their talks, 'in fact, it never existed, you'd do well to forget it. You're a different man now, you're no longer in that city out of time. The war is over.'

The cook asked who had raised him all these years. Sila told him about his cousin, about the Uncle.

'What about your parents? Your mother, your father?'

'They're not there any more.'

The cook nodded.

'They say the rebels killed half the population.'

Sila spent his free time aboard reading the only two books on the ship: an atlas and a cookery book. This is how he discovered the twin pillars of his destiny: cooking and travel.

With his finger, he travelled the world, stopping on every continent. Here were strange and fabulous names, some of which evoked vague memories. The Uncle had spoken of these continents – Europe, America – as magical places flowing with milk and gold.

One evening, Sila took from his pocket the scrap of newspaper he had kept.

'This man is from America,' he said.

Fos read the article, then opened the corresponding page of the atlas.

'He lives in the United States, a country in North America. He lives in a city called New York.'

He pointed to a large red dot on the map.

'A city by the sea, just like mine.'

Fos laughed.

'That's right, just like yours. You want to go to the United States? I should warn you we're heading for Morocco and on from there to France, to Marseilles.'

France. The touchstone. The country whose language people spoke in the City of Nowhere.

'It's smaller than the United States,' Fos added, 'but it's bigger than your city.'

Thanks to the recipe book, astonishing names tripped from Sila's lips: eggs *fino de Boffet*, painter's palette, sand roses, poached chicken with creamed lentils, spider crab *Atlantide*, rice pudding with kumquats, *tournedos Rossini*. The recipes all began the same way: Cooking Time, Ingredients. Then came elegant, carefully chosen words: 'Remove the peduncle and blanch thoroughly.' 'Singe and draw the chicken, and cut it into eight pieces.' 'Finely chop the shallots and sweat them in butter.' 'Blanch the spinach, refresh in cold water and squeeze to remove the excess.' Can you imagine the poetry of such words to a boy from the City of Nowhere? 'In a heavy-bottomed pan sweat the *mirepoix* of carrots and onions over a low flame. Add the fresh tomatoes and the tomato concentrate, the celery stick, parsley stalks and the *fond brun*.'

'I read the words but I never see the dish,' Sila protested one day. 'It's annoying.'

'You hardly think I'm going to cook things like that on a ship?'

At fifty-one, Fos was one of those unfinished creatures who have accumulated lives: a down-and-out in Liberia, he had been an artist in Paris, a student and an unemployed person in Germany, a construction worker in Brazil and a cook in a school cafeteria in the United States before taking a job on this freighter. He spoke several languages badly, knew everything and nothing, had walked the length and breadth of every major city in the world.

He loved Sila like a son because he found the boy mysterious. The boy's silence, a sort of perpetual remoteness, made him a creature apart. And the young man's beauty filled Fos with pride as though he were the cause. Sila's face radiated a strength and vitality, his eyes had an astonishing darkness, his joyful smile was infectious. As for his body, it was absolutely unique: though not as broad as a grown man, Sila was slim and muscular, sculpted like a statue. That such grace existed was thanks to him, Fos, who had saved the young man's life.

The freighter docked in Morocco. It stayed barely a day, just long enough to unload its wares and load others. The sailors worked tirelessly with the help of a few porters chosen from the crowd that thronged around the port looking for any work on offer. One of these day labourers had such astonishing strength that the others said he was a werewolf. When the moon was full, he slit the throats of women and children. Sila thought him rather a nice fellow for a werewolf.

Then the freighter set off again.

Fos had bought some spices in a Moroccan market to satisfy the captain. And so Sila became a commis chef. To monkfish, which he carefully cut into medallions and cooked for ten minutes under Fos's watchful eye, he added a coconut coulis that would for ever be remembered on this rusty, rotting hulk. The monkfish was served, needless to say, with white gloves.

Finally, the boat reached its destination.

# 2

One was called Simon Judal, which meant he was sometimes called Jude or Judas, a nickname that could hardly have been more ill-suited; the other had been christened Matthieu Brunel but had no intention of remaining so: the surname was much too common. These were the two young men who had reacted so differently at the restaurant.

Now they were walking down a side street off the Champs-Élysées, buoyed up by a sort of elation attributable to the meal, to the lightness of Simon's wallet, having treated his best friend to celebrate his new job, to their youth and to the warm June evening. The air-conditioning in the restaurant had been a little chilly and they were glad to stroll in the warm night. The world was their oyster.

'I have to say, if I'd been that waiter, I'd have smashed the guy's face in,' said Matthieu.

'You can hardly punch a customer when you're a waiter at the finest restaurant in the world,' said Simon.

'So that's the finest restaurant in the world?'

'It's the only place I could take you. There was no choice.'

'I'd still have smashed his face in!'

They emerged onto the Champs-Élysées. In the summer evening, the streetlights gave off a purple glow, forming haloes against the sky. The trees along the avenue glimmered. Light streamed from the cars, curiously silent somehow, waiting patiently for the long river of metal which stretched back to the Place de la Concorde to begin flowing.

The two friends walked down the Champs-Élysées and, when they came to the Place de la Concorde, hailed a taxi. They rolled down the windows and, silent now, allowed themselves to be lulled by the movement of the car.

It pulled up outside a large brick building in the 11th arrondissement and they took the elevator to the top – the ninth floor. Simon slipped his key into the lock. They stepped into the apartment. A hallway with a polished parquet floor led to a living room and, beyond, a covered terrace furnished in the oriental style which overhung the void. They sat down.

'That guy who hit . . .'

'Not again!' Simon interrupted.

'Well, it's not normal, is it? You don't deck a guy for taking your kid by the arm.'

'It's normal if you're a dickhead.'

'You'd have to be a very particular type of dickhead.'

'Probably,' Simon yawned.

'One with an obsession for power and property. He's *my* kid and nobody touches him.'

'Couldn't have put it better myself.'

'Do you have that obsession?' asked Matthieu.

'No.'

'Me neither, but we might be better off if we did. That absolute need to assert yourself. To mark your territory.'

'Like an animal, you mean?'

'Yeah, like an animal. To be less human and more animal. I sometimes wonder if that's not the secret to life. Allowing yourself to be guided by your instincts, your urges.'

'So you're saying we should be predators? Nice idea. Reverse the whole history of mankind and go back to being wild animals.'

'Well, I'll tell you one thing, that particular dickhead is at war. And I think people who are constantly waging war have an advantage over everyone else.'

Simon nodded.

'Maybe. But it's also because they've already lost. To me a man who's always at war is a man already reconciled to loss. The loss of everything that makes us human, but also the defeat of happiness.'

Somewhat surprised to have said something so perceptive, and fearful of a better riposte, Simon headed off to bed. Matthieu stayed for a moment, lost in thought, then he too went to his room.

They had been sharing this apartment for a year. They had met at a ball, had hit it off, though on the face of it they had nothing in common, and six months later Matthieu moved in and became Simon's flatmate. It was a three-room apartment. With the curious obstinacy he sometimes had, Simon had been determined to find an apartment with terraces. Plural. 'Which area are you looking to live in?' 'I don't care about the area. I want two terraces.' 'What's your budget?' 'I don't have a budget, I have a requirement: terraces.' This, at least, was his account of the conversation. And at the time he was far from being a wealthy man. He was working as a researcher in a maths laboratory.

Simon had scurried into the apartment on the heels of the estate agent. There was a terrace off the kitchen, and a second terrace leading off from the living room. With each new terrace Simon's excitement grew and when they came to the third terrace, he signed the deal. The third terrace, a short flight of steps up from the largest bedroom, was bordered by withered shrubs. It could hardly be called luxurious, but then neither could the apartment or the building itself, located as they were in the outskirts of the 11th arrondissement in a tangle of winding charmless streets. But this was what he wanted: it overlooked all of Paris. Though there was nothing lavish about it, it was an exceptional space, perched high up, like the crow's nest on a ship, as though isolated from the humdrum routine of the city.

'You have access to the roof if you like. It's a flat roof, it would be like a fourth terrace. You'll have the only key, you have sole access.'

Simon moved in. In winter, grey leached into the apartment from all around. The grey of the clouds, of the city. A congenially melancholy atmosphere, though sometimes a little cold. In summer, the sun illuminated the far-flung corners of every room. Simon would retreat to the roof terrace wearing only boxer shorts, and there patiently track the sun's course from morning to night, which accentuated his dark complexion. He was perfectly at home there. Alone, at peace, just how he liked it.

And yet the idea of sharing the flat had been Simon's. Perhaps because the permanently empty second bedroom troubled his sense of logic. But his decision had also been the result of the bombshell that had been his meeting with Matthieu.

Simon was a shy, diffident creature. After his parents' death in a car crash, he had been raised by an aunt, his mother's older sister. At the age of six, he had suddenly found himself an orphan, the result of a twist of fate he could not understand but nonetheless accepted. Just as he had been born, so his parents had died. It was a fact of life about which there was no point speculating. He did not cry, he was not sad, but he found himself now in a world from which all colour had drained, in a goldfish bowl devoid of life. For the most part, he did nothing; he was indifferent to books, to television, cut off from his classmates, who saw him as stand-offish and sickly, and his regular illnesses further set him apart. In this reclusive existence, through some mysterious circuitry in his brain, he developed an extraordinary memory. This inexplicable phenomenon made him a sort of memory genius and, had he displayed the least intellectual curiosity, he would have been exceptionally intelligent. But goldfish in their bowls exhibit no curiosity. Simon would lie on his bed thinking, reliving the events of his day – the pointless inanities of his life. A pear he had peeled at the dinner table, a pen he had dropped in class, a dog that had crossed the street in front of him. The polo neck of a boy in class, the frill of a dress, the texture of skin.

At the provincial school he attended, Simon had been a good pupil. He hadn't needed to study, since he remembered everything down to the smallest detail. In fact it was his prodigious memory that marked him out in his first year in secondary school. Before that, he had not been much liked. His frailness was unsettling. Other boys could not get him to play games of any kind. They could not fight with him, even a harsh word was enough to leave him distraught and tearful. Given this fact, it was surprising that he was not victimised but was left to himself, a fact that can only be explained because the school was in an affluent part of town with pupils who were not particularly cruel and who were kept on a tight leash by parents who all knew each another. The word had clearly gone out not to bother Simon but to leave him alone; this often meant him spending playtime in the classroom, extending the goldfish bowl of his bedroom, of his existence.

In his first year at secondary school, where a battery of teachers were tasked with teaching the various subjects his old schoolteacher Madame André, had taught all by herself, Simon spent his first term petrified. The different classrooms and teachers completely bewildered him and upset his routine. You had to pack up your books, leave one classroom, dash to the stairs and run to a different classroom on a different floor, careful not to get the wrong door, say 'Good Morning' to another new teacher . . . It was a puzzle. But however strange he was, Simon was not without resources and managed to adapt, though he was invariably the last to leave the class, still clumsily packing his things away while the teacher waited impatiently to close the classroom.

In the second term, in French class, they studied poetry. First, the rules of versification, then individual texts. At the end of one class, the teacher asked how many of them could remember what they had been studying for the previous hour. The poem was Victor Hugo's 'Tomorrow, At Dawn'. Everyone in the class protested. Except Simon who, as usual, did not say a word.

On a sudden whim the French teacher, a man they all found intimidating, called on Simon. Paralysed, the boy said nothing. Then, closing his eyes, he began to speak, and he recited the whole poem.

'Did you know it already?' the teacher asked.

'No,' Simon answered shyly.

'Good. So you remembered it.'

Then the teacher set another poem for the class to learn. It was 'The Sleeper in the Valley' by Rimbaud. Simon read the poem. Knew it. He leaned back in his chair.

'Simon, learn the poem!' said the teacher. 'Don't rest on your laurels.'

Simon blushed. He pored over the text again, but what could he do? He already knew it by heart. He stared into space.

Irritated, the teacher shouted at him: 'Recite as much as you've learned.'

And Simon recited the whole poem, without a single mistake or hesitation.

'Did you know that one already?'

The boy blushed again.

'No.'

'You're not going to tell me that you learned it by heart in the past two minutes!'

Simon shrugged helplessly.

'It's not my fault.'

The teacher leafed through his book and gave it to Simon open at Rimbaud's long poem 'The Drunken Boat'.

'Try and learn that while the rest of the class works on the other poem.'

Simon read the text. In his humdrum universe, the dazzling images amazed and astonished him.

Some minutes later, the teacher began asking for volunteers to recite 'The Sleeper in the Valley'. No one could recite the whole poem.

'What about you, Simon? How much of "The Drunken Boat" have you managed to learn?'

In that moment, the images swelled in the confusion of words. With impeccable, inspired delivery, Simon the goldfish recited the entire poem under the astonished eyes of the rest of the class, as though another Simon, transfigured, had just stepped into the light.

Nor did this other Simon ever completely return to the darkness. For that whole year, he was 'The Drunken Boat' kid, something that later led Simon to believe Rimbaud had saved his adolescence. Not only did his teachers no longer look on him as some pathetic creature unable to pack his school-bag who blushed or paled the moment he was spoken to, but even his classmates saw him in a different light. They would not have elected him class president, but he was the-kid-with-the-incredible-memory, the-boy-who-never-forgets, that-guy-who-doesn't-even-have-to-study, and for this they felt a certain innocuous envy. This did not mean they were jealous of him, since in every other way – his blushing, his awkwardness, the unfashionable clothes his aunt bought for him – he was utterly ridiculous.

The result of this event was that no one ever recognised Simon's true gift, which was for maths. He was never really very good at French. Since the death of his parents, silence had welled in him like a mute, infinite fountain, forever leaving him at a loss for words. He drew strength from that silence: words would never open the world to him. Truncated phrases slipped out, phrases like amputated limbs, too short, too curt, subject-verb-object constructions that never connected him to others, since nothing in his life connected.

The silent world of mathematics, on the other hand, suited him perfectly. This was his real poetry and even if his teachers did not yet fully realise it, because the problems were still too simple, they were beginning to suspect that Simon understood maths in the way that some musicians have perfect pitch, a gift, like all of nature's gifts of pure and uncertain beauty.

It was around this gift that Simon constructed his sense of self. In the reassuring world of mathematics, a field impervious to the emotions he so feared, Simon forged the personality he was to have as an adult, and would have had still if events had not conspired to destroy him. Now he moved among his peers without cowering, invisible and silent perhaps, ignored perhaps by girls (for which he was grateful since they terrified him), but at least protected from misfortune. He lived in his little bedroom surrounded by his formulae in a little apartment where meals were served at precise times, where at eleven o'clock an elderly shadowy figure in her soft, gentle voice told him to go to bed and woke him again at seven for a breakfast of hot chocolate, already steaming on the table, and two slices of bread.

Simon's schooldays unfolded as they should. He learnt formulae and mathematical problems till they were coming out of his ears. He successfully won a place at the École Polytechnique, leading him to move out of his little room and into one hardly bigger on the outskirts of Paris on a barren plain where arrogant fellow students informed him that having secured a place at the finest university in the world, it was time for him to 'make a career for himself', a concept that troubled him. If 'making a career' meant becoming an entrepreneur, he was clearly unqualified. On the other hand, he could easily imagine making a non-career for himself in a mathematics laboratory. It was a path even the least astute career guidance counsellor could not but recommend to this raw-boned young man, pockmarked with adolescent acne who could barely bring himself to look you in the eye as he shook hands. Sadly, there came a time when even guidance counsellors – fatuous fatheads who never moved from their chairs – hadn't a clue. Especially when the guidance counsellor in question took the fearsome form of Matthieu Brunel.

The university was organising its annual fancy dress ball. Simon 'the Jude', a nickname given him by his good-natured colleagues, went wearing a military uniform, and the epaulettes for once gave a certain power and form to his anaemic physique. By this point in his life, some years after graduating from the École Polytechnique, he found it easier to deal with social occasions, and the prospect of being in a ballroom in Paris with hundreds of others was no longer quite as terrifying. The uniform granted him a place, and after all, finding his place in the world had always been his greatest problem.

Stepping into the ballroom, he looked around for a familiar face. He had arrived rather early, though he knew social convention suggested arriving late to show how blasé one was about such events, and there was no one there he knew.

So he headed for the buffet table where a considerable crowd – ordinary civilians who had come to the ball for fun – was already gathering. He joined the queue. When his turn came, he ordered champagne. As the waiter handed him the glass and he was about to pay, he felt a hand on his shoulder.

'Hey, penguin features! Don't suppose you could get a glass for me and my lady-friend?'

A raucous laugh defused the insult.

Simon turned and came face to face with the last person he needed in his life. Were it not for this encounter, he would probably never have become part of a milieu that was to devastate both his life and the economy of the modern world.

Standing behind him was a tall, very elegant young man who seemed sure of his own good looks, accompanied by a slim blonde girl.

'Don't worry, I'm paying. I'll even pay for yours since you saved me having to queue.'

Simon, unfortunately, agreed. And this was how he came to meet Matthieu Brunel, his antithesis and, since they were to become best friends, also his double.

# 3

The Russian couple left the restaurant shortly after Simon and Matthieu. The man was short, with glossy black hair and slightly slanting eyes. He claimed his ancestors hailed from the steppes, that vast expanse which, over thousands of years, had witnessed a succession of nomadic empires sweeping from the plains of Manchuria to those of Hungary. Laughing, he would add that his ancestors probably included a certain Lieutenant Attila, who had brought war to the gates of Rome itself. But it was obvious that it was a hollow laugh, that his genealogical dreams indeed lay at the crossroads of the Roman Empire and Attila the Hun, in universal destruction.

His companion was also dark-haired, with a pale beauty. She, more than her husband, attracted attention, and not simply for her beauty. She was tall and had a commanding air. And that evening, she seemed nervous.

The couple headed for the Parc Monceau. They tried to go inside, but found all the gates were closed. Slowly, without exchanging a word, without touching, they circled the park. Then, heading back, they turned into the vast doorway of a luxury hotel. The man picked up their key from reception and they went up to their suite on the top floor. Through the windows, the city stretched away into the distance and perhaps, in that vastness, Lev Kravchenko's eyes met those of Simon Judal, who sat looking out at the city through the window of his winter terrace.

The woman lay on the bed.

'You should have done something back there,' she said.

'Done something about what?'

'When that waiter was punched.'

'It was none of my business, Elena.'

'That's not what you would have said once upon a time.'

'I don't know.'

'You would have done something.'

'Maybe.'

'Well I should have done something, at least.'

'Then why didn't you?'

'I wanted to. I was shocked by the brutality, the . . . senselessness, I was about to get up but then . . . nothing. No one else seemed to react, you didn't react, apart from giving the man a scornful look and, I don't know, I lost heart, especially since the waiter himself didn't fight back. All he seemed to be doing was trying not to get blood stains on the carpet or something.'

'Ah, yes. The alienation of the proletariat,' said Lev mockingly, 'we know all about that.'

'Don't joke. I found the whole thing appalling.'

'The guy should have stood up for himself. He looked like he was in good shape, too. Thin but agile, muscular. I got a good look at him.'

'While that fat pig . . .'

'Fat maybe, but strong.'

'So you were afraid of him?'

Lev smiled. 'You know very well I wasn't.'

Elena nodded. 'Yes, I know. But that just makes it worse. You didn't even want to do something. You just watched with that sort of vague curiosity, that world-weariness you increasingly seem to feel. I swear, Lev, there was a time when you wouldn't have reacted like that. I don't know if you would have done something . . . but you certainly wouldn't have watched like a passive witness, like some passer-by in the street.'

Lev shrugged. 'It's possible. But that was then, and I'm not the man I used to be any more. Excuse the cliché.'

They stared at each other in silence.

Lev Kravchenko had been Elena Matis's professor at Moscow University. A research fellow at the Institute of Economics, a hotbed of ideas where he and a few friends – none of them famous at the time – discussed radical models of economic reform, Lev had also taught a course at the university where Elena had enrolled to do a double degree in political science and literature. She admired him, as did all his students at the time, for his eloquence, his intelligence and his passion, a rare quality among the rest of the faculty.

One evening, they had met by chance in the city and he had invited her for a drink. Lev was as fascinating in conversation as he was when he lectured. He had the same energy, the same passion to persuade. She fell in love. Three months later they moved in together and within a year they married, on the very day the Berlin Wall fell. The coincidence of these two events struck them as comic, because laughter seemed to them the only possible response to the farcical collapse of the Empire.

It had been some time since either believed in Communism.

It had been some time since the succession of ageing dictators had been anything more than a ridiculous, pathetic pantomime that mirrored the regime itself. It had been a long time since they had faith in words, because words no longer corresponded to ideas: 'people's democracies' meant dictatorships, the constant mantra of 'we', of 'the people' masked the vested interests of a select few, and the 'struggle' they were constantly told about through the hot war and the cold war was simply a slow and steady defeat. Elena even considered combining the fields of literature and political science in an analysis of Communist speeches, a paper she obviously could not actually write, at least not under the dictatorship, but one which she thought might sum up the hypocrisy of the regime and the disparity between word and action. They couldn't quite understand what *perestroika* and *glasnost* meant: rightly or wrongly they believed that dictatorship either exists or does not exist, that any laxity necessarily heralds the end. Lev was convinced Gorbachev would be eliminated and things would go back to how they had been before; Elena, for her part, believed this was the beginning of the end, that before the millennium, the USSR would have ceased to exist. It was she who had been proved right, and in fact the thaw had happened more quickly than she had anticipated. Already, the huge ice floes of Communism were crashing down around them, great blocks breaking away, and the most important collapse of all, the most symbolic, was the Berlin Wall, which fell while they were getting married.

And they laughed about it, a laugh that had no real meaning, a grim laugh in absurdity revealed. But they also laughed because they were young, because they were happy. And they would have done well to go on laughing for as long as possible, because what was to come was unutterably bleak.

It was enough to contemplate Lev. It was enough to look from the lean, witty, brilliant professor he had been to the thick-set man with the cynical smirk and the screwed-up eyes of his Hun ancestors, who now gazed out of the window of his hotel suite, to realise that Lev Kravchenko would have done better to go on laughing, holding his young wife in his arms.

But Lev had stopped laughing. Not straight away, of course. No, not straight away, but gradually, as he abandoned Marx and economic theory in favour of oil and struggle. As the Hun in him gradually revealed itself and he joined the headlong rush for victory. He no longer laughed, nor did he cry. He might have wept for the loss of what he had been, but he didn't. His wife did it for him.

In other circumstances, things might have been different. Lev might have gone on working at the Institute and later, probably, taken a post with an NGO where he might have had a dazzling career, combining a few useful acts with much talk. But the collapse of the Soviet Union and the shift to a primitive, savage capitalism decided otherwise. Circumstances revealed another Lev, one neither more nor less genuine, merely the Lev of that historic moment.

In their formative stages, all societies are governed by thieves and criminals who impose themselves upon a lawless world, and it is only later, by a distortion of history and of memory, that these criminals come to be seen as great men. The feudal lords of the Middle Ages were savage plunderers, exactly as the first Greeks and the first Romans had been. Just as the millionaire robber barons of nineteenth-century America built their fortunes on steel and oil, on robbery and blackmail before rediscovering morality through the magnificent artistic and social foundations their descendants are so proud of, so Lev belonged to a savage period when crooks and robbers fought over the choicest morsels of the corpse of empire.

In this clash with his own time, Professor Lev Kravchenko died and Elena had to live with his ghost, with a man who seemed less and less like him, whose cleverness developed into a callousness that sent chills down her spine.

Lev immediately realised that the universities would be the first to be affected by the impoverishment of the state. He was already poor but he knew that, before long, he would have to drive a taxi to make ends meet. But it was not just that. Under the Communist system Lev had accepted being poor; in this emerging new world which, it seemed clear, would be utterly unlike the old, he wanted to act, to decide his own fate. The wind of change was blowing: he would make his own path through the ruined wasteland.

Lev's PhD supervisor knew Boris Yeltsin's daughter. Like Elena, Lev had first become aware of Yeltsin when he was famously sacked from the Politburo in 1987, where as First Secretary of the CPSU Moscow City Committee, having railed against the corruption, the filth, the drugs and the prostitution in the capital, he lambasted Ligachev, the Second Secretary of the Communist Party, at the Central Committee plenum, screaming: 'The corrupt and the dishonest are right here among us, as everyone here knows perfectly well.' And while perhaps everyone did know, it was something not to be mentioned. Yeltsin was sidelined and it was rumoured he had had a heart attack, but in 1989, despite repeating his attacks on Ligachev, ninety per cent of Muscovites, including Elena and Lev, voted for his election to the Supreme Soviet. Obviously they were both too astute not to notice, even in his attacks on corruption, the signs of a populism that might make him a new dictator, replacing a weakened Gorbachev, but still Yeltsin seemed like a viable solution.

And so Lev decided to get in touch with the man on the advice of Elena, who felt that in difficult times it was important to become involved in politics, to defend democracy. Yeltsin, after all, was in favour of a multi-party system. Lev, through Yeltsin's daughter, secured an introduction.

On their first meeting, he was impressed by this tall, heavy-set man with his brutal, authoritarian manner. Yeltsin was missing two fingers on his left hand, lost as a child during the war when a grenade he was playing with exploded, and his nose had been broken on several occasions during brawls. Lev would later liken him to a punch-drunk boxer: unpredictable, sometimes stupid, sometimes brilliant, driven by random urges.

'What is it you want?' Yeltsin asked.

'I want to work with you to bring democracy to Russia.'

Yeltsin looked doubtful.

'What do you really want?'

'Exactly what I said. And I'll work to get you elected President of Russia.'

'What about Gorbachev?'

'He will be President of the Union.'

'The Union? That sounds like a tall order.'

And Lev was hired. At first he was merely an administrative pawn in the team. He worked with the Democratic Bloc, of which Yeltsin was a leading light, and in an electoral landslide his mentor was elected to the Supreme Soviet as people's deputy for Sverdlovsk, which position he used to run for President of Russia against Vlasov, Gorbachev's preferred candidate.

Now President of the Soviet Union, Gorbachev still had the power to sway the Russian deputies in the second-round ballot and ensure Vlasov was elected. Yeltsin was of the view that Gorbachev would do anything to block his path and that negotiation was pointless. A campaign meeting was convened at Yeltsin's offices with the whole team present.

'We need to negotiate with his team,' Lev suggested.

'What do you mean?' snapped Litvinov, an advisor with whom Lev had a fractious relationship. 'He is the team,' Litvinov added contemptuously.

Lev did not rise to the bait.

'Gorbachev is Gorbachev, his team is his team. Gorbachev has been weakened and his men are increasingly acting on their own initiative. Mostly, they're trying to stop things falling apart. I'm convinced we can negotiate with them.'

No one said anything. Yeltsin stared at Lev curiously.

'I think the boy is right. Sort it out, develop contacts, Kravchenko will oversee this.'

If the negotiations failed, Lev knew, he would be dropped from Yeltsin's team, but he also knew that if they succeeded, it would make his name and a government post might open up for him.

Gorbachev was scheduled to make an official visit to Canada

and the United States. Lev needed to act while he was away. He met with each of Gorbachev's allies and outlined the situation. Yeltsin, he said, was the strongman of Russia, and though he might well lose this election he would win the next one because all of Moscow was behind him. His name alone was enough to bring 100,000 people onto the streets. And when he was eventually elected, he would have each and every one of them sent to the Gulag, for which he needed only to find a new name. Then, opening a briefcase stuffed with banknotes, he explained that the Russian President might prove to be generous, indeed very generous, to those who helped him.

'What about Gorbachev?' he was asked.

'Naturally, the President of the Soviet Union remains our guide, our leader,' he answered. 'It is our responsibility as advisors, allies, ministers, to ensure they work well together.'

At this point, Lev produced a document outlining the division of spheres of influence in Russia. He knew the proposal would not last two weeks and that, as President of the Russian Federation, by far the largest and most powerful state in the Union, there would be a permanent rivalry between Yeltsin and the President of the Soviet Union. Nonetheless, he proposed the paper with some success.

He did not report the details of these negotiations to Elena. He told her he was trying to get Boris Yeltsin elected but obviously without specifically admitting that he, a professor of economics, was resorting to nothing less than threats and corrupt practices.

The terms of the negotiation had occurred to him effortlessly, without the need to dwell on them, and with no sense of moral repugnance whatever. The means had come naturally to him and his first step on the path to corruption cost him nothing.

By the time Gorbachev came back, the die was cast. A number of deputies had switched their loyalties and were prepared to vote for Yeltsin.

So began a period of great expectations for Lev. He knew he had done an excellent job. Yeltsin had not actually said thank you, but the resounding clap on the back had said more than words could. Yet still there was no offer of a post. Or at least not the one he had expected. The newly elected President saw in Lev an invaluable treasure-trove of ideas, but not the minister he had hoped to be. Hiding his bitterness, Lev worked at developing Russia's power – and hence Yeltsin's – in the hope that the President's power would shore up his own. But he was aware that an advisor had no claim to power but had to content himself with that vague, illusory notion that is influence.

Yeltsin wanted Russia to be a sovereign state. This was the goal. Lev, at the head of a pyramid of experts and constitutional lawyers, was charged with finding the means. This entailed expanding his proposal on the laws and spheres of influence, proclaiming that in all cases Russian laws should take precedence over those of the Soviet Union, something that amounted to a covert declaration of war. The sheer scope of the task appealed to Lev; it allowed him to demonstrate his intellectual superiority over Yeltsin's other advisors. He alone was capable of steering this immense project, of putting flesh on its bones, without ever losing his way. His knowledge of the law – though he was not a lawyer – was considerable, and, more importantly, he learned quickly; he seemed more impressive with each passing day and within two weeks of beginning work, he could discuss every last detail with the punctiliousness of a constitutional lawyer.

Yeltsin, for his part, wasted no time. Like all good political philosophers, the ex-foreman realised that power tends inexorably towards the absolute. He held constant meetings with the Russian parliamentary deputies to persuade them to support his bid for Russian sovereignty. On 8 June 1990, the Russian parliament decreed the primacy of Russian over Soviet law, and on 12 June Russia became a sovereign state. The battle was won.

But what had they won? On the evening of 12 June, having celebrated this great victory, this was the question that nagged at Lev's brain as his chauffeur drove him home. What had they won? And what exactly had *he* won? Was the demise of the Soviet Union – and what they had done was clearly the death knell of the Union – really a victory? And if so, what kind of victory? The overthrow of a dictatorship? Would another not come along to replace it? Had he not simply worked for the victory of one man over another?

He pushed aside these questions. Forgot them because he had to forget them, because tomorrow work would begin again and because, in a month, Elena would give birth to their son Yevgeni. Just as they had married as the Berlin Wall fell, so their first child was born into the ruins of the Soviet Union.

'An epic birth,' Elena said.

Yes. An epic birth just as a new battle was beginning: privatisation. An escape route presented itself. Lev began to feel that perhaps politics did not interest him as much as he had thought.

It was something that once upon a time he had dreamed about, argued about passionately at the Institute of Economics; he had dreamed up a thousand projects in preparation for the future. Every day he was reminded of the usefulness of politics at key moments in history, but the struggle was so intense that he was already exhausted. Yeltsin drew his strength – a fighter's strength though he often reeled as much from exhaustion as from alcohol – from the conviction that he was loved, that he was indispensable to the country's fate. Standing in the shadows, Lev received no acknowledgement, no contact with the crowds and he was ill-disposed by temperament to believe that any individual was indispensable. It was probably, Lev thought sardonically, the last vestige of his Marxist beliefs: the individual was nothing, there was always someone to take his place.

The new task the government had set itself – the move to a free market economy – opened up new prospects for him: he could take over a business. Especially as those who had recently come to power included the economic reformers, like Gaidar, whose views he shared. Granted it was not the fate of a country, but at least it meant real power, actual control and the possibility of a sizeable income. After all, it was not as though he earned a particularly good living and he was a father now, a family man. And to think that Elena had given up political science and decided to do her Master's degree in literature.

'You're the one who should be in politics,' Lev told her. 'We need an idealist in the family.'

'You're already in politics.'

'I'm thinking of packing it in.'

'That's it? You don't want to influence things any more?'

'I want to influence them in a different way. And not through politics.'

'So you're abandoning your ideals?' said Elena mockingly.

'I didn't have many to start with and I have a lot fewer now, as you well know, though I like to think that I've haven't been entirely useless. And I realise that I don't enjoy politics, but I think that maybe you might. You're more than capable.'

'I've watched you at it, I'd rather not.'

Lev closed his eyes.

'Why not go back to teaching?' he thought. 'I could get a senior position at the Moscow State University. Professor Lev Kravchenko.'

But this was something Lev obviously could not do. He had had a taste of an intoxicating drug. Through Yeltsin, he had tasted power, its fears, its victories, its defeats, the constant feeling of being in the eye of the storm, at the point where decisions were made. He could not go back to being a spectator. Not yet, at least. 'Later,' he thought, 'when I've really made the most of things, when I've made my fortune and enjoyed everything the battle has to offer.'

# 4

Rousseau insisted that man is born innately good only to be corrupted by society, a theory many philosophers have striven to refute. Researchers and writers have also studied how the steady progression of Evil, in its banality, gradually changes a very ordinary man.

Clearly there have been insufficient studies in the case of the idiot.

Mark Ruffle would present an interesting specimen. The scene at the restaurant captured him in all his brainlessness, his brutality, his constant self-assertion. Characteristics further emphasised by his square jaw, his low brow and his broad shoulders. Ruffle, for his part, insisted on only one thing: 'Mark Ruffle is tough and everybody better get that through their thick skulls.' It was a theory he propounded from childhood, probably from his first day at elementary school, to the first child who dared to sit in a seat Mark had chosen.

His father was a property tycoon in Florida, an ex-foreman grown rich by dint of hard work and greasing the palms of local officials; strategies which over the course of twenty years had made him one of the most important businessmen in the state. He had built a lavish mansion with a huge swimming pool in Clarimont, a little town that was provincial, narrow-minded and pleasant, with manicured lawns and carefully tended gardens. In fact, with its elegant town centre, its vibrant colours, its upmarket stores, its polite, congenial residents, it might have been perfect were it not for the fact that sooner or later you had to wonder whether it was *real*. Whether these people were not simply being paid to *pretend*. Paid to pretend to be polite, to tend their gardens. To live.

To understand Mark Ruffle, it's important to understand the most important day of his life: Sunday. In Clarimont, Sunday was the day when football was played, the curious variant played only by Americans according to rules incomprehensible to the rest of the world which, though vaguely related to rugby, requires so much protective padding – shoulders, elbows, head – that it looks as though it is being played by robots.

On weekdays, Mark was simply a second-rate student forced to pay attention to lessons that clearly went in one ear and out the other. He was not particularly popular with other boys, who disliked his aggressiveness and his arrogance, while girls made fun of his bulldog physique. None of this mattered however: Ruffle knew no doubts. He had his own gods: his father and his football coach, whose opinions alone mattered to him and who together seemed intent on cultivating his aggressiveness and his arrogance the way you might train a pitbull.

Then came Sunday. A day prepared for by his training during the week on the football field and in the long sessions at the gym that made Mark so proud of his admittedly impressive pecs and biceps. On Sunday, one of the finest running backs in the history of the school displayed a thirst for battle, an obsessiveness and a stamina that were remarkable, to say the least. From the moment he woke on Sunday morning, he felt a feverish excitement. Today was his day. His father would make breakfast for him, his mother would ask if he felt at the top of his game, ready to win. He would grunt with conviction. His parents would drive him to the football field where his coach would ask if he felt at the top of his game, ready to win. At which point he would ball one hand into a fist and furiously thump his open hand.

He would change into his football gear, put on his pads, listen to the pep-talk of the coach, fleetingly aware of the man's flushed cheeks, look round at his teammates, then the team would troop out onto the field.

And then Mark would hurl himself into the fray. And he could not have demonstrated greater passion in the kickoffs, greater ferocity in the tackles. What was most surprising was that despite his heavy build, he was very fast, easily managing to outrun much leaner opponents. And in these bursts of speed, as he raced down the gridiron, his wiry legs supporting a heavy, muscular torso made all the more impressive by his warlike gear, a cheer would go up from the stands. Yes, Sunday was his day. The roar from the coach's bench and from the crowd – admittedly just players' families and a handful of fans from Clarimont, but it was enough, especially when his mother clapped, when his father leapt to his feet yelling above the cheering of the crowd – this was what filled him with joy, what reminded him that life was worth living, that he was Mark Ruffle, powerful and admired by everyone in spite of his fucking teachers. He felt a vital spark kindled in him, the exhilaration of self and of the struggle and, the roar from the stands accompanying him like a victory parade, he would run, swift, strong, invincible towards the Grail that was the goal-line and, with an animal cry, score a touchdown.

And that cry, when he was sixteen and had his first girl-friend, that cry was an assertion of masculinity addressed to the whole world and in particular to the big-breasted cheerleader he thought of as his reward for his role on the team. She was the sister of one of his teammates, the sort of girl who in middle school wouldn't have given him a second glace but now, spell-bound, would jump up and down clapping and giving little squeals of delight.

Yes, Sunday was his day. The exhilaration of anticipation. The pleasure of a victory won by sheer force, the one feeling he truly gloried in, the one he would have liked to be able to experience every other day of the week without being forced to pay lip-service to duty, respect and education.

But Sunday drew to a close. And with it the match, the vic-tory, the post-match analysis and congratulations as his father drove him home, having hugged him hard as he came off the field. In spite of his efforts the next day to talk about his win or at least his perfect performance on behalf of the team, the feeling wasn't the same. Off the field, his enthusiasm seemed excessive or stupid or simply laughable to others. And as the voices of his teachers grew louder, drowning out the roar from the bleachers, the vital spark within him flickered out.

What could he do to keep Sunday alive?

What could he do but go on to play pro football so he could experience to the hundredth degree the glorious feelings he had tasted?

What could he do but explain his plans to his father, whose reaction was enthusiastic, though the enthusiasm seemed a little phony, as though other plans had already been made for him, as though – a hideous thought – *they didn't believe in him?*

What could he do but prolong his high-school career at a university to which he was admitted by virtue of his sporting prowess and – though he didn't know it – a generous donation from his father to the institution. Curiously, though not the one he had applied to, it was a good college, and the coach there had known his high-school coach for years.

What could he do but try to keep the flame of Sunday alive now when, more often than not, he found himself sitting the game out on the bench, when in spite of his aggressive temperament he found himself crushed by monsters who were bigger, stronger and faster than him?

What could he do but grunt confidently when his mother asked if he felt at the top of his game, ready to win, to become a pro footballer?

What could he do but constantly reassure his father that he would win, but that he was finding it tough, a confession which filled his father with a secret satisfaction as though some carefully hatched plan were coming together?

What could he do but work at it, work harder, take everything that was dished out and more, take something to help him out, it wasn't doping, just a little boost, not some rubbish?

What could he do but tough it out while other players gained ground until they were completely out of reach and even his place on the bench was doubtful?

'I'm gonna win, Pop.'

Doubt. Crippling doubt. The terrible feeling that his father had always denied him.

And then deliverance.

'I got injured. During training. It was tough, really tough because we had a big match that weekend, the semi-final against Boulder. Big bastards. Well, obviously I was training hard, I wanted to get on coach's good side. He's been talking seriously about putting me back on the team. But then in this tackle I put my knee out. My knee. I swear, Pop. I completely fucked up my knee. Tore all the ligaments.'

'Yeah, it's all over, the doctors all say the same thing. I'll never play again. Never. They say I'll be lucky if I don't end up with a limp.'

'Yeah, it's definite, like I said. It's over.'

'Work with you? In real estate? After college? Sure, Dad, I'd love to work with you. And I'll work hard, I'll earn my place. Don't worry, I'll make you proud of me.'

You're a winner, Ruffle the tough guy. You're right where everyone expected you to be all those years. You'll fulfil your destiny, this is what you were raised for. The real battle: business and money.

So why are you crying?

Why did you put down the phone, lie back on your hospital bed, alone, shaken by sobs as if you'd been lied to and betrayed your whole life, as if your part had been written for the end-of-year school play?

# 5

Ruffle had finished college. He was heading home to take up a job in his father's business, a phoney career path that was to lead from the foothills to the dizzy heights and allow his father, head held high, gripping his son's arm, to declare with a proud, beaming smile: 'Mark started at the bottom and he's worked his way to the top; he is now worthy to take over the family business.'

We weren't quite there yet. Ruffle Senior, the portly father whose flushed face and bow legs made it look as though he had just climbed down from his horse – a Ford four-wheel-drive – threw a huge party to celebrate the graduate's homecoming to which all his friends and his son's were invited. It was a casual party, a barbecue. So everyone dutifully pretended to be casual as they waited for alcohol to do its work, peeling away airs and graces. They had been careful to wear jeans and shirts that were at once casual and cost a small fortune. Their host, after all, was a millionaire.

Ruffle had completed his university education, which is to say he had drunk too much, gone to as few lectures as possible, studied a number of practical examples, attended a few seminars on management where an overpaid – hence respectable – CEO smugly spouted platitudes. He had sniggered during marketing lectures, like many people, but had made an attempt to understand the basics of accountancy since it might come in useful, hankering for the world of finance while quickly realising that, at least from a technical viewpoint, he wasn't cut out for it. But after all, he thought, the technical aspects were always handled by the juniors.

Thanks to understanding professors who were much more lenient than the high-school teachers who had insisted on filling his head with rubbish, he had managed to get a degree, and from an Ivy League college at that. Now he could go home, the graduate's laurel wreath like a halo of wisdom perched atop his bulldog face. Curiously, despite his laziness and his fecklessness he had acquired an indefinable flair for human relationships, a sort of easy-going directness that masked his deep-rooted aggression. All in all, he was perfectly equipped to slip into the business world.

When he arrived back at his house – his father, as usual, had met him at the airport with his girlfriend Shoshana who, despite various fumblings with girls at college, still had the most beautiful breasts he'd ever seen – the assembled guests, casually gathered around the swimming pool, yelled 'Surprise!' though it was anything but. They hugged him, congratulated him, shook his hand, kissed him, everything, in short, to give him a fitting welcome while he puffed himself up, laughing nervously, thrusting his chest out and making clucking noises as he chest-bumped his buddies.

Fist gripping a huge chicken drumstick which he regularly dipped into a jar of mayonnaise, he strolled through the assembled crowd, leering, with a sort of dazed smile impossible to interpret.

It was with the same dazed smile that he listened to his father's speech: 'Brilliant university career . . . first in the family . . . his considerable talents as a jock and a scholar . . . but the sporting world's loss is the business world's gain . . . the same energy . . . in the service of others . . . doing for society what . . . joining the family business, putting his keen mind at the service of . . . climbing the company ladder . . . now, let's party!'

As he wandered around, grabbing a beer bottle to replace the chicken drumstick, Ruffle listened to an old friend of his father's, nodding at just the right moments, smiling as the man patted his arm. Now well and truly loaded, he barrelled a couple of guys from his football team like bowling pins and knocked them into the pool and was immediately rewarded with his own dunking, his fat, ruddy face staring wide-eyed underwater. The music was louder now.

An hour later, eyes vacant, he was slumped in a chair, silent, motionless, chugging a bottle of beer.

Lev entered the Moscow restaurant where Councillor Litvinov was celebrating his birthday. The Councillor had rented the whole space, which was decked out in red and lit by thousands of candles. Tall, thickset men in black suits turned away passers-by. This was Litvinov's *krysha*. Yeltsin's most important advisor and Lev's fiercest rival had become a shrewd businessman – which is to say ruthless, frenzied and dangerous. And to protect his business interests from competitors, Litvinov had set up an umbrella of protection – a *krysha* – in this case calling on the Slavic Brotherhood, the most powerful gang in Moscow. The brotherhood had five men posted on the door and three more working the room. The party would go off without a hitch.

They had done sterling work, Lev, Litvinov, Gaidar, Chubais and the others. Yeltsin's team, known as the 'kamikaze cabinet', had liberalised prices, privatised the economy, opened the country up to capitalism. And, inevitably, Russia had immediately crumbled. They knew 'the transition' as they called it, resorting to the economic euphemisms that quickly replaced Communist slogans, would be difficult but they had not anticipated the ferocity of the maelstrom that would engulf the country. They had fought hard, and there had been unforeseen events: Yeltsin's car crash, which Gorbachev exploited to regain the upper hand; the August putsch in which hardliners tried to stall progress by arresting Gorbachev and attempting to seize power. Yeltsin's stroke of genius had been to rise from the dead, climb up on a tank and harangue the crowds *in support of Gorbachev.* The loudmouth clambered onto the tank and, in the hoarse voice of a drunken boxer, delivered his speech in favour of resistance; and the people had rallied to him, the army had deserted the hardliners. Democracy – which in this case meant delivering the empire into the hands of thieves and criminals – was saved. But Yeltsin had saved Gorbachev the better to crush him completely. On national television he forced Gorbachev to admit that his own ministers had been behind the coup and to replace them with Yeltsin's men, leaving Gorbachev with only a fig-leaf of power. Yeltsin had proved to be the stronger. Alcoholic, easily influenced, but stronger. Most of the time his advisors manipulated him like a puppet, but every now and then the fighter in him would stir, the broken-nosed brawler who knew how to lead his people.

Yes, there had been unforeseen events, but they had triumphed: Yeltsin was still in power, master of the largest country in the world, a sprawling continent of boundless energy resources.

If Yelstin was master, his advisors were princelings. And now they had to be rewarded. And so came the time of thieves. All those close to him, all his advisors, all those who, by hook or by crook, could find a way to loot the empire set themselves up in business and fought over a plunder unrivalled in history. A few hundred men helped themselves to a treasure out of the Arabian Nights, a treasure no fairy-tale sultan could even have dreamed of. For a song, making the most of subsidised prices thirty or forty times below world market rates, they made off with vast reserves of gas, oil, diamonds and metals. These men came to be called oligarchs and the West marvelled at their wealth and their vulgarity, putting them in the same category as the *nouveau riche*, oblivious to the criminal source of their vast riches. At such prices, even the idiot on a corner with a begging bowl could have become rich as Croesus: these men were buying oil for one dollar a barrel and selling it for thirty dollars!

But the struggle to be a part of this little circle was vicious. And Litvinov was among the fiercest fighters. He had always wielded considerable influence over Yeltsin and, from the first, had never strayed from his strategy: establish Russian sovereignty, eliminate all opponents including Gorbachev and set Yeltsin up as master. He was consistent. While others were still thinking in terms of the empire, of Yeltsin and Gorbachev ruling together, of liberalising the regime, Litvinov had already put the past behind him: from the ruins of empire, he insisted, a capitalist Russia would rise. And this is what happened. At the time of the August putsch, Litvinov had been on all fronts, fighting the power of the KGB every inch of the way. He resisted everything: pressure, threats, promises. He played the Yeltsin card. No one quite understood why, since it was obvious that he had never been moved by idealistic motives, but he dug his heels in, displaying a mixture of patience and ruthlessness. He was everywhere, at every meeting, however important or trivial. He sat at the table, fist clenched, his massive bulk bent double, spoke rarely but always succinctly, he was resolute, unshakeable. A fighting bull respected by all. One by one his rivals were eliminated or sidelined to minor roles while he had become Yeltsin's primary advisor. The man of dirty deals and low blows.

And Litvinov had become master of Russian oil. Yeltsin entrusted him with the major Siberian reserves. He was now the head of the largest company in the country and one of the richest men in Russia.

Litvinov dismissed Lev as 'a pencil-pusher' but he found it impossible to sideline his chief rival completely. Lev was too useful. True, he did not have Litvinov's decisiveness, the almost incredible combination of self-assurance and ruthlessness. But he was much more intelligent and Yeltsin, like everyone else, knew this. The redistribution of power he had negotiated with Gorbachev's people was proof in itself, as was his ability to get Yeltsin elected President before the introduction of universal suffrage. People needed him. Unbeknownst to him they mistrusted him for obscure reasons that had to do, not with his loyalty, but with an almost imperceptible aloofness. The disquieting sense that, unlike the others, he was not wholly engaged in action, in power. 'A pencil-pusher.'

And yet in the division of the spoils of empire, Lev had fared rather well. Unlike Litvinov, the pencil-pusher did not get the choicest cut. But from the bloody carcass, he managed to steal a meaty haunch with sufficient oil reserves to create ELK, the tenth-largest company in the country. Like the other oligarchs, he stood tall as gold rained around him, and like them he bought a palace in Moscow and a Mercedes 600. Like them, he could buy a restaurant simply because he liked his meal. Like them, through the miracle of money, he could fulfil his every whim by simply clicking his fingers. And, like them, he had been invited to Litvinov's triumph, to the lavish birthday celebration intended to crush Yeltsin's ministers and advisors by its sheer opulence.

Women of miraculous beauty glided about the room; the most miraculous of all sat next to Litvinov, attesting to a power that could even buy beauty. Lev thought of Elena, who had refused to accompany him since she despised Litvinov and all the oligarchs. She had become a teacher, though it meant her yearly salary amounted to what Lev earned in a couple of hours, because her independence was important to her and she was happy to be working, to be thinking. Lev, even as he suggested she give up working, was proud of her, as though through her he preserved some part of his past. Like most Russians, she considered the oligarchs to be thieves but she never thought too hard about her husband's case. Lev seemed to escape her opprobrium.

Greeting a former councillor whose career had been less

meteoric than his own, Lev noticed the plates were made of gold. 'I flaunt therefore I am,' thought Lev. On the tables were bowls piled high with caviar, tall granular peaks of translucent purplish black, a nod to Litvinov's little sideline on the Caspian buying caviar from fishermen for a few dollars and reselling it in the West at a 100,000 per cent profit, all the while depleting stocks of sturgeon. The oligarch was blessed with a boundless imagination, a limitless ability to plunder. Russia was being bled dry.

Litvinov came over to Lev.

'Good of you to join us, councillor. The party should be magnificent.'

Litvinov had gained a lot of weight and lost a lot of hair.

'I don't doubt it,' said Lev. 'You always did have a talent for doing things on a large scale.'

'You can say that again,' Litvinov gave a booming laugh. 'A very large scale!'

The woman standing behind him laughed too, just for the sake of it. Lev smiled politely. Litvinov continued to circulate, welcoming newcomers.

The champagne was being served by two waitresses in short skirts, who, though young and very pretty, were less striking than the tall, extravagantly dressed blonde women now gradually moving in on the men in the room. Lev took a glass. He noticed one of the women looked a little like Elena but with blonde hair.

Seeing his look, the woman came over to him.

'Good evening, Councillor Kravchenko.'

'You know me?' Lev asked.

59

'Who doesn't know Lev Kravchenko, one of the most powerful men in Russia?'

This unalloyed flattery pleased him.

'And your name is?'

'Oksana.'

'How do you know Litvinov?'

'Knowing the most powerful men in the country is part of my job.'

'And what is it that you do?'

'I bring pleasure to the most powerful men in the country.'

'A noble profession.'

'I think so. Aren't you tired, Councillor? Tired of the constant struggle? It can't be easy having to constantly fight to stay at the top, to remain number one. Don't you ever feel in need of relaxation?'

'Of course,' said Lev, 'but I'm married.'

'Of course you are, Councillor Kravchenko. To the beautiful and brilliant Elena, the esteemed professor of literature. An exceptional scholar. I would have liked to study with her.'

'I see you know all there is to know.'

'As I said, it's my job. And the fact that you're married does not pose a problem. All the powerful men in this country are married, but they still need to relax. They are fighters. They have the right to a little pleasure too.'

Her voice was languorous and yet she sounded slightly mocking.

'So this is an offer?' said Lev.

'A formal proposition.'

'Am I rich enough to keep a beautiful woman like you happy?'

'Very few men in Russia are,' said Oksana. 'But you are. And I'd like to add that for me, spending time with one of the most brilliant and handsome men in the country would undoubtedly be unforgettable.'

This time, she really was teasing him. Lev laughed.

'I'll give it some thought, Oksana. I've never had a proposition so tempting.' He added, 'Or so candid.'

'Don't think too long, Councillor,' said Oksana, gliding away, 'that weariness might become too great, too overwhelming . . .'

She gave a little wave.

'This is what Russia has become,' thought Lev. 'A country of thieves and whores where anything can be bought, where even the most beautiful and intelligent women can be had if you're willing to pay.'

The women circled their prey. One by one, the men were cornered. They drank the champagne, wolfed down the caviar, bared blackened teeth and slipped rough paws round the women's delicate waists. They had hit the jackpot.

Lev studied the bodyguards. Three hulking men with shaved heads, guns bulging in the left-hand pockets of their suits. Gang rule. Even the police force had been destroyed. Private police forces had to be created. The State and justifiable violence? Which state? What justification? Everything had been destroyed. Force was necessary. They were nothing more than state-of-the-art warlords, plunderers who had appropriated the empire through violence and could survive now only through violence. Overnight, the whole edifice might crumble. It needed only someone more powerful to appear. Someone more cunning, more violent. Hence, they all had the same goal: to steal money and spend it by the million, by the billion. To amass fortunes and squander them. To put their money in offshore tax havens, in the Cayman Islands, Switzerland, the Channel Islands, before a change of government changed everything.

The men in the room got to their feet. Hands abandoned caviar spoons, slipped from around the women's waists, each lifting a full glass. On a stage that towered over the assembled company, Litvinov picked up a microphone.

'Thank you, my dear friends, for coming to help me celebrate my birthday. Fifty-three. Life begins at fifty-three, it's the time when a man begins to enjoy the good things in life, the fruits of his labours. A time for family and for dear friends.'

His every word was tinged with his distinctive sarcasm. His guests, all of whom he had wronged at one time or another, took it in the spirit it was intended.

'To those of us who have given so much to our country, I would like to propose a toast to our Holy Mother Russia! To the country of our ancestors freed from the yoke of Communism!'

They raised their glasses.

'To Holy Mother Russia!'

'I'd like to propose another toast,' Litvinov went on, 'a toast to someone without whom none of this would have been possible, someone who cannot be here tonight because he has urgent business abroad, but who is with us in spirit. To the man who made our fortunes, Boris Yeltsin!'

They raised their glasses.

'To Boris Yeltsin, the man who made our fortunes!'

'And lastly,' Litvinov said, coming to the front of the stage, 'let us raise a glass to our God.'

The guests looked at each other, dumbfounded. The oligarch took out a thick wad of bills and waved it.

'To our God, the Almighty Dollar!'

He took out a lighter and torched the wad of bills, which quickly caught, and soon Litvinov was holding only a flame, which he contemplated with a sort of grave joy. A dozen people in the assembled company also pulled out wads of money and set them alight. Litvinov tossed the burning sheaf of banknotes on the ground and stamped it out.

'Now let's party, my friends! The drink is flowing, the women are stunning and we can do anything we please. This is our day!'

Lev had seen enough. He ventured into the night. He considered walking for a while, but no sooner had he stepped outside than his two bodyguards approached as the car silently drew up.


Matthieu became Simon's flatmate in the terraced apartment. Their timetables were very different. Simon worked during the day at his laboratory while Matthieu, who handled PR for a nightclub called Le Miroir, was only just surfacing when his friend came home at night. People found it somewhat strange to see how easily this elegant bourgeois Parisian, raised in the finest neighbourhoods and educated at the finest schools, melted into the very different world of the nightclub. But though his elegance and gentility gave him a certain air of superiority, deep down Matthieu was a creature of instinct with savage urges. Both men – one in the sterile, cold, colourless setting of the laboratory, the other in the pulsing pandemonium of a nightclub – had found the ideal environment in which to thrive. On the face of it, it seemed nothing short of miraculous that two such different people could share a flat, but it was their differences that brought them together: Simon, the introvert, was fascinated by Matthieu, the womanising extrovert who, through some vestige of innocence, was extremely fond of this maths geek who had the good taste to admire him. He relished this admiration all the more because Simon was a graduate of the prestigious École Polytechnique while he, Matthieu, had never even got his degree – a glaring lapse in the eyes of his bourgeois family. He had enrolled to study law, but he was one of those people who see no need to work unless compelled. He could read and write, was bilingual thanks to his English mother, and his education – in his own opinion – was more than adequate. So he quickly abandoned his studies and moved into PR, a profession for which he proved to have a remarkable flair. All the more so because, as he defined it, Public Relations was a wide brief: he considered clubbing to be PR work, since he invariably found new contacts to add to his address book. When he was taken on by Le Miroir, he invited his friends, a raft of casual acquaintances met while clubbing, organised a number of moderately successful marketing exercises and indulged the journalists and the starlets. And it must be admitted that his talent for having no job – no one would have imagined that the friendly, irrepressible young man clapping them on the back was doing so out of self-interest – verged on perfection.

Matthieu wanted to celebrate moving in to the terraced apartment. Being an expert in such things, he decided to do something *quirky*, something that had nothing to do with Simon or with himself. He settled on a Moroccan couscous. He talked about it to their cleaner, a young Moroccan woman, who assured him she made the finest couscous in the city. Being both wary and a connoisseur of couscous, he insisted on a sample. Convinced, Matthieu sent out invitations to his friends, as did Simon, though he was more anxious about the results.

And so one blissfully sunny Saturday in June, as three Moroccan women took over the kitchen, from which wafted intoxicating smells, two civilisations collided: the Matthieusians and the Simonians. Solemn, serious, somewhat dull creatures came face to face with neurotic, superficial fashionistas.

After some attempts at arranging things, like an artist arranging forms in a disastrous composition, Simon quickly realised that the guests were not mingling. One side of the living room was a sea of shapeless T-shirts and jeans, the other a riot of garish colour. Overcoming his crippling shyness, he forced himself to go over and join the Matthieusians.

'God, look at all the spotty geeks . . .' he heard someone say behind his back. 'It's like an IT convention.'

He turned round.

'Would you like a glass of champagne?' he asked a guy with a shaved head who stared at him surprised.

A gulf opened between the two camps, a gulf which Matthieu and Simon courageously crossed and recrossed.

The doorbell rang. Simon went and opened it to find a member of his own camp who, strangely, was accompanied by a graceful young woman.

'Welcome!' he heard Matthieu call from behind him. 'Pretty girls get special treatment here!'

The Simonian started slightly but the girl next to him smiled.

Matthieu had already taken her by the arm to show her around the apartment.

'She your girlfriend?' Simon asked his friend.

'No, just a friend, but who the hell's that guy? He swooped on her like a vulture.'

'That's Matthieu, my flatmate,' Simon said, a little embarrassed. 'He's actually a nice guy.'

Face flushed, the Simonian stepped into the apartment. Matthieu had clearly scuppered his plans. Simon took his coat, doing his best to compensate for this awkward first impression.

A few moments later, the couple were back.

'Julie loves the apartment, Simon. I think she's already planning to move in,' Matthieu teased, laying a hand on the woman's shoulder.

'Thanks, but for now, I think I'll just stay for the party,' she said.

Julie and the newcomer, Nicholas, went into the living room and, miraculously, stood right in the middle, between the opposing camps, in the yawning gulf, as though they belonged there. Simon was happy they had come. Not only did he find Julie pretty, but Nicholas, with whom he only had a nodding acquaintance at the lab, was much more relaxed than he had expected. He chatted to the Matthieusians. Nicholas joked that, having spent his whole career working on abstruse subjects nobody could understand probably explained why he was awkward and alone at parties. In fact, he added, it probably explained why he didn't get many invites any more.

Talented and self-deprecating, thought Simon. Emphasise your strengths and then make fun of them. He went over to Julie whom Matthieu had abandoned for a moment.

'You got everything you need?'

'Absolutely. The place is fabulous. All those terraces . . .'

'Would you like me to give you the tour?'

He was astonished to find himself so effortlessly suggesting the idea.

'Matthieu already gave me the tour, but I'd be happy to take it again.'

Simon ushered her through his bedroom to the largest of the terraces, which was crowded with guests. It was dusk, though the sky was still light. This was his favourite time of day.

'It's fabulous,' Julie said again. 'Matthieu told me you were the one who found the apartment.'

'I walked into the estate agents and I said "Find me terraces", and they found me terraces.'

'You only had to ask.'

'Exactly.'

'So you work in the same lab as Nicholas?'

'Yeah.'

She hesitated.

'And you went to the same university?'

'Yes. We were in the same year at the École Polytechnique.'

He tried to find the appropriate tone, simply stating a fact, eager not to sound pretentious. For once in his life a pretty girl seemed interested in what he did.

'That's impressive,' she said, smiling. 'I've just started my maths degree and I'm already struggling.'

'Really? I could help you if you like. You just need to get into the right frame of mind.'

'That would be great. Nicholas already offered but two

heads are better than one. You'll quickly get tired of it, take my word for it. So was Matthieu in your year too?'

'Matthieu? In our year?'

The very idea of Matthieu at the École Polytechnique was bewildering.

'No, he wasn't . . . You know, Matthieu isn't exactly the academic type . . .' Simon went on in an underhand attempt to discredit his all-too-charming friend.

'That's what I thought. He doesn't look the type to spend his nights poring over books.'

Matthieu appeared in the doorway.

'You sneaking off on your own?' he asked.

In a mocking tone he said to Simon, 'Stop trying to pull girls and go and look after your guests.'

He made it sound like a joke, though it clearly wasn't. Simon flashed him a bitter smile.

'Chatting with one's guests is a host's duty.'

The retort seemed about right. He was rather proud of it.

'I'll leave you to the tiger's tender mercies,' Simon quipped to Julie as he left. 'Call me when you've had enough. And if he attacks, just yell and I'll come running.'

Very proud, in fact. His casual tone surprised even Matthieu.

In a particularly good mood, he did the rounds of his guests, slipped into the kitchen, inhaled the wonderful spicy aromas of the two huge saucepans of vegetables, lifted the tea-towel covering the couscous.

'We can serve up in half an hour,' he said in a tone he hoped was firm and then worried it sounded officious.

'Up to you,' said his cleaning lady, radiant, barefoot. In her kitchen she reigned supreme and clearly considered her boss a fool.

A cool breeze blew through the living room. The guests had moved out to the terraces and the yawning gulf had dissipated into indifference. The guy with the shaven head was chatting to a female researcher who was staring at him too insistently, too intensely. In short, the party had begun.

When the three women carried out the platters piled high with couscous, there was a burst of applause. Everyone sat around the table on the big terrace, squeezing up to make room, passing each other plates. The skinhead, brandishing two bottles of red wine, began filling glasses.

Sitting next to Julie, Matthieu smiled at his success. Simon appeared, bent double from the weight of the huge stockpot which elicited a roar of approval. He set it in the middle of the table.

'I'll serve.'

When he had finished he went inside and checked the living room, where he found a dozen people chatting. 'No need to go out to the terrace,' he said to them, 'I'll sort you out.'

He picked up some plates and with the help of the three cooks piled them with food and passed them around.

By the time he went back out onto the terrace, everybody was eating and joking. No one had saved him a place. He considered the people. If the two camps did not quite form a harmonious whole, the food and the wine had clearly created bridges between them. In the gathering darkness, differences melted away. Simon was thrilled with his success until he saw Julie, staring into space, smiling at Matthieu who was talking to her in a soft voice, verging on a whisper, the dangerous tone of seduction. His shyness boiled over.

'Matthieu,' he said, his voice quavering slightly, 'aren't you going to look after your guests?'

His friend did not hear. Raising his voice, he said again, 'Matthieu, could you help out a bit?'

'That's what I've been doing.'

'What about the people in the living room?'

'They're old enough to take care of themselves.'

'Really? I just served them.'

'Chill, man. It's a party!'

Then, in a magnanimous tone, he said, 'Come on, join us, help us eat this delicious couscous!'

People moved up to make space and Simon squeezed in beside his friend. Matthieu turned away from Julie for a moment to liven up the general conversation. Simon sat in silence. He had nothing to say. He would have liked to talk to Julie about maths. Would have liked to ask about her professors, talk to her about his research, discuss the pros and cons of different universities, bring up her maths degree again, maybe suggest some way they might work together. He would have liked to be interesting, to be attractive. Attractive to her.

But right now the whole table was roaring with laughter at one of Matthieu's jokes and he felt so small, so drab, so boring, a dreary *lab rat* . . . Why would this beautiful young girl be interested in talking about professors and mathematical theorems? How could she talk to him without yawning?

Simon drained his glass of wine, hoping for some miracle, for a warm rush of Dutch courage.

'Anyone want more couscous?' he asked pathetically.

Nobody answered.

Reaching behind Matthieu's back, he touched Julie's arm.

'Are you okay? Would you like some more couscous?'

'Perfect, I'm all set,' she said politely before turning away.

Simon gazed up at the sky. Wisps of blue still streaked the darkness. The moon had risen. He stared at the translucent circle, longing to join the tranquillity of the stars, far from frustrations and humiliations. To become one with the heavens.

But it was not he who melted into the heavens. Some hours later, high above the party, as the evening wound down and the last notes of the music faded, as the guests sat or sprawled on beanbags sleeping off the wine, as the cooks, having tidied the kitchen, headed home with the serving dishes, happy to have been feted and handsomely paid, up on the roof terrace Julie, naked, stared into the heavens, in the passion of a fleeting embrace, quivering with the pleasure of this single, ephemeral, never-to-be-repeated evening, her eyes taking in the moon, the stars, the bright nimbus of the city lights and Matthieu's face, contorted with pleasure.

No, it was not Simon who became one with the heavens.

Sila lived in a derelict warehouse in the suburbs of Paris, in a quiet neighbourhood not far from the Bois de Vincennes. There were about a dozen people living there, and since most of them had papers, police raids had become desultory and rare. When there were raids, Sila would quietly creep down into the cellar and hide in an old oil tank. The cops, bored and tired, would try to work up a little aggression for the occasion to prove that they too could be hard men, like the Robocop units who dealt with more difficult suburbs. But they had no riot helmets, no boots. At the end of these courtesy visits, there was always someone who would shout: 'See you soon, guys. Nice of you to drop by.' At which point the cop in charge of the squad would nod and say, 'Watch it. Don't go taking the piss. And I've told you a thousand times, this warehouse isn't safe. One of these days it's going to collapse on top of you and you won't be laughing then.'

For some time, the local council had been planning to evict the residents of 14 rue de Verdun in order to demolish this dangerous warehouse which was unfit for human habitation, but two associations had complained and taken them to court and so, in spite of the mayor's aggressive posturing, discussions dragged on from one council meeting to the next. Given the usual swiftness of the law and the city council, the residents at 14 rue de Verdun could probably expect to stay for another decade. This was a good thing, because the warehouse was a convivial place, even if the makeshift communal showers and the Turkish toilets set up in one corner of the building, though they were scrubbed down every day, did not quite provide the level of comfort modern man has come to expect. The warehouse had been partitioned to create comfortable rooms, most equipped with televisions, whose only drawback was the lack of soundproofing, which meant it was impossible not to overhear people having sex and, nine months later if contraception had failed or been forgotten, the wailing of a healthy newborn baby. The best room was on the first floor where Roger lived with his wife, a Cameroonian woman of about forty with a noble, thoughtful face. Roger behaved as though he owned the ware-house – though no one knew whether he actually did – and he had picked the best space. His apartment of bare breezeblock walls, well furnished and pleasantly warm compared to the ground floor, which was freezing in winter, had lovely views over the city and the rolling expanse of the Bois de Vincennes through the huge window of what had clearly once been a large office. Sila liked to come up in winter to enjoy the warmth and thick, richly coloured rugs which Roger had acquired through one of his dodgy business dealings.

As any estate agent would have pointed out, one of the features of the property – besides being preferable to sleeping under a bridge – was its proximity to the Bois de Vincennes. After arriving on the cargo ship, Sila had got a job washing dishes in a tourist restaurant in Montmartre. Fos, who had contacts all over the world, had put him in touch with a friend whom he had asked to find the boy a job and somewhere to live. Then he took his leave of Sila, telling him, 'Don't worry. You'll be fine. I'm sure of it. You have the light.'

The exact nature of this 'light' was difficult to understand. And given Sila's fate, Fos's prediction might seem like a mocking laugh. But it is true that for a long time, Sila seemed to benefit from the light. It took Fos's friend less than a month to find the boy a room in the warehouse and a job at the restaurant. At first, Sila was grateful to his employer – he was, after all, employing an illegal immigrant – until he realised that the man was simply exploiting him, paying half the minimum wage and no social security. In short, Sila cost his boss a quarter as much as a French employee. Even so, Sila grew accustomed to his

job. He became a perfect illegal immigrant, commendable in
every respect.

But still Sila missed the natural world. Surrounded by a sea
of concrete, he felt suffocated. He took deep breaths, tried to
suck in lungfuls of air . . . but it didn't work. Everything was
so polluted, the crashing waves of grey concrete and stone were
impossible to escape. So the Bois de Vincennes was not simply
an estate agent's talking point. In these woods – though criss-
crossed with man-made paths that were often deserted during
the week - there was air, he felt he could breathe. Sometimes
one of the other residents at the warehouse would go running
with him, but who could keep up with Sila when he ran? How
could anyone measure up to that natural energy, that boundless
ability to run? Sila was indefatigable; running to him was as
natural as walking. He would set off along the paths, jogging
slowly so as not to leave his running mate behind, but as time
passed and the other runner began to tire, struggling to keep
up, Sila would suddenly take off, flying like an arrow for the
sheer thrill of the speed, crashing through thickets, hurdling
hedges. No one could keep up. 'Sila's a champion,' they said
in the warehouse. 'He shouldn't be a waiter, he should be an
Olympic runner.' And Sila would smile and shake his head,
then go back to the basement of the restaurant.

It was on his return from one of his runs that he discovered
Roger's wife, Céline, was celebrating her birthday 'upstairs'.

'Which birthday?'

'We don't know. But it's her birthday. She's been cooking since
this morning, making dinner for everyone in the warehouse.'

'Dinner? With what?'

'We don't know. It's a surprise. We'll find out soon enough.'

Sila, who was not without a certain pride in his appearance, washed himself carefully, slicked down his hair with a cream that made it look even blacker and shinier, put on his best clothes and, at the appointed hour, appeared in the apartment upstairs.

'Sila!' his hostess greeted him. 'How handsome you look. I'm honoured.'

The others laughed and poked fun at him but he didn't get annoyed, he simply sat down; he knew they all liked him. Through the window, beyond the city, beyond the motorway, he could make out the trees of the Bois de Vincennes.

'Did you have a good run?' asked Céline. 'You were out there for hours apparently.'

'Yes. I caught a rabbit.'

'A rabbit?'

'There are lots of them. They're hard to catch because they're fast and they zigzag in a way that's difficult for a person to copy. But I cut him off a couple of times and eventually I caught him.'

'Did you bring him back? We could cook it.'

'It's just a game. I let him go as soon as I caught him.'

'Sila's fast,' they whispered to each other.

They drank a toast to Céline. With a sparkling wine that tasted a little bitter but not bad.

There was a sort of philosophical serenity in the incantatory tones of the Cameroonian woman, in the stillness of her face that made even the most banal phrases seem profound. She constantly seemed to speak in epigrams, her language refined

75

and old-fashioned with classical twists as though all the wisdom of the world were being expressed through her.

People chatted. Everyone was on their best behaviour, carefully groomed and dressed to the nines, as though self-conscious at finding themselves 'upstairs' with the owners. In fact Roger asserted his status as landlord by being casually dressed in an old pair of trousers, a yellow shirt and braces.

They sat at the large kitchen table in the spacious, bright room crammed with bric-a-brac.

'I've made typical food from my country,' said Céline, 'food that is maybe a part of your own culture . . . or maybe not.'

Céline served a spicy fish dish and the smell stirred memories in Sila. He began to eat, attentive to every sensation, chewing carefully to extract from the flesh images of the past, to conjure in the spaces between flavours the memory of a fish he had once watched the Uncle fillet in the City of Nowhere. The flesh had been firm, pinkish near the backbone and had no sharp bones, only a profusion of small spines which the Uncle had patiently removed for the child. As Sila looked up, his eyes misting over, lost in this memory of the past, he saw others around him staring into space as though this humble fish had reconnected each of them with their past, with their homeland, with beginnings made half unreal by the glorious memories of childhood.

'In my country,' someone said, 'nothing worked. Everything was always rotten. Everything crumbled and every year the whole country crumbled a little more.'

He said this tenderly, as though talking about a wayward child. Then each in turn began to talk about his past.

'How did you get here, Sila?' asked Céline. 'You've never told us what happened.'

Sila sidestepped the question. He said only that he had stowed away on a ship.

'You were lucky not to be thrown overboard,' said someone. 'And to get into France.'

'Things aren't easy in France. They've gotten tougher.'

'These days you're better off going to Canada.'

And everybody nodded. 'Oh yes, Canada is the place to go.'

They talked about Canada. As it was a country none of them had been to, they had a lot to say.

Céline interrupted, her sing-song tone even more pronounced.

'That's not true. France is a good place. I'm telling you, France is good. Look at the police when they come here. They are nice, they wish us no harm. When I had my first child, I had no papers, but in the hospital, they asked no questions. France is a good place, I'm telling you. But they don't want people to know that, so they shout and they talk tough and they say they don't let anyone in. But tough talk is nothing.'

Everyone hesitated. Céline's words had an air of authority. Besides, when you came down to it, they knew nothing at all about Canada. It was simply that someone had mentioned it. They didn't care about it now.

'Anyhow,' a Congolese man said thoughtfully, 'many people still try to come here. You know about the man who was sent back? The one with the bandages?'

This was a story that had done the rounds.

'Tell the story, not everyone knows it.'

77

'This guy,' the Congolese man went on, 'he knew that people who were injured were always allowed in. The doctors never deported them, or at least not until they were well again. So this guy, he wrapped himself in bandages, he looked like a mummy, and he was being pushed in an old wheelchair. But the cops, they weren't fooled, they peeled away the bandages and the guy took off like a rabbit.'

'Like a rabbit,' someone echoed, 'wearing nothing but his underpants, running around trying to get away from the cops.'

Everyone laughed at this story that was so much like their own.

'Wait, wait. What about the man who fell from the plane . . . He was hanging on to the wheels, and when they got to Charles de Gaulle airport and the pilot lowered the landing gear he wrapped his arms around the axle and hung on for dear life, but in the end he let go and he fell from all the way up there.'

'All the way up there?'

'I don't know how high, but I know he fell, he couldn't hold on, every bone in his body was broken.'

'Broken?'

'Shattered in a thousand pieces!'

The man doubled up with laughter.

'But at least he's in France now like the rest of us. They treated him, put him in a plaster cast up to his neck, but he's fine, he's happy as Larry, they feed him well at the hospital.'

'Happy as Larry,' they all roared in unison, smiling and laughing, as though this terrible story was the funniest thing in the world.

# 6

'We need to look at the big picture. We need to start making money.'

Simon, still half asleep, hardly reacted. They were having breakfast on the big terrace. Matthieu stood up, wearing only boxer shorts, looked out over the city and adopted an imperious air.

'Money! Lots of money! We are the masters!'

Matthieu's grandiloquence when he talked sometimes verged on the ridiculous. Simon shot his friend a questioning look, wondering if he was being ironic.

'I'm telling you, I'm not going to keep working for them for ever. I'm sick and tired of working for a bunch of arseholes.'

'Arseholes?'

'Yeah, arseholes. They pay me nothing when I've given them everything.'

'Everything?'

'Everything. The contact list they've got is thanks to me, no one else would have given it to them. And how much do they pay me?'

'How much do they pay you?'

'Peanuts. And you're no better.'

'No better?'

'Stop repeating everything I say and listen. You're a great scientist, Simon. Probably the best in your lab. I'm sure one day they'll give you the Fields Medal.'

'I'm not sure about that.' Simon puffed out his chest. 'That's like the Nobel Prize for maths.'

'I'm telling you, you'll win it. But what good will that do you? You'll go on working on your little equations, you'll go on being a researcher earning fifteen thousand a month . . .'

'No way, I'll be Research Director at the CNRS taking home twenty-five thousand a month!'

'Same difference, Simon. I'm talking about a different world, I'm talking about real money, my friend. I'm talking filthy lucre. Enough money to fulfil all your desires.'

'I've fulfilled all my desires. I like my job, I live a comfortable life in an apartment I like and I don't deny myself anything. Life's fine, thanks very much.'

'You've got no ambition, Simon. I'm talking about a different world. More exciting, more thrilling. No more equations.'

'Maths is very exciting. You know nothing about it.'

These conversations, or rather these monologues delivered by Matthieu, had been happening with increasing frequency. The line of attack varied a little, but in the end they all came down to the same thing: money. Matthieu didn't have enough of it and Matthieu wanted lots. Simon could sense in his friend a dark desire, a dissatisfaction, a thirst for recognition which fired him up with this protean ambition – something all the more strange since Matthieu did not have expensive tastes. True, he liked to dress well and he liked the terraced apartment. But that was all. And yet, having no personal ambition, he wanted what other people wanted: money. The word summed up a different life, a different world, one that was indefinable but surely happy.

Simon didn't listen. Or rather he tried not to listen. But into his carefully circumscribed universe Matthieu's words trickled their acid like the vague, inchoate hope of some new horizon. The chimera of desire, that mythical and modern monster, cast its huge shadow. Simon's temperament had so many flaws that he needed to stay in his simple, abstract universe. If he strayed outside, he would be lost. But steadily the acid was eating away at the restraints . . .

'I don't know anything about it, but I can imagine.'

Matthieu, belly pressed against the guardrail, flexed his biceps.

'Has anyone ever told you you're preposterous?' said Simon.

'All the time. Dozens of girls have told me that. And half an hour later they were in my bed.'

Simon thought of Julie and felt a twinge in his stomach. 'Are you going to see her again?'

'See who?'

'The girl from the other night. Julie.'

'No. We had a good time, but she doesn't want to see me again. She said she has a lot of work. Said she likes me, but she's got too much on. And she's afraid that if she's with me she'll get nothing done. She's not wrong.'

He flexed his biceps again.

'Are you sorry not to see her again?'

'Yes and no. I enjoyed our time together on the roof,' he said with a smirk, 'I'll remember it for the rest of my life.' His voice returned to its usual emotionless tone. 'But I think it was the fact that it was short-lived that made it special.'

Matthieu lay down and closed his eyes, soaking up the sun. His body, hardened by long hours at the gym, was tanned from his many sessions out here on the terrace. But now he lay down because he could feel one of his black depressions coming on. Matthieu was possessed of a strange, convulsive energy that alternated between periods of intense brightness and bouts of bleak darkness as if a light had suddenly gone out. The same anxiety that led him to pontificate about money could sometimes crush him and leave him in a stupor. He was a creature with no foundations, constantly trying to shore himself up by flirting with women and dreaming of money.

He spent that whole day brooding, tormented by God knows what thoughts. He got up only to get a drink of water and put on sunscreen. At lunch, he barely ate and seemed agitated.

Simon was used to these moods and did not take offence. He had some work, which he did in his room, then watched the Tour de France on television. Late in the afternoon, he changed to go running. As a boy, even as a teenager, he had never played sports; for the most part he had been excused from playing since everyone thought him permanently sickly. But in late adolescence, for no particular reason, he had become much stronger and it was simply out of habit that the ageing family doctor went on writing sick notes. Simon had not become an athlete, but he found that certain things like running suited him, and in fact he got into the habit of running once or twice a week. The Bois de Vincennes wasn't far from the apartment, so he regularly went running there.

He took his Dutch bicycle down in the lift, rode out onto the avenue and down to the woods. There, after a few conscientious

stretching exercises, he began jogging slowly, paying no attention to the faster runners, who passed him, of whom there were
quite a few that Sunday. He ran for thirty-one minutes, a private
joke he'd shared with Matthieu. 'The body starts to burn fat after
thirty minutes,' he said, 'so I run for thirty-one  and burn one
minute's fat. It's not exactly like I've got much fat to lose.'

At some point, a black arrow zoomed past Simon, leapt over
a tree trunk and disappeared in a flash. The speed was incredible and astonished the various other runners in the area. 'The
guy must be an Olympic champion,' thought Simon. INSEP,
the training centre for professional athletes, was near the Bois
de Vincennes. Simon found this a satisfactory explanation. He
went on running and completed his circuit within the time
allotted. Then he headed back to the apartment on his bike.

Matthieu hadn't moved an inch. He was lying naked on
the terrace, soaking up the sun. When the sun finally began to
set, he stood up, shook himself and went to take a shower. He
walked back through the apartment, still naked.

'You could throw a towel round you,' Simon said.

'Why bother,' muttered Matthieu. 'It's not like we don't
know each other.'

Then he watched television, something he rarely did.
Surprising as it seemed, Matthieu preferred reading to watching television, and in fact he had excellent taste, much better
than Simon, whose taste in books had changed little since he
was thirteen.

Then he got ready to go to work. He did not have to go to Le
Miroir every night but frequently went just the same, though
Simon didn't understand why, since Matthieu was constantly

telling him it was boring. He emerged from the bathroom slicking down his wet hair, a familiar gesture that marked his entry into the fray. Every night was a battle to be won. Against all comers.

He arrived at Le Miroir just before midnight and chatted to the bouncers on the door. There was no queue yet, Sunday was usually a quiet night. But the club was hip enough to attract a crowd every night.

Tonight was no exception. And Matthieu Brunel rose to the challenge. He smiled, he strutted, he joked . . . He was everything he had not been during the day. He waged his daily war and it was impossible to tell whether the man who had spent all day on the terrace was merely a double or whether the real doppelgänger was this charming, beaming puppet moving easily among the crowds. In fact, there was no double, there was only this character of shifting moods and appearances in search of his reflection.

He headed down to the toilets. The stairway was wide and carpeted in red. Anyone who wanted a little peace and quiet came down here and it was always heaving. A tall, elegant young man turned to him.

'How's things?' Matthieu asked.

'Banging night. Bet you're happy.'

Matthieu nodded. A very young man emerged from the toilets, eyes shining, and high-fived Matthieu, who gave him a smile. For the past couple of months, almost by accident, and at first simply as a favour, as he put it, Matthieu had set up a coke-dealing service in the club toilets and now checked that everything was running smoothly. Le Miroir, like every club, had customers and dealers. Matthieu merely facilitated contact between the groups. In return, he made a decent percentage.

Call it a service charge. He liked the dealer, who was well-mannered and refined. Qualities that seemed sufficient to Matthieu. Who wouldn't want an upmarket dealer?

He went back upstairs. He crossed to the bar and ordered an orange juice. The pulsing strobe lights swallowed up the mass of bodies and spat it out again. He should, he thought, dive into the throng, find a girl. But, as often these days, he didn't. As often, he realised that he didn't want to chat, to joke, to do the rounds as usual. He was better off on his own. He knew that a quick drink or a trip downstairs would put him in the mood, but he found even the idea exhausting. The surge of energy he had felt as he emerged from the bathroom back at the apartment was already starting to fade. But all it would take was one drink. Just one glass of something other than orange juice. Just to get the spark going. After that, it would be plain sailing.

But he stuck to his orange juice. He did the rounds again, greeted people, shook hands. He really should go running tomorrow, he thought. Like Simon. It would be good for him. A tall, pretty girl was dancing. Their eyes met. He wanted to go over and talk to her. The problem was the first word. All he needed was the first word. Matthieu always claimed with a sort of innocent, infantile arrogance that, for him, girls were easy. Offer to buy them a drink, find somewhere to sit, job done. But tonight, he couldn't think of the first word. Serious writer's block. What was the first word? Their eyes met again and Matthieu realised he didn't need to be a great writer, just a mediocre hack, a pencil-pusher.

But he did not say the first word. He went home early. And he didn't go running the next morning.

# 7

'Mr President, you simply don't have the resources. We are everywhere. Give us the power and we will restore order in Russia and the CIS.'

Lev remembered the words on the poster he had been shocked to see on the streets of Moscow. The Russian mafia brazenly flaunting its power a few short years after the collapse of the police state.

Communism had crumbled and the instruments of power had not survived. The Red Army's vast resources had been sold off to conflicts around the world by corrupt administrations, arms dealers and the Russian mafia while former KGB agents sold their services to the highest bidders, often joining the gangs. The black hole. Here was the black hole again, engulfing vast swathes of the former empire, breaking down borders, depleting resources, swallowing up men and souls in a universal entropy.

And now here was this fat, half-bald man, head shaved, standing in front of him, the embodiment of the shift of power. Here he stood in Lev's Moscow office, in his tower, amid all the trappings of power, in front of Lev's staff, making this dangerous proposition without a flicker of hesitation.

'I could have you kicked out. I could call my bodyguards.'

'Of course, Councillor Kravchenko,' the man said, smiling, 'but I'd simply come back through the window.'

On his thickset face, the smile was a rictus. 'A wrestler,' thought Lev, 'they seem to have a lot of them.' He remembered the wrestling tournaments he used to go to with his father, a fervent enthusiast. He had stared in admiration at these colossal men with their scars, their heavy, lumbering strength capable of extraordinary speeds. These days, he was meeting many of the idols of his childhood. But there was nothing admirable about them any more.

'And why would I trust a Chechen?' asked Lev.

'I anticipated such a question, Councillor, though, if I may say, it does you no credit. The first reason is simple: Chechens are highly competent, a fact recognised around the world.'

'They've flooded Western Europe with cocaine, amphetamines and ecstasy,' thought Lev, 'they're in every nightclub.'

'We can offer you absolute protection,' the wrestler continued. 'Private security firms, as you know, are not always very trustworthy. They can be poorly organised, too small and employ individuals of a somewhat flexible morality.'

'Whereas you on the other hand are of the utmost integrity?'

'Absolutely,' the man said without a trace of irony. 'We guarantee our clients' security at the risk of our own lives.'

On this point at least, Chechens had an excellent reputation, so much so that they had sold Slavic gangs the right to use the term 'Chechen' as though it were a franchise.

'So we come to the second reason, which is ... more delicate,' the man went on. 'But everyone knows that Councillor Kravchenko is a man of great delicacy. It concerns your friend, Councillor Litvinov.'

'What's the connection?'

'Everyone also knows that your friendship is . . . tenuous.'

'I still don't see the connection.'

'Of course you see the connection, Councillor, you see it perfectly clearly. You simply want the fat oaf in front of you to spell it out. You want to see the fat oaf getting in deeper. You are familiar with your friend's *krysha*?'

'The Slavic Brotherhood.'

'Our most serious competitors. They are tough, organised men with intelligent leaders.'

'Yes, and they're Russians. Why shouldn't I go to them?'

'Go to the men who protect your friend, the men he pays so handsomely they have raised an army for him? Would that not be a little dangerous, Councillor? After all, Litvinov's means are virtually limitless. And he is a personal friend of President Yeltsin. Put your trust in men in the pay of such a tenuous friend? That seems to me a very dangerous course of action. Whereas if you put your trust in the Chechens, the enemies of the Slavic Brotherhood, you can put yourself entirely in our hands. Your interests are our interests.'

Lev studied the man.

'My interests? With the sort of money you demand?'

'Of a man such as yourself, Councillor, we demand nothing. We are simply proposing an alliance. We consider the sum we ask fair compensation for our services. After all, it is a matter not only of ensuring your personal safety, but also that of your various businesses, including those projects . . . currently in development.'

'They really do know everything,' thought Lev. The poster was right: they were everywhere.

'I'll think about it,' he said.

The big man got to his feet, deferentially saluted and left.

'Protection rackets now. There's no limit to how low this country can sink. And they have the gall to take me on. Oh, they sound servile, but the results are the same. And what choice do I have but to accept their little proposal of marriage? There's no state any more. Litvinov has already made his marriage of convenience; everyone has made a pact of some sort. But how do I know that the Chechens won't bleed me dry?'

More than 800,000 men worked for security firms all over the country, mostly in Moscow and St Petersburg. They had usurped the powers of the police, who were incapable of carrying out their role. They enforced the law – at the cost of countless murders. They made their presence felt by any means necessary. Sometimes however, as with Litvinov, people approached them to create a private army, partly to protect themselves, partly to muscle in on other people's territories.

'Warlords. Armed thugs trying to invade rival kingdoms – though these days the kingdoms are multinationals. It's the Middle Ages.'

Lev went home to his Moscow palace, the former palace of Prince Ehria. Oligarchs had replaced princes. Outside the railings stood two men. Bodyguards. They would have to be replaced. He'd have to make the Chechen gorillas wear suits instead of their hideous tracksuits and baseball caps. A Russian resorting to Chechens . . .

Standing motionless a short distance from the bodyguards was an elderly man, a beggar with a long black coat and a walking stick. Lev asked the driver to stop next to him. Through the tinted window, as the car purred gently, he contemplated the man silently, with a sort of dreamlike attentiveness. He contemplated the man's pallor, the deep furrowed wrinkles, the hungry face consumed by misery. A victim of neglect, but most of all of self-neglect.

'A *muzhik*,' thought Lev. 'A character straight out of Tolstoy. This country has gone from being an epic to a seedy thriller with gangs and criminals and militias. But the *muzhik* remains, still exploited, enslaved, humiliated.'

He rolled down the window. The old man looked up, his eyes weary and clouded by cataracts. His head swayed, trying to make out the person in front of him. What could he see? What could anyone see in Lev Kravchenko who, even after a hard day at work, presented an expression of icy perfection, as though it was vital to reveal nothing, as though his safety depended on the poker-face, the perfectly knotted tie, the immaculate white shirt with its starched collar?

For a moment, the two faces remained motionless, facing each other. Then a hand appeared, opened, placed a banknote in another hand, and the tinted window silently rolled up again as the car drove towards the gate, which was already opening.

Lev got out, walked up the steps to the entrance. A maid took his briefcase and he headed into the living room. Elena came over to him, wearing a somewhat artificial smile. As so often, he pictured her as the student she had been, and as so often dismissed the image because the Lev he had been back then no longer existed either. Or rather he no longer had the right to exist except in the ghostly form of a dream tinged with remorse. A sort of rain inside him, the drizzle of memory, persistent and a little sad.

Elena kissed him. She was wearing a black dress. Lev thought of the beggar's long black coat. Elena was always elegant, always dressed up to greet him.

'Good day?' he asked.

He knew he had to start the conversation. Their relationship required these platitudes, the seemingly futile words that began the process of bringing them together again, like the flourish of a proffered hand before a dance, words that were all the more necessary since their days were utterly different, especially given that he had just had a Chechen gangster in his office. What had she spent her day talking about? Which French, Italian, Spanish writer? Stendhal, Rabelais, Cervantes, Dante? What scholarly interpretation had she been elaborating even as he had been trying to weigh up the threat posed by the sudden incursion of a protection racket into his life, into their lives? It was not the sort of protection racket a shopkeeper faces when some thug teaches him the harsh realities of business, but one that heralded the beginning of a dangerous and menacing alliance. A menace contained in a neck that, though meekly bowed, was like that of a bull, in a smile that, though humble, was fraught with ominous undertones. An alliance for better or worse, until death . . .

Lev stroked Elena's hair. Surprised, she drew back. He so rarely touched her . . . Usually he behaved in a cold, controlled manner that could be charming but was icy for all that. Then she came towards him. He breathed in her perfume, kissed her hair. Then he drew back with an awkward smile. She looked at him, puzzled. He nodded his head and smiled again.

'Are the children in bed?'

Always the same question, though he knew the answer. Of course they were in bed. How could they not be at this time? They had two children now. Two boys he did not see grow up. Two boys who would be strangers to him, like everyone except Elena.

They went upstairs to kiss their sons. In the palace bedrooms. Rooms so vast they were absurd. Lev thought of the two-roomed apartment where he had grown up, of the strange grey, colourless world in which he had been raised in which *things* were so scarce, so drab they seemed to wince. Now, his children had so many *things*, an orgiastic accumulation of *things,* filling the rooms with an expensive clutter that even Elena made no attempt to curb.

Elena opened the bedroom door of the older boy, Yevgeni, who was sprawled on his huge circular bed. He was breathing regularly. The boy was tall and thin, a beautiful child who looked a lot like his mother.

'Two parents watching over their child,' thought Lev. 'It's as moving as a soap opera.'

They moved on to the younger boy's room. A small cot with bars at the sides. For the hundredth time Lev thought that he did not know this child. Mikhail Kravchenko. It sounded good. But who was this boy? Lev knew Yevgeni a little, the boy had been born in a different period of his life, back when he had been one of Yeltsin's advisors, when everything still made some sort of sense. Now that every day was a struggle, now that all his energies were devoted to clinging on to what territories he had and trying to annex others, he found it terribly difficult to look at his wife's child, this helpless little creature, so fragile and so delicate. Who was this Mikhail Kravchenko? A baby, later a child that he sometimes held in his arms, a boy he rarely saw awake since he was so rarely there in the daytime. But a child he would have to get to know if he were not to have another stranger in his midst, someone vaguely familiar, someone to whom he would smile, address a few platitudes, to whom he would bequeath a part of his fortune so he in turn might carry on the struggle.

He kissed the child. His skin was soft. Then, carefully – and to some extent they were both playing a part – they stepped out of the bedroom and went back to the living room.

'Would you like dinner?'

'That would be lovely.'

The table was laid. The cook, as always, had prepared dinner but Lev did not like to be waited on by servants. Sometimes, Elena would insist on serving him. More often than not, she had already eaten by the time he got home but even so, it was a shared moment. She would sit next to him, sometimes sipping a glass of wine, and here they wove the ties of their relationship, the tenuous ties that had to be rewoven every day, not because they did not get along, nor because they no longer loved each other, but because of the ghosts.

The ghosts of their first meeting. The professor and the undergraduate. The brilliant intellectual, the young, beautiful student. The girl who took notes during Professor Kravchenko's lectures and who, after they had a drink together, fell in love with her professor. Elena was still beautiful, but she was no longer young. She was a wife and mother, she was a professor who taught at the university where once she had studied. She no longer took notes from Professor Kravchenko. In fact she did her utmost not to take notes, not to register the cynicism in his voice when he talked about his businesses.

The ghost of the professor. The ghost of a man who had never been an idealist but who joked about the empire with such caustic, such acerbic wit that Elena had thought him brave. He was not brave. Not that he was a coward, but he did not believe political courage was a valid concept because he did not believe in anything. He had not believed in Communism, nor had he any greater faith in capitalist democracy. 'It's the rule of money,' he would say, 'that's all there is to it. We've gone from being ruled by bureaucrats to being ruled by accountants. And the Russian people are neither more nor less happy.'

But more than that, the ghost of a man more cheerful, more amenable, more *alive*. Not the Hun, no, not the Hun. How could she not miss the Lev she had once known? How could she not go on looking for this ghost in some fleeting look, in his infrequent smiles, in some deft, eloquent phrase?

Lev ate in silence. Elena toyed with a glass of red wine.

'You know, I had someone try to extort money from me today.'

He said it as though it were a joke. Immediately Elena was on the alert: he rarely talked about business.

'Extort money? In the street?'

Given he was permanently flanked by two bodyguards, this was improbable to say the least.

'In my office. Easier that way, not so many witnesses.'

'Who?'

'The Chechens. One of those security firms, you know, there are lots of them. They offered to protect me. In exchange for money, obviously.'

'Did you have them thrown out?'

She used the same words Lev had used when confronted with the Chechen.

'No. Actually, it was just one guy. An ex-wrestler making a comeback. He was very polite. Couldn't have been more polite. I told him I'd think about it.'

'Think about it? They're trying to extort money and you're going to think about it?'

'Yes. Because if I refuse protection – from them or from any-one else – then we would really be in trouble.'

'What trouble?'

'At best,' said Lev, sounding detached, 'they attack the drill-ing operations or the pipelines. Though I suppose they could easily plant a bomb in the ELK Tower in Moscow. At worst, they kill me.'

'How could they kill a man as rich and powerful as you?'

Lev looked at her curiously. She was so intelligent, so inde-pendent yet here she was thinking like everyone else, thinking solely in terms of money and power.

'I wouldn't be the first,' he said. 'Berezovsky's enemies set off a bomb in the middle of Moscow as his car was passing – and he was one of the five most powerful oligarchs in the country. His driver was decapitated; Berezovsky escaped with only minor injuries. No one is safe. Anyway, I have no choice. I need to form an alliance, with the Chechens or with someone else. But I can't carry on by myself.'

'There's always a choice,' Elena protested. 'There's still a police force in the country.'

'Poor Elena,' thought Lev. 'Choice. She thinks of it in terms of something you learn at school: the nature of choice. Philosophers agree that we always have a choice so, like a good little student, she thinks it follows: we always have a choice.'

'The police are weak,' he said simply. 'But you're right. I'll take my time. Weigh up the situation.'

But that night in bed while Elena was sleeping, the word rattled around in his head. Choice. What choice did he have? He could resign, of course, he could walk away. That was the choice he had. Give up. Give up the crippling weight of business, the worries, the problems, the responsibilities. Responsibilities . . . What did that mean? What responsibilities did he really have? What exactly was he responsible for? His business? It would be swallowed up overnight. His family? Of course. But they could always leave the country. He had so much money . . . They would only need to take a fraction of it. But was that a choice? Was giving up a real choice? He wanted to carry on. He was caught up in the system and now he had no choice. Otherwise he faced defeat or death. He might win, end up in prison or wind up with a bullet in his head. That was how it was. Because things had taken a strange turn. Because his life had become the strange violence of this ruined country.

Choice.

What choice did he have?

# 8

In life, the problem is reinventing oneself. Becoming someone else. Especially since when we try to reinvent ourselves the real work begins, that of sustaining the illusion; a powerful force that compels us to go on being ourselves such that the metamorphoses ravel and unravel and we come to the terrible realisation that we are still ourselves, only more so.

And it's quite possible that the ghost of Lev was merely an illusion, that the oligarch was already latent in the professor. The irony and caustic wit were the first inklings of a disenchantment, a prelude to cynicism, bitterness and cruelty. The long process of decline.

But Lev was older than Simon, Matthieu, Ruffle or of course Sila, and business had made him old before his time, if not physically, then morally. His role as Yeltsin's advisor at precisely the point the empire blew up – at the point when the kamikaze team, believing it necessary to destroy the ancient, ossified carcass, had deliberately blown it up – had not helped.

As for Sila, he did not consciously reinvent himself because he was still young. He was content to change. He was entering into the real, becoming more ordinary. And yet his aura had not yet completely disappeared: as Fos had predicted, Sila had luck on his side. What Fos had called the light. And it is true that he attracted people, men and women, possibly by a sort of impassivity. Sila expected nothing of anyone – or of life itself. He set no store by predictions, by wishes or hopes, he simply lived. A rare talent. And this pure presence, this harmony, combined with his great beauty was like a magnet to others, especially to Westerners eaten up with frustration, tormented by unquenchable desires.

One evening when Sila was covering in the restaurant for a waiter off sick, he was called over by a man with a shock of white hair and an affected manner who was drinking at the bar.

'I've got a job for you, if you like.'

'I've already got a job,' said Sila.

'I'm the greatest restaurateur in the world. You'd be working in a unique environment, you'd be well paid and you'd truly learn the trade.'

Sila considered the man with amusement. Pretentiousness had always made him smile.

'Give it a try,' the man went on, 'you've got nothing to lose. I'll pay you three times what you're earning now.'

Sila shrugged.

'I couldn't even if I wanted to.'

The man looked at him.

'No papers, huh?'

Sila nodded.

'The President of the Republic is a regular at my restaurant. I'll have a word with him. What do you say?'

Sila tossed his dishcloth onto the counter and walked out

with his new employer. Anyone can promise the moon, anyone can claim to be on intimate terms with the President, but the man who, by some quirk of fate, happened to be having a drink in Montmartre that night was indeed one of the foremost restaurateurs in the world, and like all restaurant owners, he was constantly complaining about his staff. Sila's physical appearance and his impeccable demeanour were considerable assets. In short, the light had done its work.

So began the period of his apprenticeship: Sila studied during the day and worked in the evening. Gérard Lemerre, true to his reputation as restaurateur, artist and philanthropist – a combination that could only exist in France – became Sila's mentor, much as Fos had been but with infinitely greater means. He got his protégé a work permit, enrolled him in a hotel management course where Sila learned the business and acquired the basic knowledge he lacked. It was here too that he was first introduced to English, a language that would later prove invaluable to him. He was entering the real world.

For Ruffle, reinventing himself meant finding himself. Over and over he told the story of the promising football jock whose career had been cut short by a knee injury. A one-shot story, always the same, like the feeble pop of a cap gun. This was his life, his lie. And his whole family colluded in the story. His mother often tearfully spoke about him coming home after the accident, hobbling on crutches, devastated that his career was over. And his father, adopting a more positive tone, backed her up. 'He was a tough kid. He could have been a pro footballer, but it wasn't to be, God decided otherwise, but he went on to become a champion businessman, because he had that same fierce determination, that same fighting spirit. I've always said, life's like a football game. You run straight for the end zone and you give it all you've got.'

The problem with lies, even when you believe them, even when you revel in them, is that they become strangely, subconsciously unsatisfying because the disparity between mask and truth resonates like muffled guilt. With Ruffle, this disparity took the form of a persistent, recurring, nebulous feeling of never being equal to the task. He was a man with no Sundays. With no one to cheer him, to admire him, to praise him. With no public, no fans. He felt as though he were invisible.

If he could only get Sunday back ... It was something he couldn't quite explain, but this was the nub of it. Why did he have no more Sundays? Shoshana had stuck by him and he was proud to be with the cheerleader he had dated as a teenager, the girl with the big breasts who had cheered him from the sidelines, but her admiration, which had once fascinated him, given him confidence, spurred him on, was gone now. She still loved him, he didn't doubt that, but perhaps all they had in common was a comfortable life where money was no object, a nice house (not as big as his father's, but nice) with a pool (not as big as his father's, but nice) and a European car, a BMW (not as big as his father's, but nice). Yes, he had things, he owned things, but ... And that was the problem. *But*. A life filled with buts was a satisfactory life but was constantly undermined. Like himself. Spoiled by the bad taste in his mouth.

Maybe the bad taste came from the fact that a 'satisfactory life' was not really living. Not being Mark Ruffle. On those faraway Sundays, in the roar of the crowds, he had been Mark Ruffle and everyone he passed would say 'Good game, Mark, good game.' 'You're the best, Mark, you're the best, champ.' The intoxicating feeling of living, of being noticed.

What was he now? Mark Ruffle Jnr. On the football field, his father had been Mark's dad. In business, Mark was his father's son. Daddy's boy. Oh, he had started at the bottom, he had mopped floors, run off photocopies, made coffee. Of course. He had to work his way up, climb the company ladder on his own merit. It was taken for granted. He played along. He mopped offices that had already been scrubbed clean by workers who did not want the boss's son to think they were dirty. He had played the coffee boy with admirable sincerity. For a whole day. He had spent time as a real-estate broker and the branch manager worked him hard. Obviously. The boss had said, 'No favouritism. I don't want you treating him any different just because he's my son.' So it must have been out of sheer respect for his talent that Mark was given the best properties to sell, the ones where you only had to open the door for the client to sign a cheque. The branch manager told his boss, 'I don't know how he does it. It's like he only has to open the door and he's got the client eating out of his hand. All that's left is for them to sign the cheque.' And Mark Ruffle Snr gave a proud satisfied laugh . . .

Mark was a winner. A natural, whether on the football field or with a client. Every job. Every rung. On his own merits. He was appointed manager of the real-estate agency. Everything was going fine. He hadn't got Sunday back, but Monday was now his glory day, when he walked into his agency, got his team all fired up, got his tired employees to work.

'Come on guys, you can do it. These are your targets . . . any-one doesn't make his target gets a personal ass-kicking from me!'

And he'd laugh. Everyone laughed with him. He was a good guy, the boss's kid. A bit of a hothead but a good guy. Always got someone pulling strings for him, but a good guy. He was the boss's son . . .

Monday, Tuesday, Wednesday, Thursday, Friday, they were all Sunday now. So why did he still have that bitter taste in his mouth? Why could he still hear that *but*? Why did he still feel incomplete, like someone watching his own life, someone who has not found himself?

It is always difficult not to have a first name.

This is perhaps why he became a young father, to the delight of his own parents. It was such a wonderful story . . . Everything glided so easily through the shimmering of these perfect lives: a site foreman becomes a property tycoon, marries a dependable, faithful wife with whom he has a son who grows up to be a football pro, or would have if it hadn't been for the accident, and a pro in business who quickly proves himself and will one day take over the family business and expand it further. And now the champion has fathered a child, and with a beautiful girl too, Shoshana, yes, that's right, his childhood sweetheart. A handsome strapping child. Nine and a half pounds.

No longer his father's son but his son's father. Hearing him-self called 'Dad'. Rediscovering Sunday for someone. Through the eyes of his son. Being a former champion, a boss, a husband, a father. Accumulating the symbols of respectability. Having the house, the pool, the BMW. Strolling the streets of Clarimont with his wife and his child.

Mark Ruffle's lawns were immaculately mown, watered on spring and summer evenings by sprinklers tracing perfect arcs. The child, growing up now, loved to leap into the spray. It was one of his favourite games. The child would pass through the liquid fan, laughing at the coolness of the water, the sweep of water, making rainbows against the setting sun before returning to its usual course.

And everything glided through the shimmering.


But no one felt this desire for reinvention as keenly as Matthieu. He could not stand himself. From the beginning and perhaps to the end. He needed, like a snake, to shed his skin, his life. He would say that things around him had started to smell, to rot like a life losing its youth and its drive.

'It stinks, Simon. We have to get out of here. This country isn't for us any more. We need new horizons.'

The country stank all the more given that his dealer had been arrested. Matthieu had read it in the papers. He had been calmly eating breakfast when he stumbled on a sly, mocking article in *Le Parisien* clearly delighted at the fall of the 'bourgeois gang', as the police had nicknamed it. A nightclub owner Matthieu knew well had set up a drug-dealing racket, initially in his own club, later in other clubs. Since most members of the gang, like their customers, came from rather posh families, in locking them up the police had enjoyed a very pleasant social settling of scores. And it would be several years before they got out. One of them had been Matthieu's dealer.

'There's no decency left,' he joked to himself, reading the

paper. 'To think that he was working for the competition. How completely immoral!'

But even as he joked, Matthieu worried. He knew he could very easily have been one of them. For two months, he panicked every time the doorbell rang and hated going to Le Miroir. Thankfully the dealer kept his mouth shut.

Even so, the episode heightened the sense of guilt that ate away at him and fed his desire for change. Despite his arrogance, Matthieu constantly felt himself in the wrong, diminished, and this was another reason he was constantly boasting and trying to impress. He felt threatened by the police and, deep down, by all forms of authority. He found hierarchies intolerable and could not bear a boss's stare. Even the slightest degree of power was unbearable for him because he constantly felt guilty. While he was arrogant towards lesser mortals, sneering at servants and lashing them with a contempt verging on insult as often as possible, he reserved an almost equally surly disdain for their masters, which though less aggressive, and akin to pretension, clearly marked out the social no-man's-land he inhabited, dreaming of summits without having the means to attain them while living in a permanent fear of disparaging looks and confrontations.

But Matthieu was not devoid of character. And when he made a decision, it was final.

'We need to be in finance. That's where the money is.'

'What are you talking about?' said Simon. 'You don't know the first thing about finance and neither do I.'

'So what?'

'If you're going to work in a profession it's better to know something about it, don't you think?'

'Stop thinking like a civil servant. You're intelligent, you can adapt.'

'And why finance rather than something else?'

'Because the world changes. And because if we want to stand under the rain of gold, that's where we need to be these days.'

Simon rolled his eyes.

'You don't get it, Simon. You don't get it because you don't monitor things. The world has changed. It changed over ten years ago, but since the fall of the Berlin Wall it's become more marked. Huge tides of money are flowing around the world – legal and illegal, but money just the same. Russia has exploded, Asia is waking up, everything's changing. Even France has got into deregulation. Markets are being deregulated. Because we need money. People have got things the wrong way round, they think we should make the most of opportunities. Actually, it's the reverse: we have to make opportunities that suit us. People needed money so we found a way to create it. By throwing open all the doors, we found a way to make some cash. That's what finance is: people want to get rich and they find a fantastic way to do it, they make money work. They make money with money. We're going to get into banking.'

Simon said nothing.

'I've given it a lot of thought,' Matthieu went on. 'I'm leaving.'

'What?' said Simon, taken aback. 'To go where?'

'London. The English really understand how money works. I'm joining them.'

'But have you got a job? Anything?'

'No, I'll sort something out when I get there. I'll check things out, worm my way in and then mount an assault.'

'You're just going to desert me?'

The heartfelt cry of an abandoned child made Matthieu smile.

'No, but you have to move your arse. I've always told you you've got the brain of Einstein but the arse of a diplodocus. So I'm going to move for both of us. You'll join me later.'

'In England?'

'You know how to catch a train, don't you? I'm leaving tomorrow.'

There was a degree of arrogance about this sudden departure. Matthieu wanted to have a story to tell, the story of the determined man who is capable of uprooting himself overnight. But he was sure about it, the time had come for the snake to shed its skin. He had been going round in circles for years, late nights and one-night stands, he needed a new world, needed to be a new person. In a city where no one knew him, in a different language, he would be able to reinvent himself.

The next day, in London, when his landlady asked him his name, he answered: 'Matt B. Lester.'

And this is who he became. The abbreviation of Matthieu, the American B. and his English mother's name. A different man.

# Part Two

# 9

The man ate. The courses kept coming, graced by curious names carefully articulated by waiters: murex, tuna tataki with obsiblue prawns, lacquered pork belly, Sicilian snakes, Buddha's hand, *merinda* with rare herbs, goujons of sole in a cornflour veil, white summer truffles . . . Precious poetry. And the flavours, mingling delicate ingredients into a coherent multiplicity, melted on the tongue in explosions of flavour, constantly conjuring new subtleties.

But the man, who was about thirty, heavy-set and broad-shouldered, was as insensitive to words as to taste. He consumed this culinary bliss with complete indifference. From time to time he exchanged a few words with his partner, a young woman with a careworn expression, or glanced over at his son, a boy of six or seven wearing a baseball cap who was finding it difficult to sit still.

'That guy isn't really eating, he's just guzzling,' said Sila, coming back into the kitchen.

'And he doesn't look like a big tipper,' said another waiter.

'He's about as friendly as a rattlesnake. Not a smile, not a thank you. And the kid seems like a chip off the old block,' said Sila.

'Like father, like son,' said an elderly head waiter sententiously.

'He's not getting any,' interrupted a tall, thin, brusque waiter.

'Whatever.'

'I'm telling you, he's not getting laid. That's always the problem.'

'I'm working the Russians' table,' said another waiter as he came back in. 'Russians are big tippers and this guy, he's the jackpot.'

'That's Kravchenko,' the maître d' said gravely, 'one of the oil oligarchs. He's filthy rich.'

'Where do you know him from?'

'He always comes here when he's in France. His wife speaks very good French, actually, she teaches it.'

'A teacher?! With all the money her husband's got?'

'She's something of a genius, apparently. She does research or something . . . She told me she gives lectures at the Sorbonne.'

'She can lecture me any time,' quipped the tall thin waiter, 'she's hot.'

The door swung closed. Sila had already left, carrying a large tray.

At precisely that moment, Matt was raising his champagne glass.

'To your new job.'

Simon smiled diffidently.

'And at Kelmann. You couldn't have done better.'

It had taken a little time, but Matt's influence over his friend was such that Simon finally took the plunge. The decision had been made easier by the fact that his career at the maths laboratory was stagnating. He hadn't managed to get a post at the CNRS – and though he suspected that recruitment for the research post had been rigged in favour of another candidate, the result merely confirmed what he already suspected: he was not a first-rate academic, he would never win the Fields Medal. He was a good, maybe a very good mathematician, but would never rise beyond the level of a decent researcher. He was careful not to mention any of this to Matt, preferring to preserve his brilliant reputation, but it was what he believed.

The day he found out he hadn't got the job at the CNRS, he contacted the École Polytechnique's Alumni Association.

'I want to work in banking,' he said.

'Now that's original!' sighed a voice on the other end of the line. 'Anywhere in particular?'

'London.'

'A French bank?'

'It doesn't matter.'

'What year did you graduate?'

'1986.'

'What have you been doing up to now?'

'Maths research.'

'Oh, okay . . . so, financial engineering, then?'

'Yes,' said Simon, who didn't know what this meant.

'I'll give you the numbers of three students from your year. They're at J.P. Morgan, Kelmann and SocGen. They might be able to help.'

Simon carefully noted down the names, job titles and phone numbers.

'Good luck,' said the drawling voice on the phone. 'Polytechnique forever!'

Simon phoned J.P. Morgan where he was coolly received by a fellow-graduate who in a smug, disagreeable tone informed him that his profile was too parochial, not sufficiently international.

'You've never worked the markets, your whole life is a maths lab, you've never even been out of France. Forget about J.P. Morgan.'

He was told he would be better off contacting SocGen, who were always interested in the Polytechnique graduates. He called the Société Générale but the woman he spoke to there clearly remembered him as a nerd just about capable of spouting formulae.

'I don't think SocGen is right for you. Maths would lose a first-class researcher and you wouldn't gain anything. I don't think it would work out. You know, I think what you're doing is very noble. The best Polytechnique graduates have devoted themselves to research, not to making money.'

At Kelmann, his fellow-graduate gave him a warm welcome.

'Hey, Rimbaud! So you want to work in finance? Well, it'll make a change from reciting *Les Illuminations*, that's for sure, but I'm happy to do anything I can to help.'

Once again Rimbaud had saved him. Sometimes at the École Polytechnique, when he felt particularly isolated and helpless, unable to communicate with the other students, ill-equipped to join the casual, urbane conversations which to him seemed so Parisian, he would start reciting Rimbaud. This idiot-savant routine sometimes had him bracketed with the idiots, sometimes with the savants. His classmate, it seemed, had fond memories.

He told Simon that there were openings at Kelmann, that the financial sector was attracting the best brains on the planet and that this was just the start.

'They're buying up everyone. No one says no to the banks because they're the ones with the money and they're prepared to pay top dollar. Everyone who gets sucked into the system likes money and that's what the banks count on. They're going to get everyone, apart from the saints and suckers. But there's a hefty admission price to pay.'

'How do you mean?'

'First off, Kelmann is very particular, they'll scrutinise you like you've never been scrutinised. You'll have to pass a series of gruelling interviews and, take my word for it, even then nothing's guaranteed. On top of that, to make senior grade you'll have to work like you've never worked in your life, even for the Polytechnique entrance exam. You can kiss your private life goodbye.'

'That's handy, I haven't got one.'

'Perfect. Lastly, and this might be a sticking point for a poet like Rimbaud – you have to accept the rule of the game, the single rule.'

'Which is?'

'Money, money, money. Making money for the bank, making money for the team, making money for yourself.'

'I'm no Rimbaud. But then again I can't say I'm obsessed with money.'

'Okay, first, that's something you keep to yourself. You never admit it in interviews. Second, you say that now but in a couple of years, you'll be like the rest of us. Money will be the only thing you talk about. You'll be constantly talking about the level of your positions, thinking about your bonuses, you'll be a money-making machine. Either that or you'll be out on your arse,' concluded his mentor.

Simon worked on his English in preparation for the interviews. The bank had done some research on him, talked to his fellow Polytechnique graduate, scrutinised his career, grilled him about concrete examples. Bizarrely, he came through it all with flying colours. Perhaps it was the years spent with Matt, and Simon's chameleon-like efforts to be more like his friend, to emulate his quick-wittedness, his poise. He surprised himself. Without being brilliant, he managed to answer satisfactorily – without blushing and in English – questions that would previously have left him speechless. Only one question genuinely flustered him: an elderly man in glasses asked pompously whether he played sports. Simon managed to stutter that he loved sport.

'Do you row?'

He stammered that he had rowed a little but that he was very interested in it as a sport. The old man had gone on staring at him as though waiting for some revelation.

The final interview was conducted by a man and a woman barely older than he was. The woman, who was English, questioned him about his mathematics research. He was surprised to discover she completely understood his frame of reference and followed up with more technical and probing questions. The interview was becoming an exam.

After twenty minutes, she said: 'Welcome to Kelmann. You'll be working on my team. Together we're going to do great things.'

And this was how he and Matt, having come back to Paris for the weekend, came to be celebrating his new job at the restaurant. Simon took a small sip of champagne, thinking that at these prices he needed to savour it. He felt happy he had lived up to his friend's expectations but – and this was more surprising – he also felt a certain pride. He had been *chosen*. He took more pride in this than he had when he was accepted at the Polytechnique because, though the entrance exam had confirmed his aptitude for mathematics, it was not as though the Polytechnique had specifically chosen *him*. And in fact, in his years at university, it was obvious that most people thought of him as a likeable half-wit, just as they had back in school. And girls hadn't paid him any more attention. But now a girl – and a pretty English girl at that – had chosen *him*. And it was his personality, he thought, that had made it possible for him to get through the interviews. He had been able to answer, to persuade, in a word, to seduce. He, Simon Judal. The spotty boy in glasses sitting in the front row near the blackboard. He was very much his aunt's nephew, he thought, feeling pangs of guilt that he hadn't been to see her for a long time. Now here he was, wearing an Armani suit, rich with the proceeds of a salary he was yet to earn, treating his best friend, the most fascinating man he knew, to a meal in a restaurant whose prices were obscene. The ballet of waiters traced a sinuous curve around him, eager to satisfy his every desire.

At the next table was a foreign couple. Simon was more or less sure the maître d'hôtel was speaking to them in Russian. A short man, with a woman somewhat taller than him who was now chatting pleasantly to the waiter.

In fact Elena, who made a point of speaking in French, was telling the maître d'hôtel that they loved Paris and that whenever their work brought them to France, they always made the most of it and spent a couple of days in the city, and always had dinner in this restaurant, which was their favourite thing of all. And the maître d'hôtel, overjoyed yet solemn, not knowing how to express his contentment, wandered off with a rictus he intended as a smile but looked like the ecstasy of suffering, like Saint Sebastian pierced by arrows of pleasure.

Elena had been invited to contribute to an international symposium at the Sorbonne under the evocative title 'The Fortunes and Misfortunes of the Balzacian character in European literature'. Though not on the level of Tomashevsky, Bakhtin and Russian literary critics of the past, Elena was nonetheless a good researcher, and most of all she had exceptional charisma, which meant she was much in demand at university seminars. Everyone knew she was extremely rich and that fact alone filled the researchers with awe and, bemused by her presence among them, they vied with each other to sit next to her. This Russian woman who was something of a mystery, since she was the wife of one of those men with obscure fortunes who had emerged from the ruins of the empire, was like something out of a novel. They imagined terrible crimes and reprisals, and those few who had been introduced to the poker-faced and perfectly polite Lev Kravchenko gave terrifying accounts of him. And so, switching effortlessly between Russian and French, the foreign language she spoke best, and between Italian and Spanish or English, the beautiful critic impressed her entourage. Indeed, during this conference at the Sorbonne, which focused entirely on the greatest chronicler of capitalism, the first writer to portray, in novels of overwhelming vision, the power exerted by money and society over an individual forced to adapt or die, Elena was probably the only person who understood Balzac's works in her very core.

As the waiter presented the next course, stiff-backed, his elegant description of the food like some high-flown poem incomprehensible but pleasing to Lev's ear, Elena contemplated the squat man sitting opposite her and thought about that eminently Balzacian notion: did Lev really have to adapt or die? Obviously, Russia exhibited all the characteristics of nascent capitalism at its most brutal, and Lev, in order to make a name for himself, had demonstrated both his strength and his intelligence. But at the same time, was he really obliged to adapt? He had pre-empted things, he had wanted to work with Chubais, Gaidar and Yeltsin, he had taken his share of Russia's riches. Of course his pact with the Chechens, this alliance that seemed to her so dangerous and which she had repeatedly warned him against, might be considered Balzacian given Lev's insistence that he had no choice, but surely he had willingly got caught up in the system years before? Wouldn't they have done better to stay in their modest little corner, teaching, thinking, not participating in the carving-up of the empire? They would probably have been poor but they would have had no need to adapt. Possibly some small compromises at the university, she thought, but nothing major, not the fate of the largest country in the world.

She noticed a young man staring at her. She met his gaze and he looked away, flushed with embarrassment. He had an olive complexion, an indefinable fragility. A drawn-out adolescent, scrawny, too quickly grown. Opposite him was a man of the same age, his features cruder but pleasing. The other man, feeling himself observed, looked up and held her gaze. 'A ladies' man,' she thought, 'the sort of Casanova so common in France. The playboy and his stooge.'

'She's obviously Russian,' thought Matt, 'though she doesn't look the part. Now the man on the other hand . . . he's the epitome of the Russian businessman in all his glory. But she doesn't look like a whore. Strange. A class act.'

This thought, one of the clichés he was fond of because he thought it true, was interrupted by a sudden commotion. A child had jumped down from his chair and run into the middle of the restaurant, where he stood, stock still. Then, just as suddenly – like in a farce – he dashed back to the table where his mother, a heavy-breasted woman, grabbed his arms and, speaking to him in English, clearly gave him a talking-to.

'Give him a break,' said the man sitting opposite her, 'he's just having a bit of fun. This has to be boring for him.'

The triumphant boy sniggered.

'It just isn't done,' said Shoshana.

'So what? He's not bugging anyone,' said Ruffle, shrugging, 'it's what kids do. I'm sure you were the same at his age.'

'I was not.'

'Well, I'm sure I was. He takes after his dad, that's all.'

Matt jerked his chin towards the table.

'Have you seen those rednecks?' he said to Simon. 'Incapable of bringing up their child properly.'

Simon, who understood nothing about such things, having

not been 'properly brought up', especially since he barely moved a muscle after his parents died, did not reply. Matt, who had been very strictly brought up, felt personally insulted by this permissiveness.

'And the guy's clothes! Jeans hanging down round his arse. At his age! Trailer trash like that shouldn't be allowed in a restaurant like this.'

Sila quickly stepped to one side. The boy had jumped down from his chair again and the waiter had almost walked into him. Lev watched the scene with a vague interest. The child looked the waiter up and down, then quickly dashed back to his seat. He could have upended the tray, thought Sila. What a nightmare. He imagined the plates strewn across the floor, the shame, the comments of Lemerre and the maître d'hôtel. He could even have lost his job. People had no business to bring a child into a restaurant if he couldn't behave!

Ruffle, Shoshana and their son Christopher had been visiting Paris for three days. They had done the Eiffel Tower, the Louvre, the Musée d'Orsay, Notre-Dame and Versailles, and though Shoshana had found the visits interesting, they were all tired. This tiredness manifested itself in her as a vague melancholy, in Christopher as hyperactivity and in Ruffle as a pent-up aggression. So, not wanting to start an argument, Shoshana said nothing to her son when he came back to the table. Instead, she thought about the gargoyles of Notre-Dame. She had been entranced by the soaring majesty of the cathedral but in the context of such grandeur and beauty she had found the gargoyles shocking, like a sort of lapse of taste; they had a medieval brutality and malevolence that firmly restored this timeless church to a precise and, to her, largely unfamiliar period of European history. The demonic at the heart of beauty.

She wanted to confide this thought to her husband but his attention was fixed on a young man who was glaring scornfully at Christopher. She herself felt hurt. Her eyes flickered around the restaurant, finding those of the little man with slanting eyes and olive skin; she fleetingly sought out those of the tall dark-haired woman sitting opposite him, also a mother probably, someone who could understand her, then looked back at her husband. He was crimson with rage and this worried her: though she suspected the stare was not sufficient provocation for Mark to get to his feet, but if the young man were to say something . . .

Christopher was crumbling up his bread on the table, which was now covered with little brown and white balls. She grabbed his hand and, with utter indifference, he carried on with what he was doing with the other. She let his hand drop. Immediately, as though she had released him, he leapt down from his chair and went back to his little game, getting in Sila's way.

This time Sila was not surprised. He grabbed the child by the arm and told him to go back to his seat. But at that moment a large, bellowing face appeared before him and a moment later his head exploded with pain as his nose was smashed and everything crashed to the floor with a terrifying racket.

The maître d'hôtel rushed over to Sila. Staggering, he got to his feet, took a handkerchief and pressed it to his nose. Out of the corner of his eye, he saw the man sit down again, filled with a barely contained fury that was not yet sated. He felt humiliated but completely devoid of anger, stunned by the inexplicable violence and numb with pain. Torrents of blood pulsed into the handkerchief.

Lev considered the scene without reacting. He was anxious for things to return to normal. For order to be restored and, with it, silence. Such displays of force always seemed to him somewhat ridiculous, especially in such a situation. The poor guy with the overdeveloped torso ... He wondered whether it had been wise to come out without his bodyguards. Elena couldn't bear to have them around, especially when they were abroad.

Ruffle, for his part, was still flushed with rage, filled with a combination of satisfaction and shame. He wanted to say something, to mutter something like 'Jesus, the nerve of the guy!' but Shoshana's horrified expression pleaded with him to say nothing. So he remained silent, trying to shut himself off in his gorilla-like posture, though acutely aware that the other asshole over there, doubtless a French asshole, elegant and well dressed, probably a faggot with his boyfriend, was looking him up and down with an expression that dripped contempt, the same expression that had driven him mad with humiliation. He deserved respect, that much was clear, but it was the other asshole whose face he should have smashed in, with his faggoty aristocratic airs. As for the other faggot sitting opposite him, why doesn't he just up and help the nigger instead of squirming in his seat thinking about whether he should do something? And what's the Russian woman doing staring at her husband, waiting for God knows what? Staring at him like he's got a duty to do something? The guy clearly didn't give a fuck, besides, everyone knows the Russians hate blacks, they kill them in the streets of Moscow.

Meanwhile, Sila had stumbled back to the kitchens and the doors had closed behind him.

'I told you that guy was an arsehole,' said one waiter.

'Don't make a fuss,' the maître d'hôtel interrupted. 'Nothing happened. We carry on as normal.'

'What? We're not going to do anything? Have you seen the state Sila's in?'

'If Sila wants to make a complaint, he's free to do so. In the meantime, nothing happened.'

A hotel employee got his car and drove Sila to casualty. On the way, Sila did not say a word.

At the restaurant, everything went on as normal. The waiters recommenced their ballet unmolested by the child, who sat in silence. Only Shoshana remained petrified. She did not eat, she no longer spoke, no longer thought. Overwhelmed, she stared at the gargoyle sitting opposite her, like a stone animal guzzling the food she had not touched. In the timeless structure of marriage, the yawning fracture of violence had just opened up.

# 10

The lights of the city infused the curtains with a soft glow. A thin, insistent beam breached the gap where the heavy drapes met. From the bed where Lev lay sleeping, Elena stared hypnotised at the life swelling beyond the window, the slow throb of a city that never really slept but whose energy was dispersed, separated by patches of latent darkness in areas which, at this hour, were peaceful villages of deserted streets, and focused on a few vivid, luminous spots. She could not get to sleep. She and Lev had walked together in silence, come back to this hotel suite where they always stayed when in Paris, though they could have stayed in a different hotel every time, something she would have preferred as it would give her a chance to experience other places. Other hotels, smaller, more anonymous, more charming than this *grand hôtel,* which, though elegant, was cold – a perfect example of the French monumental classical style aimed at foreigners. But she was convinced that Lev did not like France as much as he said he did, because he only truly loved Russia. In other countries, he knew the skyscrapers, a handful of monuments and museums and the *grands hôtels.* In China, in Brazil, in Venezuela, in the United States, in Saudi Arabia, throughout Europe, all over the world he knew the five-star hotels. And were it not for her, he would never experience anything else, especially since, with time, he had become increasingly indifferent to things.

She turned her head towards him. His tense face, his torso stripped of muscle. Wasn't that a poem by Ronsard? *Fleshless, stripped of sinew, muscle, pulp* . . . Ronsard, at the end of his life. But Lev was anything but fleshless; on the contrary, his body had filled out. Yes, his body was round, with round feet, round calves, a round belly . . . a rotundity so different from his former wiry thinness . . .

This evening had been a terrible defeat. Why had Lev not done something? Why had she not intervened? Obscurely, without quite understanding why, she felt that this indifference in the face of a man being beaten presaged terrible things. She took it for granted that terrible things had happened in the long years while Lev had been making a name for himself, because she despised the oligarchs and could not entirely dissociate her husband from this milieu of lies and brutality, but it was this trivial incident that had revealed to her Lev's inner corruption. A young waiter going about his job had been punched for no reason by a thug simply for trying to get his son to move out of the way, and not only had Lev done nothing, he had not even felt the need to do something. He didn't care. It seemed clear to her that if a man had been killed in the street he would still not have got involved. He would merely have registered that same disdainful contempt. True, no one had done anything, because people are naturally cowards, they go about their business, they don't want to stand up for other people, but no one else in the restaurant had shown the same utter indifference. She had been indignant, as had the young man, the man who looked like an overgrown teenager, as had many of the people in the restaurant. Only Lev had remained impassive. Lev the intellectual, Lev the professor, Lev the democrat. A man eager to get back to his dinner.

It was not fear, it wasn't even the natural reluctance to get involved. Even she had to admit that Lev was afraid of nothing. He wasn't rash, wasn't foolhardy and he often gauged the dangers of a situation, but he wasn't afraid. No, it was simpler than that: he didn't give a damn.

In the light of this incident she found herself reassessing all her husband's traits. The extreme politeness which, like his impeccable suits, she had always considered a form of elegance, she now saw as characteristic of his indifference, like a high wall set against others, against the world, a polite statement marking his retreat. I am not one of you. I am nothing but these indifferent words, a readymade mould to fit every situation. Even his sense of order, which mapped out his days, was an outward sign of a machine well-oiled and, deep down, inhuman because it did not connect to the rest of humankind.

Lev gave a deep breath and turned over. On his back, his birthmark. Elena stared at it. A dark stain. The coarse, slightly scabrous skin hypnotised her. This, perhaps, was his corruption. A dark blemish, small at first, then gradually getting larger like a single water lily constantly doubling in size until it fills the lake, suffocating all life in it. A throttling, a suffocation that, little by little, would destroy him, or at least destroy everything about him she had once loved. And if she was truly honest, perhaps the water lily was already there, already spreading out over the heart of this man, stifling his pity, his tenderness, his humanity. And in that case, what was she doing with him? What was she doing with this poisonous water lily?

Not far away, in a room at the Hotel Cane, above the restaurant where she had had dinner, another woman was also having trouble sleeping. In the shadows, she too was staring at her husband's sleeping body, a body that was not round like Lev's, but pumped and muscular – the upper body at least. She was not staring at a blemish, but at her very own gargoyle, the man she used to cheer from the sidelines of the football field, this infantile creature that, as a bubbly cheerleader, she could not help but love and even admire not realising that he was already a gargoyle in the making, a self-infatuated idiot plagued with frustrations, irredeemably infantile, slave to the pathetic demon of appearances, turning endlessly in circles in his thwarted illusions of power and greatness.

And so, high above the slow pulse of the city, a former cheerleader in rumpled socks gradually shrank back into the darkness of her feelings, as did a slightly older woman from the other side of the world, both of them staring at the dark back of a man abandoned to the sleep of folly and cruelty.

# 11

Simon loved London because it was here that a new life had begun for him. Completely by accident, since he had been perfectly happy with his previous life, Simon Judal, now known as Jude, has also reinvented himself, like a puppet slipping on the costume of a banker at an American bank. It never ceased to amaze him. He thought about it all the time. The boy with the glasses sitting in the front row. The boy everyone made fun of. The swot. He was a *banker*. And it was with the joy of a child dressing up at Christmas that in a cold, elegant boutique decked out in marble he had bought several dark pinstriped suits which he felt made the best impression, and into the pockets slipped his ivory-white business cards, which were soft and felt like cotton. In the shoe shop to which Matthieu had taken him, a salesman had asked him with a grace he found moving: 'Is this your first visit to John Lobb?'

And this loss of virginity, veiled in a highly instructive speech about the respect due to shoes, which after being worn for a day should be allowed to rest for three days, so that a true John Lobber should own at least four pairs, had fascinated him because he felt as though he had become a member of a brotherhood of initiates, probably much like those who owned a pair of Berlutis. A brotherhood prepared to spend one, two, even three times an average monthly wage on a pair of shoes. And if he felt any remorse, it was drowned out by the purchase of fifteen dazzling blue and white shirts of that silky softness that now constituted his material world.

Of course he'd found it strange that they'd changed his surname and he was now called Jude, like his nickname, his team leader having insisted no one called Judal – a name dangerously similar to the biblical Judas – could work in banking, a profession based on trust and loyalty. But after all, it simply amounted to following Matthieu's example without the domestic and psychological implications.

Every morning, like brushing his teeth, Simon with his pathological memory, recited something he'd learned years before while studying to get into the Polytechnique, which claimed that every man dreams of being a gangster. Because this was exactly how he felt when he put on his suit and knotted his tie. He would roll his shoulders a little, say good morning to Matt who, if the weather was fine, still breakfasted on the terrace – even in London, Simon had managed to find a terrace, which though not as big or as high as the Paris apartment, overlooked a beautiful, green square. Then Simon would head down the stairs – silkily carpeted as though the whole building were a single apartment and the communal areas as important as the most elegant living room – pick up the newspaper on the doorstep, carry on down the stone steps guarded by a pair of lions rampant, and find himself in a large, tranquil square in Chelsea surrounded by small houses like his. In this haven of materialism, which endeavoured simply to cosset and pamper every banker on the square (almost everyone here worked in the City) Simon felt *at home*, his every desire satiated. Nor did it feel as if he was living in the financial capital of Europe, living for and through the City, which was in the grip of a financial frenzy, drawing young people from across the continent to the Grand Casino; on the contrary, it felt as if he was living in a quaint, charming country town which smiled tenderly upon its residents like a grandmother. And here in the peaceful – and extortionate – surroundings where they lived, as he hurried towards the Tube station which would suck him and the other besuited men into the bowels of the earth, he felt exactly like the gangster in the book. He was earning money, he would earn a lot, if all went well a hell of a lot; he had a job people envied; he was part of a team who called themselves 'the Kelmann mafia' the way people refer to the 'Morgan mafia'; all this in a bank at once admired and feared, just like a gangster in the movies.

'Kelmann,' the young English woman Zadie Zale, known as ZZ, informed him, 'is not a bank, it's *the* bank.'

This is how she began her speech, before explaining that Kelmann was feared because it was powerful, because it demanded absolute loyalty, because in the Kelmann tower in Manhattan, a symbol of power were the 300 all-powerful partners, invisible, selected through a ruthlessly competitive process, who left their jobs only when invited to join the US Treasury Department where, in hushed tones, they gave the best advice. Best for the government and best for Kelmann, since no one ever truly left the firm.

'At Kelmann, in Europe at least, we're the shock troops. We're new, we're young, we're the best. We're hired to created the financial instruments of the future, the ones that will make money for the bank, make money for us, the ones everyone will imitate. We are the future. We're the ones who will dream up the derivative products of the third millennium and I really believe that when we've finished nothing will ever be the same.'

This grandiloquent but inspirational speech, which had young Zadie with her blonde curls all but panting as though in the throes of religious ecstasy, greatly worried Simon but as a team leader the Englishwoman was exceptional: forceful, charismatic and charming. Her position and her skills were undisputed. The most important trader on her team was a likeable, good-humoured American guy of about thirty called Samuel Corr, who dressed with studied elegance like a marquis at the court of Louis XIV, clothed from head to foot in the most lavish and costly designer labels. But then, in the modern world, were they not the courtiers of another Sun King, diffracted in a virtual world of bank accounts, bills, cheques and credit cards? The Money King, worshipped and magnificent, to whom, at the moment, they were lowly equerries at best but to whom, in time, they would become important vassals.

Samuel had studied at Harvard, Zadie Zale at Cambridge and Simon at the École Polytechnique. Each believed they came from the finest university in the world, Samuel because Harvard was the richest and the most famous, Zadie because Cambridge gloried in a tradition without peer and Simon because he was the result of a terrifying selection process. If all three were the products of the most elite schools in their respective countries, they were not of equal value. Samuel was a banker with a glittering future, at once charming and grasping, gifted with limitless self-confidence. He was the brokers' blue-eyed boy, and they constantly invited him to the finest restaurants. Simon, for his part, was still an idiot-savant whose talents were almost entirely in the field of mathematics. This was another reason Zadie had hired him: she had nothing to fear from him. Simon was not management material and found it difficult to manage himself. He was not permitted any real responsibility. But he could play a major role in a subordinate position because within his circumscribed domain – applied mathematics – he was quite brilliant. The real power on the team was Zadie. This woman, with her sometimes wild-eyed stare, her all-consuming ambition, was exceptional. Zadie was single – men were terrified of her, they could not compete, they found her speed and her energy at once alluring and emasculating – and she possessed a breadth of vision that Samuel utterly lacked. The man who hired her to work at Kelmann, after her decisive interview, had thought: 'She'll crush us all.' But he hired her even so, for fear she would go over to the competition, and in the secret hope that she would remember him one day.

At the end of her speech, with the panache of a film director, Zadie got to her feet, strode briskly down the corridor, flung open the double doors of the trading room and announced: 'The whole world is here!'

She was right, the whole world was here. The world in microcosm, in this hive of computers, mapping the world by translating it into numbers. The best access point to the modern world: money. Intangible digits whizzing from London to New York, Singapore or Shanghai, Paris, Frankfurt or Tokyo, clouds of numbers trailing money like swarms of bees targeting a particular area, a particular passing fad. And the men, young, rich, aggressive, and eager to make fortunes for themselves too, following the tides of the world, of money across the global currency markets.

Standing in the doorway, hesitant to cross over, Simon absorbed the sounds of the room, the shouted orders of buy and sell, the concentrated fury of hundreds of traders crowding into the space, filling the space, waiting for the slightest variance in markets round the world to make an offer, take a position.

'Go in, Simon,' Zadie said gently as one might to a child. 'This is the world, it's your world now. Go in.'

And he had gone in. He had moved cautiously, breathing in the smells, taking in the sounds, soaking up the energy of the room. He had stopped, and in a blinding revelation, understood what he was going to do. It was something he already knew, of course, but he suddenly felt it inside himself. This confusion of instincts, voices, sounds, products, places, he would crystallise just as he had done throughout his terrified childhood. Just as, after the death of his parents, he had engulfed the terror of the world with silence, projecting his fear onto numbers, so from this confusion he would create data models based on the reassuring combination of statistics and projections. He would create perfect models, calculating the lows, the highs, the volatility, the correlations, thereby providing his bank and his clients with the infallible winning formula which would protect them from all unknown factors, for a fee, naturally. Basically, he would be doing what he was best at: seeking out security in a world fraught with risk, converting fears into figures, something that was the very core of his being. Contrary to what he first thought, coming to finance after working in research was not a change, it was in fact the crucial meaning of his life. It was what he was born to do.

Though she could not read his thoughts, Zadie noticed the radiant look on his face and it reassured her in her decision. No one had wanted Simon. 'Leave him to his lab,' they said, 'he's not cut out to work in a bank. He's a complete loser.' Samuel had been brutal: 'Nice enough. Bit like a toilet. Very white.' But she had seen possibilities in him, notably a capacity for synthesis she'd rarely found even among the 'quants' – the quantitative analysts – working for her. But she was drawn to this 'toilet', to the sort of mathematical innocence, an almost childlike purity on which was inscribed – dazzlingly, in her opinion – the whole breadth of mathematics. It was equally clear that Simon would never be a team leader.

'It remains to be seen whether he gets shat on from a great height,' quipped Samuel alluding to his 'toilet' comment. This same Samuel was the first to come up to him every morning and shake his hand, nor was he being hypocritical: an uber-geek like Simon would never have been his preferred candidate, but now Zadie had hired him, they had to work with him.

In fact, Simon fitted in well with the team. The schoolboy mentality reminded him of the Polytechnique. Clever people who only ever talked trash. A mixture of sarcasm and sex. Over the weeks, over the jokes and the lunchtime sandwiches, he discovered a number of very different characters. In fact, they came from everywhere, from every walk of life, every country, and though rallied to the banner of the Almighty Dollar, they conserved something of their otherness. A Danish archaeologist barked his offers as though betting at a high-stakes table;

a Russian Hebrew scholar whispered them with an intense
solemnity as though he were risking his soul for his clients; and
an elegant Frenchman, an aficionado of the *nouveau roman*,
was reputedly one of the bank's best traders. Of course, most of
his colleagues were utterly dull, young fund managers who had
decided at the age of ten to work in banking so they could make
as much money as possible as quickly as possible. But there
were also those who had wound up here by chance, gravitating
towards the centre of the world, following the crowds without
quite knowing why. And they were not the worst, like Simon,
who had accidentally discovered a fundamental vocation.

Fundamental and quite enjoyable. Simon was among the
horde of zealots who sat trembling in front of a bank of moni-
tors and phones, their voices metallic as though tempered by
stress until they became like steel. Simon worked at his own
pace, he produced his data models, studied derivatives suggested by the team, aggregated statistics, calculated possibilities.
For every product, he assessed risk – not in the way an Indian
agribusiness client trying to protect himself against a devastating monsoon might do, but with that naive, confident conviction that what he was doing at his computer was good work.
He interpreted uncertainties, evaluated the future, examined
the variables to fit statistically rational curves.

'You're a good worker,' he was quickly informed by Samuel,
who had changed his mind. 'You should be making more
money.'

'I'm making too much as it is,' said Simon.

Samuel, assuming this was a joke, burst out laughing. He
mentioned it to Zadie.

'You should give him a pay rise, otherwise he'll leave.'

'He said that?' asked Zadie, astonished.

'Well, he was joking about how much he earned.'

'Maybe, but he's just starting out as a quant. We can hardly put millions his way.'

'He makes probably a twentieth of what I earn.'

'You're overpaid.'

'If you gave him £5k a month, I think he'd be all right. With his bonus, that would be fair and should keep him happy for a while.'

'He really said this to you?'

'Absolutely. And I felt bad for him.'

Simon was offered another £1,000 a month. He went home shaking his head.

'They've given me a pay rise! I mean, I was already earning three times what I made at the lab, and here they are giving me a rise. All this just for calculating risks on a computer!'

'And you earn nothing compared to your boss,' said Matt, 'who earns nothing compared to some of the traders and they earn nothing compared to the fund managers.'

'It's obscene.'

'No, it's irrational. Welcome to the kingdom of the absurd. Let the living begin!' said Matt flinging his arms wide.

That night, they had dinner at The Fat Duck, one of the finest restaurants in England, not far from London.

# 12

Mark Ruffle would probably never have become a father had it not been for Dario Fesali. He was already the father of a small child, but he would not have been a father as he understood it, meaning a man with a fully-fledged identity, including a first name, were it not for the help of Fesali and of television.

At the Ruffle house, the television was permanently on. It was both a background noise and a familiar, even a familial presence. Mark and Shoshana's son Christopher, who naturally had a TV in his bedroom, was an addict and only in front of the screen did his face, which bore the profoundly vulgar expression of all spoiled children, light up. It was this addiction that saved – or possibly doomed – his father.

Arriving home from work one day, Mark saw a man on TV with an over-tanned face and white hair whom he mistook for Hugh Hefner, the founder of *Playboy*, a magazine he liked to read. Doubtless both men had the same ageing vitality, a product of greed and cosmetic surgery, but it wasn't Hugh Hefner, it was Dario Fesali.

The name Fesali, which means nothing in Europe, first became famous in the USA in the mid-nineties, only to become infamous some ten years later. Dario Fesali was a man of about sixty, of Italian origin and, as he liked to remind people, he was the son of a grocer and a child of the Bronx, and now CEO of D.F. Investment. But above all he was 'The Man who Built the American Dream'. And it was when he heard this motto that Mark became a father and the begetter of his own name. The moment he heard it, he found his true religion and through it, his identity.

According to the news report, Fesali was the man who had started the subprime property market in New York back in the late '60s. The principle was simple. The ambition of this admirable philanthropist was to put the means of home ownership within reach of the poor and the minorities who had no capital of their own. To do this, the loan was made by the bank in exchange for the title deeds to the property. And since property prices kept rising, the borrowers grew rich. At worst, if they couldn't make their payments, the bank would sell the property and, prices having risen in the meantime, the lenders benefited. Of course, since risk was an important factor for the lending establishment, it felt compelled to charge very high interest rates, especially as there was no cap on the rate charged in the United States where usury limits do not exist.

D.F. Investment was an unqualified success. It had a six billion dollar turnover, tens of thousands of employees, hundreds of area offices offering loans across the whole of the United States and making healthy profits. In fact this documentary about Fesali had been shot on a vast estate in California, in a house whose living room made Ruffle's father's lavish mansion look like a garden shed. The camera, lovingly lingering on the trappings of financial success, followed him as he went about his business, exploring his vast limousine with its cream-coloured seats, his private jets.

Ruffle listened spellbound as the man talked about the little kitchen table back in the Bronx in the 1960s where he had
started his business; then suddenly Fesali's catch-phrase, the
insistent leitmotiv that had made him famous – like the 'little
phrase' from Vinteuil's sonata that haunts Swann in Proust's
*In Search of Lost Time* – appeared in the brilliant sky of the
television: 'Give me your poor, your huddled masses, I want
to share my fortune with them.' And just as Swann reclined
in a thrill of sensual pleasure when he heard the famous 'little
phrase', savouring the subtle fragrant essence of the music, so
Ruffle, his boorish heir, discovered the meaning of life when
he heard his mentor's words. This base, vulgar creature whose
spiritual interest had never strayed beyond the end zone of a
football field felt a thrill as intense as that most rarefied dandy
in all of literature. And he was not stirred by the talents of some
great musician whose art, in Proust, that great tormented soul,
is depicted as the quintessence of his suffering, but by the two-
bit philosophy of a wily old fox.

Ruffle finally realised what he had to do. His vocation in
life was not to be his father's son, to take over the family business as and when his father saw fit – which would be as late as
possible – but instead to set himself up in the high-risk mortgage market. He would turn the houses and the apartments
his father had built into fabulous high-yield investments. Like
D.F. Investment, he would lend to the poorest of the poor and
become the high priest of American prosperity to everyone.

This, in the end, was what it was all about. What the former
Clarimont running back was searching for was not so much
money as a role, a voice. He couldn't stand it any longer, he

needed to find a way to talk about his football triumphs again and the interview with Fesali had just given him the words. He needed so badly to talk, to talk about himself, to have an audience, to find recognition. From others and from himself. If he pulled this thing off, he would be rich without needing any help from anyone then he too could claim he was an American dream maker, he too could welcome the poor, the huddled masses. Like Fesali he would pose, hand on his heart, and his words would coil around him like so many beautiful garlands.

From that moment, things moved quickly for Ruffle, and he experienced what was without doubt the happiest period of his life. No security and no particular authorisation were necessary to set up a loan company, he could have worked out of a shack on a patch of waste ground as long as he could find borrowers to trust him. But he didn't need to. Banks welcomed him with open arms and he found several Wall Street investors, people he'd met during his years working for his father's firm, who were happy to help him set up in business.

In 1996, with his wife and son, he moved to Miami. He had briefly considered New York but the global city, its universal appeal, a magnet for the whole world's talents and desires, made him nervous. His Fesali-like armour was not yet strong enough; behind these steel plates, as thick and tough as the football pads of his teenage years, lurked the anxieties of the uneducated provincial boy from Clarimont. He feared the eloquence, the intelligence of the big New York entrepreneurs, whether American or European. Miami was an ideal stopover between Clarimont and the world. It was a large, cosmopolitan city but bore no comparison with the gigantic proportions of the truly big American cities. A city shot through with water and sunlight, nestled in the tropical atmosphere of his childhood, bordered by swampland. And a region where, thanks to his father's wealth and connections, his name was not completely diluted by the vastness. What's more, for the first time in his life Ruffle proved to be genuinely clear-sighted. Miami was at a turning point in its recent history, midway between the ravages of the hurricane of 1992 and the property boom of the 2000s. Everything was possible, and before the construction cranes became a permanent part of the landscape, before skyscrapers, each taller than the last, rose above the Miami skyline, there were vast fortunes to be made.

Ruffle set himself up in offices of worrying size, which marked out his ambition from the get-go. He hired brokers to scour the poor neighbourhoods and from that point, anyone who was not already a client of D.F. Investment signed up with Ruffle Universal Building, the company he founded.

Over the years, Ruffle had come to recognise his father's top agents, the ones who could be friendly, cheerful and reassuring. The consummate professionals who could sell the dingiest, ugliest properties. Offering them more money than his father ever had, he lured them to Miami and at a huge meeting for ever known in the company as 'White Thursday', promised colossal bonuses to the highest performers. And being the new Fesali, Ruffle entrusted them with a mission to go into every home, into every seedy building, every hovel, and save these people in spite of themselves.

'People don't want the American dream, they sit around on their asses because they haven't got the balls to change their lives. So you're going to kick down the door of their nightmare and turn it into a dream. You'll move in with them and hang out in their shit-tip kitchen until they sign the fucking contract. You are the architects of the American dream. Thanks to you, thanks to us, these people's lives will be transformed and, as you drive down the coast to see them, remember that this is a mission, a mission to do good.'

And the brokers, seeing dollar signs flashing, kicked down the doors, and if they were sent packing they went back again the next day. Like vultures, they hung around stairwells asking the kids playing in the street when their parents would be home. Since they worked all hours, they had all the time in the world. They sensed their time had come, that Ruffle Junior would pay for their beachfront houses, their Mercedes convertibles. They sensed that the life they'd dreamed of was theirs for the taking if they could only get names on contracts. They knocked on the doors of the poor, of Blacks and Hispanics in run-down neighbourhoods, they exploited every Cuban contact they had in search of newly arrived immigrants. Then they camped out in their kitchens. They went one better than Fesali in the Bronx. They persuaded the senile, the feebs and the drunks to sign up, but they also convinced the young couples and the gullible. They talked like they'd never talked, their smile sunnier, their manner more reassuring than it had ever been in their lives. They offered thirty-year variable interest mortgages with the first two years *interest free*. Eyes fluttered at the thought of these two glorious years with nothing to pay; the most clear-sighted minds were opened and they signed up, even those who had been suspicious from the start, thinking it didn't matter, that they would sell on, that property prices were constantly rising, that they had nothing to lose. They'd sell on because trees did grow to the sky, because the world had discovered a universal winning formula, one that guaranteed everyone could be rich and sustained growth could carry on for ever. Life was a cinema screen. They had zero earnings? It didn't matter. All they had to do was sign a little contract, and two years from now, they'd earn big time. Two years in the USA was a lifetime. So what if they only earned 15,000 a year? They deserved a 200,000 dollar mortgage. And those first years weren't just interest free, they could be *payment free* if necessary. The money was theirs, all they had to do was sign. All they had to do was surrender, here at their kitchen table, finally worn down, just append their signature to the bottom of the contract. And then it was all over, all the brokers had to do was smile and say, 'You made the right decision. It's for your own good.' Then they'd have a drink, a toast to their future prosperity, their beautiful houses. And the realtors would say goodbye, close the doors behind them and dash down the stairs. Picking their way through the ravaged streets, past kids skulking on street corners, thinking it was best to get gone before they had their tyres stolen. The day was a success because the contracts kept piling up, because they'd sold the American dream by the truckload. And all this was right and good.

What Ruffle truly wanted was a transformation: he wanted it enshrined in bricks and money. His house in Clarimont had been nothing but a pale imitation of his father's wealth. His house in Miami shattered any possible notion of comparison, scotched any idea that the son would be happy to follow in his father's footsteps. Instead of a big suburban house, the Ruffle family opted for a white dream on the seafront with a vast, blue swimming pool some distance from downtown Miami. This was the word Ruffle used to described it, the only word on his lips now: 'This is my dream.'

The dream in question was wide and low, a little like a flying saucer, with a projecting roof supported by pillars like animals' paws. Inside, everything was white, dazzling, shimmering with sunlight with wood fittings of staggering richness. Ruffle had preferred this house over Shoshana's choice, a colonial mansion in the European style. Still he had hesitated, both because Shoshana had developed a passion for Europe since their trip to Paris, and because he wondered whether a more classical building would confer on him the air of sophistication he so clearly lacked. But in the end he rejected the colonial house which was so unlike him. The circular spaceship on the other hand, modern and luxurious, surrounded by water, perfectly embodied the spirit of Miami: a young, constantly developing city, a crossroads between worlds where people of every nationality melted into an immaculate modernity.

There was one thing to be said in Ruffle's favour: he had felt no fear. His faith in the future was such that he had racked up debts for several generations to come. He was supremely confident: he sold credit and he lived on credit. His business was connected to the banks by a constant IV drip. Expenses were colossal but he believed in his own success.

When his father came to visit, in a rental Chrysler from the airport, he stood open-mouthed, staring at the house. Then he sniggered, his fat paunch jiggling as though someone had just told him a dirty joke, and announced boorishly: 'Now that, my son, is some house, that's really some house.'

And it was impossible to tell whether he was thrilled by this spectacle, which humiliated him and made the Clarimont house look like a ridiculous suburban monstrosity. But perhaps it was simply his ingrained common sense as a foreman – however wealthy he'd become - protesting at such Pharaonic extravagance. For all its glittering, brilliant appearance, the house before him was neither as substantial nor as lavish as he had imagined; on the contrary it was open, gossamer-like, luminous, something that obscurely disturbed his small-town American values forged by dogged years of hard work, as though all this were tainted by the sin of excess. This house, so white, so modern, as though *wafted* onto the seafront . . . This business with its absurdly pretentious name, Ruffle Universal Building. Ruffle Senior was a working man, crafty and cut-throat, obscenely rich, yet he was still rooted in the clay of the first house he had built with his own hands, still deeply committed to ensuring the survival of his business, of his family, and now here before him loomed the new America, a globalised country where no one spoke English any more, where he was met at the airport by a babble of languages, Spanish, obviously, but Russian, French and Chinese too, a wild, extravagant land, completely out of kilter; and now here was his own son moving into this gewgaw, this *thing* nestled by the sea, as though the whole country was doomed to be swallowed up with all its delusions of modernity.

Perhaps somewhere in the wrenching anxiety he felt a stab of pride, since both father and son agreed on the essential values:

business and money, they whispered the hallowed word 'entrepreneur' between them like a secret code. Nonetheless, now, as they all gathered in the dining room to be served exotic, ostentatious dishes by copper-skinned Cubans, the former building-site manager, huge elbows planted on the table, exchanging worried glances with his wife, could not help but feel a vague sense of impending ruin which was simply the portent that a new world, one utterly alien to him, was emerging, one in which men like him, men of the old generation, would be nothing but dinosaurs.

The following morning he was astonished to find they had been joined for breakfast by a past pupil of Clarimont High School, someone he didn't recognise and who Mark had barely known at school but who, through the convolutions of the city of Miami, like the coils of a snake, had ended up in touch with his former classmate. Ruffle Senior did not know that Mark had invited him in order to crush him with his wealth and opulence, by his extravagant display of friendship, because the head of R.U.B. still saw him as the cruel teenager whose mocking laugh had been genuinely hurtful. And Mark had been good enough to invite him round like a buddy to talk about old times in this spaceship about to blast off, and to watch this man struggle in order to exist, to sell *his* story, his scheme, his dream here on the lip of this vast swimming pool, this guy who'd got into fashion and was running the local franchise for a French jeans company and trying without much success to launch a line of distressed vintage T-shirts. Oblivious to this secret settling of scores, Ruffle Senior gawped at the tall gangling man in front of him in his ripped jeans and his paint-spattered T-shirt, who talked like a teenager about the 'raves' he went to where he mingled with famous stars. His boss in France, he explained, the man who owned the franchise, used stars as a marketing strategy, he knew a lot of stars and paid them to come to his parties so people would talk about him, talk about his jeans, because it was all about the stars. And since people wanted to look like stars, they started wearing his jeans and the brand was really taking off big-time. He and Mark high-fived and Ruffle Senior, who'd never met a *star* and never had the slightest interest in that world, stared at them in astonishment.

'My question is this,' he said later to his wife. 'Is that what passes for a man these days? You saw the guy, he had paint splashes all over him, he talked like a teenager, all that stuff about stars and nightclubs and parties, and his clothes – you couldn't leave the house dressed like that . . . He was a sort of mutant, you know, with his tattoos and his stories about fashion. He's not what I'd call a man, I can tell you. All this stuff, it's not good, and I'll tell you something else, it's not making Shoshana happy. And you know me, I can sense these things, I can tell when something's not right in the family.'

Was something not right with Shoshana? Marooned in this dazzling white spaceship, did she spend her days longing for her lofty European mansion? Let's just say that with the move to Miami, she'd lost the reference points she'd had in Clarimont. There was nothing here for her to hold on to. If nothing else, the dreary little gardens of her home town brought back memories of childhood, and even if these gradually faded, at least they were a familiar backdrop, garlanded with the glory of memory. The monotony of her life was marked by memories of her childhood, her adolescence, her first tentative steps as a young woman.

Clarimont was where she had grown up. But here in Miami she had lost her bearings, trapped as she was between a child so gripped by television and tantrums that he didn't do what he was told, didn't even listen to her any more, and a husband, a gargoyle bloated with rage, whom she had come to despise over dinner in that Paris restaurant. Oh, there was the house to take care of, but she had lots of help, what with the cook and the maids; who really needed her? What was her purpose in the world, with no career, living with a husband whose whole life was taken up with his search for recognition? His life as the football pro of business, playing a new game every day. From time to time he noticed her, but only when he wanted her to make herself beautiful, to dress up, so he could have the pleasure of seeing her, of flaunting her, showing off her breasts, like a camel being paraded for tourists. This obsession with her breasts he'd had since they first met, his constant comments about how beautiful, how firm they were, his suggestions that she wear tight sweaters to show them off, contrasted with the slight reluctance in his eyes now when she was naked, when he saw them limp and sagging, his faint embarrassment as though for a faded star. Time and motherhood . . . It was true she could catch his eye when she put on a bra, and under her sweater her breasts were as firm as they'd ever been. But when she needed love, when she finally needed to make an intimate connection with someone she loved, she couldn't turn to Mark because what she felt for him was no longer really love, more a vague affection soured by irritation and contempt. No, it was her son, this pasty, blond child that she wanted to kiss, to hug.

'Chris, baby! Sweetie!'

She smiled hopelessly, unconsciously remembering his early

childhood when the bond between them had seemed natural, almost organic, but the pale robot who now turned to look at her was not the child he had been, his eyes were vacant, apathetic, already jaded as though sated with love.

What could she do? How was she supposed to fill her days? Apart from keeping herself in shape, obviously, swimming in the pool and taking aerobics classes in town, which meant she got to meet other women. For half an hour, to a musical soundtrack, Shoshana sweated and panted, shaking her body, finishing off with slow stretching exercises on the floor, chatting to the women next to her. She liked meeting women who were as idle as she was, and preferred to avoid the midday class at which there were too many businesswomen skipping lunch for a quick workout before heading back to the office. Too many busy, strong-minded women whom she assumed were much more intelligent than she was, and not as lost.

When she came out of her fitness sessions, she'd walk around down town, gazing in the shop windows, frequently buying things and coming home with bags full of clothes which she used to fill the yawning wardrobes in the house.

One day, leaving the leisure centre at noon, eager to avoid bumping into her hard-working foes, she took a stroll down Lincoln Road. She was wearing dark glasses and luxuriating in the warmth of the sun. Strolling past a French restaurant, she stopped, thinking perhaps she and Mark might go there some night. She took off her sunglasses and peered through the window to see inside. Suddenly, she froze.

The man in the suit moving between the tables; it was the waiter her husband had punched.

# 13

Across the vast steppe, huge metal insects siphoned their plunder from the bowels of the earth. With regular movements, the horse-heads rammed into the soil; as far as the eye could see these steel monsters slashed the ground to bring the oil to the surface.

It was late 1997, and Lev had come on an inspection visit. He stood, motionless, fascinated by the spectacle, gazing across this mechanised plain where the very earth itself seemed to shake with strange, incessant spasms, as drills pounded the boreholes, and rock-bits hacked and chewed away the rock and sucked up the precious liquid. There was nothing now but these insects, they stretched across the horizon, a vast swarm of predatory locusts. Hundreds of metres down, they ate and drank, soaked up the crude oil, bringing it to the surface to be transferred to the refineries of ELK, Lev's company.

The oilfields need to be inspected regularly. Lev was constantly checking the company figures, particularly the productivity of the wells. He knew that he had to constantly reassert his authority with the managers of the oilfields, with the foremen and the workers. Oil seeped out everywhere. A steady leak. Everyone stole, and without rigorous checks, they would steal it by the tanker-load. This was especially true in Garsk,

the largest of the oil fields and the principal source of his revenue. But in fact the threat existed right across the supply chain,
something the company controlled from prospecting to distribution. This was why he had contracted the Chechens to provide security. Lev had had no choice. Armed guards patrolled
the oilfields. At regular intervals, a figure would emerge from
the twilight, a dark machine-gun barrel clearly visible above
the shoulder. The Chechens had made their presence felt on
every ELK site, at Lev's Moscow palace, even in his car. They
were a private militia of which he was at once master and pris-
oner. Gusinsky – one of the biggest oligarchs who'd made a
fortune in property and later in television through his close ties
with Moscow mayor Yuri Luzhkov – had a militia which num-
bered a thousand men, a private army run by a former KGB
general. But Lev had left it too late, by the time he tried to raise
troops the gangs had formed, had become too powerful: they
would never have allowed him to raise an army. Besides, rich
though he was, Lev did not have Gusinsky's money.

So far, things were running smoothly. The Chechens had
proved obedient and efficient. The silent, deferential bodyguards who accompanied him everywhere did not wear tracksuits but dark, well-tailored suits, with only the slightest bulge at
the breast pocket. The muscular ex-wrestler always addressed
Lev with the utmost respect. And yet beneath this meek exterior, behind the well-oiled, perfectly regulated rounds of bodyguards, even in the impeccable manner of the Chechen in dark
glasses who acted as his chauffeur, Lev could not help but see
a threat. Lev Kravchenko was neither alone nor free. He was
no longer really a man, he was a conglomeration of interests.

And if things should take a turn for the worse, what could he do against these men?

Standing stiffly behind him, the foreman in charge of the oilfield waited for Lev to finish his thoughts.

'Did you make the offer?' asked Lev.

Some fifty kilometres away was another oilfield, a family operation. A farmer who had struck oil on his own land. A primary development well from which pressurised crude oil spurted from the ground with no need for pumps to bring it up from the depths. The man had set up three derricks and money was flooding in. ELK usually handled refining and distribution. But, like many others, Lev thought that field contained major oil reserves with much of the crude easy to extract. He wanted to buy the field, but the farmer had refused, either because he was hoping for a better offer or because he wanted to develop it himself.

'Yes. We made another offer. It's been rejected.'

'You think he's had other offers?'

'It's possible, but I don't think that's why he's refusing. He wants to hold on to his land, simple as that.'

'Well then the offer isn't big enough. Wait a while, then up the offer 15 per cent. Tell him that's our final offer. Make that clear. He needs to understand this isn't an auction.'

'He's stubborn. Very stubborn. I don't know whether he'll sell.'

'He'll sell.'

Lev turned around. He contemplated the vast steppe. It was colder now, the sun was sinking. The reddish glow slid from the steel frameworks already thick with shadow.

'I'll go and talk to him myself,' Lev added.

He strode back to his car, which immediately roared into life. It was not far to the farmer's house. What was his name again? Riabine? He'd persuade the man. It was in his best interests. This peasant had no hope of setting up a new company. While that might have been possible during the transition, there was no place in the market now for start-ups. Saturation point had been reached, and the big corporations were buying up the regional companies. There were barely a dozen companies now and the process would accelerate until there were only three or four. Maybe only two. Buyouts, mergers. Obviously, ELK's size made it vulnerable, being midway between the local companies and huge conglomerates like Litvinov's company Liekom, which was already planning foreign oil takeovers, as far away as the United States. In the rush to achieve critical mass, ELK needed to buy up every small business it could, even fledgling companies like Riabine's miraculous potato field. Expand or die.

Overlook nothing. Not even Riabine.

Through the car window Lev contemplated the Siberian steppe. A desolation both sad and fascinating. Headlights on, the car sped through the empty space yet in this territory shorn of landmarks, it seemed to make no headway for all its speed. As usual when he found himself alone, Lev felt overcome by exhaustion, by a sort of unrelenting weariness, a vague disgust for others and for himself that had nothing in common with Litvinov's cynicism. Just the weariness of the words that had to be said, the energy that had to be summoned to persuade the farmer, the shifting threats and promises of endlessly repeated arguments.

Overlook nothing. Not even Riabine.

When surrounded by others, Lev was decisive, he acted quickly, he was a consummate leader, but when they scuttled away like crabs on a beach at high tide leaving him alone to do what had to be done, he suddenly felt overwhelmed. What was it all for? This was the question that had haunted him since his time with Yeltsin. What was it all for, all the work, the effort, the stubborn, relentless determination in the face of adversity? For money? He had money enough for several generations. For power? Lev was not interested in power. Without him truly understanding how, things had been set in motion. He had been one of Gaidar's circle of economists, joined in the heated, hypothetical discussions about the future of Russia then, suddenly, by a fluke of history discussions became decisions, words became power. When Gaidar's government imploded, Lev, like many others, had profited from the privatisations. Since then, he'd managed his company to the best of his ability, struggling not to be swallowed up by the others, trying not to die. But he had wanted none of this, foreseen none of this, planned none of this. Things had been set in motion, that was all there was to it. Dominoes falling one after the other. The pieces of his life, time racing alongside the dominoes as they fell, he himself running in an endless race, doing his best not to stumble. But he was increasingly breathless and every time he found himself like this, sitting silent and alone behind his black-suited body-guards, their thick necks and broad shoulders rising above the leather seats, the long, voiceless gasp of his blind headlong rush welled up in his chest.

Overlook nothing. Not even Riabine.

Night had fallen over the steppe. The car devoured the road, they would soon be there, even as the solid mass of shadow pooled into an impenetrable blanket of darkness. The beams of the headlights sliced through this thick blanket. And Lev felt himself being engulfed by these futile thoughts. It was not as though he felt out of place in a game of dominoes. No one was aware of the panicked, headlong rush. And besides, a whole society was rushing ahead, in an accumulation of virtual money and debt. Even the oligarchs, despite the vast reserves of energy, despite the desperate need of the country, were amassing colossal debts, throwing themselves into ever more ambitious projects, straining towards the future, towards future profits. And there was an exhilaration, a thrill in this headlong rush that held him hypnotised. But now he was not alone. Now he was in a car being driven to talk to a farmer as lucky as he was deluded. Yes, he felt completely at home. He had reached an enviable position in this game. He was rich, powerful, respected. It was a position he had earned, he believed, not through work but through natural superiority. Because this was another aspect to Lev. The deep-rooted self-assurance of the aristocrat. A paradoxical aristocrat, at once conscious of the chance nature of his position and yet convinced he was superior by virtue of his birth. He had acquired his importance through inheritance. And he had to prove he was equal to it, in spite of the weariness, in spite of the feelings of futility. And now, as the car slowed down before parking in front of a ghastly house of bare breeze-blocks, he would have to assert himself before Riabine. Have to speak, to persuade. Get back into working order.

His feet sank into the foul-smelling mud, a mixture of dirt

and oil probably. The black, liquid gush, invisible in the darkness, made a constant, oppressive roar like giant blades turning in a rustle of steel. A rectangle of light was carved out above the doorway of the house. Riabine welcomed them, toting a shotgun. The two bodyguards stepped forward, forming a shield in front of their boss.

'Kravchenko!' Lev introduced himself.

'What do you want round here at this hour?' grumbled the farmer, a man of about fifty wearing filthy denim overalls and a baggy vest.

'To talk to you.'

Riabine shrugged.

'Got nothin' to say.'

Lev considered the man, who held his rifle in front of him like some sort of armour. He knew what they wanted from him and he was not prepared to give it.

'Why don't we have a quiet conversation,' suggested Lev, 'it doesn't commit you to anything.'

The man shrugged again.

'Suit yourself.'

He went inside and Lev followed. In the main room, he glimpsed women. Fleeting flashes of white and pink dressing gowns, of flaxen hair. The room was furnished in typical Soviet style, a combination of poverty and poor taste, and was dominated by a huge TV, evidence of the new-found wealth brought by oil. It was sweltering, the radiator on full. The two men sat down at a table covered by some sort of oilcloth with two glasses and a bottle of vodka. The farmer filled the glasses, sullen and uncommunicative.

'Nice TV,' commented Lev.

The farmer sighed. Lev knew what this meant. 'I know you look down on me, I know you're a fucking oligarch, you live in a palace and you own a Rolls and a couple of planes, I know my place is a hovel but fuck you because it's my hovel, it's my oil.' Yes, Lev knew exactly what it meant. But it didn't matter. The farmer's hostility was like a wall. But he would tear down that wall with his eloquence and his wealth.

He explained the reason for his visit, he said the time had come to think clearly, reasonably, that magnificent offers had already been made for the land, offers which Riabine had refused. It was perfectly acceptable, of course, to try to push up the bidding, but all good things had to come to an end, trees did not grow into the sky, it was time to make a deal, it was in both their interests, a deal that would make him rich and free him from all concerns. He could enjoy life, spend time with his family, after all, he'd been fortunate, finding oil on his land, it was a stroke of luck, a genuine gift from life, at his age he should make the most of it instead of working himself into the ground on a difficult field.

The farmer looked at him without a word. Lev went on. He smiled, joked, then with a flourish of his hand, like a man offering all he possesses, he named a figure. And he waited.

The two men sat, stock still. The farmer said: 'You're not the only one to offer.'

Lev felt a slight shock but did not let it show.

'Good for you. But need I remind you that you're already working with us, ELK is already buying your oil. You'd be better off sticking with your partners. You know you can trust us.

And I suspect that our competitors' offers aren't as interesting as ours.'

'They've got money. Loads of money.'

Liekom? It was possible. Strange, given the size of the corporation, to take an interest in such a small field, but maybe, like him, they believed it was a promising deposit.

'Anyway,' said Riabine, 'I want to stay independent.'

Suddenly, Lev understood Riabine. He wasn't sly, he wasn't trying to drive up the price, he had none of that cunning people attribute to farmers, he was just stubborn, determined to hang on to his little plot of land whether the crop was crude oil or potatoes. Fiercely attached to his land, clinging like an animal to his territory. His hands, gnarled from hard labour, his rotten teeth, his thin, wizened body, his expression at once ferocious and frightened, everything marked him out as an animal in his lair.

Lev wanted to try again. He leaned forward, then suddenly something inside him crumbled. What was it all for? The nagging question returned right in the middle of a negotiation. This was a first. A warmth spread through Lev. It had no right. Not now. Not the tiredness. And yet, he also knew it didn't really matter. That Riabine wouldn't give up. You couldn't argue with animal instinct. Lev tried to collect his thoughts. He opened his mouth. The farmer's claw-like hand held him spellbound. A savage, primitive man who would never surrender.

'I understand, Riabine. I completely understand.'

He got to his feet.

'Maybe in your place I'd have made the same decision,' he said. 'To be your own master, for better or worse.'

As he spoke, the feeling of unease faded. No, he hadn't failed, he hadn't been beaten in the negotiation. He had simply happened on an animal, a farmer who was a brute beast. There was nothing shaming about that.

He went outside. The chill night fell around him. He straightened up. The tiredness left him. It must have been the heat. He hadn't failed. Just too much heat and a stubborn farmer. A real *muzhik*, that one. A fine example.

The car door opened. He dived inside. The lean farmer stood on the doorstep, still wary, a little dazed by this abrupt conclusion.

Riabine watched the car drive away. The black mass moving into the distance, the red and yellow lights punching holes in the darkness. In the silence of solitude, the rush of crude oil continued to make its reassuring roar.

# 14

Sila turned. A young woman was looking at him through the window of the restaurant. He wondered if she was a customer. As she simply stood, frozen, staring at him, he moved towards her. He opened the door of the restaurant.

'Can I help you?' he asked in English.

The woman didn't answer. Instead, she adjusted her sunglasses.

'Would you like to reserve a table, madame?' he spoke again.

She nodded her head with difficulty.

'For what date?'

'I'm not sure yet,' she said weakly.

Sila smiled. 'Take all the time you need to decide. We're at your service.'

Suddenly, Shoshana was no longer sure. What if it was someone else . . .? After all, this man didn't look like he'd had his nose broken. And his pleasant, affable manner was nothing like the stunned, shattered expression of the waiter on the floor.

Sila went back inside. Shoshana slowly crept away. But for the rest of the day, she thought about the encounter. What if it really was him? What was he doing in Miami? Could he have followed them? But why?

The truth was that Sila had followed them, for no particular reason, the simple, chance movement of a leaf buffeted by the wind. With no intention, no purpose, only the unfathomable curiosity of a wanderer coming from Africa, passing through Europe, deciding to spend some time in the United States. A week after being discharged from hospital, where he'd had an operation on his nose, he had announced that he wanted to go to the States.

'But why?' the maître d'hôtel asked him. 'Are you not happy here?'

'I am, but I want to see the world.'

'So why the States?'

'Because the guy who punched me is American. I want to see what the country is like.'

'You get arseholes the world over. He could just as easily have been from France or Belgium or Venezuela.'

'Maybe. But the fact is he's American. It interests me. I want to see the country.'

Lemerre called him into his office, asked him if he was sure about his decision. When Sila insisted he was, Lemerre said he would go on helping him. He owned twenty-three restaurants around the world, three in the United States - in New York, Miami and Los Angeles. He would make him maître d'hôtel.

Sila had seen from his hotel registration card that the American came from Florida.

'I'd like to go to Miami.'

'Is this why you've been learning English?'

'No, but I'll get some use out of it.'

Everything had been simple, as always for Sila. All he had had to do was wait a few months for his work permit. When he left the restaurant, one of the waiters said: 'The guy's an idiot.'

'No,' said Lemerre, 'he's a prince.'

And no one quite knew what he meant by this.

Sila settled in Miami. He took a studio apartment down-town, and adapted to the restaurant which, while it didn't have the prestige of the flagship restaurant in Paris, had skilfully developed the concept of a fusion of flavours from all over the world, something that initially disconcerted the clientele but quickly became one of the hottest tables in the city, all the more so since Lemerre's name and the glowing reviews for the res-taurant quickly reassured them. What was needed now was to manage this success, especially during the day, since business lunches attracted a hurried clientele ill-disposed to waiting.

The staff, in the kitchens and in the dining room, came from all over the world. To the various people from North Africa, Sila spoke French. But they preferred to speak English, even if badly, to leave their former identity behind, to melt into the new language of their new lives. And Sila himself eventually felt completely at ease speaking English.

One day, he asked one of his colleagues: 'Are we really in the United States?'

The man clearly didn't understand. 'Of course.'

'It's not like I imagined it. The sun shining every day. It's like being at the beach. No, honestly, this isn't how I imagined it. All this dazzling whiteness, all this money, it lacks truth.'

'Truth? I don't know what you're talking about, but I have to say I love Miami. It's just one facet of the States, one face. You can find others if you travel around.'

Time passed. Sila grew accustomed to living in this white seashell that was Miami, its whorls and layers like a huge cake.

And he was happy there, though he had already decided he would move on, to catch a glimpse of the other faces of this country. But if the strange, absurd word 'fate', which had fascinated him since his far-off adolescence, had any meaning, here it had re-entered his life, since one of those beautiful, inconsequential, humdrum mornings, Shoshana had stopped, frozen, in front of his restaurant.

The day after their meeting at the restaurant, Shoshana was still thinking about the Parisian waiter. She was plagued with doubts. Hypnotised by the memory, her thoughts constantly returned to him, she couldn't shake them off. She had to know. She went back to the restaurant.

The moment he saw her, Sila went over to her.

'So you've decided to come.'

She smiled self-consciously.

'Would you like a table?' he asked.

'Please. A table for one. I'll be having lunch alone.'

It was very early. The crowds had not yet arrived. Sila led her to a small table by the window.

'A waiter will come by to look after you.'

The young woman nodded, then said suddenly: 'Excuse me. Would it be possible for you to serve me?'

Sila looked surprised.

'It's just, I don't know, I just like your French accent, it's so lovely.' Shoshana gave a theatrical smile which she felt was completely fake but actually came off quite well. 'I love France. In fact I've been there,' she added sitting up, proud of herself, like a diligent schoolgirl. 'And since we're in a French restaurant, I would really, really love it if I could be served by a man with a French accent.'

'I'm not sure my accent is particularly French, madame, I suspect a real Frenchman might disagree with you, but if I can be of any service, I would be only too happy.'

'He's not French. So it can't be him,' she thought, relieved.

Sila brought the menu.

'You choose for me. Whatever the specialities are. I trust you. You know I once went to Lemerre's Paris restaurant. A great chef. He owns this place too, doesn't he? It was an unforgettable experience. And you didn't get to choose. If you ordered the tasting menu, they just brought you everything. It was delicious, no, it was more than that, I can't explain it, it was, you know, sort of a whole experience, like it was art, or a mysterious journey, and the flavours were sublime. I had no idea what was on my plate, it was like magic, and with flavours that blended perfectly or that contrasted perfectly depending on what the chef was doing. I'm sorry, I can't really explain it . . .'

'You describe it very well, madame,' said Sila, who was not staring at her.

'Really? Oh, I'm so glad . . . Have you . . .' Shoshana went on, increasingly nervous now, 'I mean, do you know the restaurant?'

'I worked there before I moved here.'

The young woman's face fell.

'Oh, really? You worked there?'

Then she stopped and stammered: 'It really was a wonderful, wonderful experience.'

'It's him. It's got to be him. I was right. And he recognised me. I saw it in his face. I'm sure he recognised me. I feel so ashamed. Why did I come here? He must really hate me.'

'A wonderful experience,' she said again.

'I'll bring you a selection of our specialities,' said Sila. 'It may not be as good as Paris, but we just might surprise you.'

He walked away a little abruptly. The customer's comments had reminded him of the other arsehole, the lunatic who lost it. Why? The young woman had been rather nice, but, without knowing why, the memory came flooding back and with it a feeling of unease.

Shoshana's embarrassment was tempered with relief. She felt horribly guilty, as though she were the one who had hit Sila, yet at the same time she was happy to know she had not been wrong because here, perhaps, was a chance for her to put things right, to get to know him, to explain, apologise, to finally do something in her husband's stead. After all, it had been his thuggish behaviour in the restaurant in Paris that had shattered the balance of the relationship, and transformed Mark into a gargoyle, so much so that she could no longer consider him rationally. It had been this brutality which had set in motion the breakdown of her marriage, which had distanced her from Mark's infantile play-acting, whereas before that they had made rather a good couple; they rarely argued; of course they rarely argued even now but the arguments weren't the worst, the worst was the awkwardness between them which meant that everything rang false, as though drowned out by the silence and mutual incomprehension. And maybe, by some magical gesture, something that would have to be creative, harmony could be restored just as a broken nose could be reset. And though it was strange to run into this man in Miami as though he'd followed them, at least it was still an opportunity to put things right. Obviously, it was something she couldn't talk about to Mark, he had other things to do and he'd already forgotten the whole story, but behind his back, by some luminous, magical gestures, perhaps she could restore unity as though by some voodoo ritual. Of course, nothing can repair the shattered pieces of a vase smashed in anger. Nothing except a gesture of conciliation, a plea to the man sprawled on the floor, a man who seemed good and kind, who had an innocence about him and would surely not reject her gesture of peace. No, he couldn't refuse, all she had to do was speak to him frankly, with the sincerity of an honest heart, and everything could be put right. Between Mark and her, between Chris and her, between them and the waiter and perhaps, she thought obscurely in the naive, instinctive way she had, in the world itself. All that was needed was to replace this piece that had been dislodged by violence, this tiny piece that was crucial to the equilibrium of the world.

She waited. She felt both nervous and impatient because this man could not refuse to listen to her, because honesty and sincerity were bound to be respected. A sunbeam lit up her hair and her left hand. She felt embarrassed by it. It felt rather warm. Sila personally brought her a plate of *confit* and caramelised meats, small sweet mouthfuls. She thanked him.

'It looks delicious,' she said.

And she couldn't say another word. Sila left and she tried to enjoy the dish he had brought, though she wasn't even hungry. She devised phrases and readied herself to say them. But when Sila returned, she found herself unable to do so.

She wanted to say, 'I just have to talk to you.' She wanted

to say, 'My whole future depends on you.' would have said: 'Would it be possible to discuss a matter that's very important to me?' But she said nothing. Honesty and sincerity remained silent. With an absurdly enthusiastic smile, Shoshana asked, 'Do you like Paris? I just love the city! I love it!'

Sila gave a polite smile. What could he say?

And so the lunch played out, between silences and ridiculous, incongruous excesses. Sila would come to the table and Shoshana would suddenly be all keyed up with excitement, while inside she was tormented by the confession she could not make.

It came time to pay. She could already see herself getting up, leaving the restaurant, stepping out into the street, only for the confusion of thoughts and regrets to start again. She would go home and replay the scene ten times, a hundred times, dream up perfect scenarios for other encounters. And so, desperate, mustering all her courage, in a whispered confession that sounded as though it had just slipped out, she said: 'I'm the wife of the man who hit you.'

Sila froze.

'I'm the wife of the man who punched you in Paris. I'm so sorry. I came to apologise to you.'

Sila said nothing. He was astonished and yet at the same time he understood why this woman had come, why she had needed to talk to him. He hadn't recognised her. In fact, had he even seen her before? All he remembered glimpsing was a face, savage, baboon-like, a face he wasn't sure he would recognise. So the woman sitting with him at the table . . .

He extended his arm, opened his hand. He did not know the

reason for this gesture. In itself, his raised hand meant little. A gesture someone might use to stop a car. Or a hypnotist placing his palm on a subject's forehead. A black hand spread wide, the fingers splayed, the pink palm proffered, naked, vulnerable. But at this simple gesture, Shoshana felt calm. She did not interpret it as a refusal or a dismissal, but as a sign of peace. Perhaps because all she had hoped for was a silent, perfect reconciliation, something like this open hand.

'Thank you, thank you,' the young woman stammered, rushing out.

And as she fled, she took with her the iconic image of this man, one hand raised, like a saint or a healer.

## 15

Lev considered the man he was speaking to with suspicion. It had been a long time since they had met. He knew the Chechens were occupied elsewhere. They were having problems with the Slavic Brotherhood who, for some years now, had been fighting for supremacy in Moscow. This was a turning point in the war between the gangs. The decentralised structure of the Slavic Brotherhood, affording considerable autonomy to local gangs and taking no interest in their trafficking and racketeering in exchange for a bond of fealty by which they freely provided men in times of armed conflict, proved to be stronger than the strict centralisation of the Chechens. There were always more gangs prepared to ally themselves with the Brotherhood, while the Chechen franchise, in spite of its reputation, attracted fewer. And the disparity in numbers was becoming glaring although, since the 1993 turf war when a machine-gun battle between the gangs in a Moscow cinema had left one of the leaders of the Brotherhood dead, both sides had favoured skirmishes over all-out confrontation.

But the man with the wrestler's neck standing before him, the same Chechen who had first come to his office to make the 'proposition', had good reasons to be here.

'Riabine's had an offer from Liekom. We're sure of it. And

that means Liekom have as much chance of getting the oilfield as we do.'

'*We?*' Lev snapped.

'We, you, however you want to put it. But the Chechens share your interests. We're connected now.'

'Like Litvinov and the Brotherhood?' asked Lev.

'Sure,' the wrestler grumbled, 'but that's obvious. Things have changed. The gangs have allied themselves with the oligarchs, we're not mafia any more, these days we're businessmen just like you.'

Or these days we're all mafia, thought Lev.

'Anything that hurts Liekom, hurts the Brotherhood,' the wrestler went on. 'And anything that's good for ELK is good for the Chechens. We can't lose that oilfield. Liekom is taking over everything, and pretty soon they'll be taking us over.'

'Not a chance,' Lev interrupted, 'I'll never let that happen.'

The wrestler fell silent. And in the silence, Lev understood. Things really had changed. If they had to, the Brotherhood would eliminate him, and launch an all-out war to exterminate the Chechens.

Lev's voice grew fainter. He tried to stick to the subject of Riabine.

'I made him a decent offer. He refused. It's his loss. It's not like it's a particularly large oilfield. I mean, it's only three wells.'

'That's not true, as you well know!' said the Chechen in a tone that had none of the humility of their early meetings, when he had been all fake deference. Now, he knew that Lev's life was safe only by virtue of his connection to the Chechens.

'That field has serious possibilities. It could be a major

supply. And Riabine should never have been in a position to refuse. It sets a bad precedent. You accepted defeat. And in our world, that's not good.'

Lev angrily got to his feet.

'There was no failure on my part! I'm president of ELK and I'm head of the Chechens since I'm the one who pays you. Without my money, the Chechens would be nothing any more, and it's not like the diminishing returns from your rackets or your humiliations at the hands of the Brotherhood are going to save you. Your money, your reputation, it's all me. If it weren't for my money, the Chechens would be nothing! The Brotherhood would hunt you down on the streets of Moscow and slit your throats.'

The Chechen lowered his head.

'I'm sorry if I offended you,' he said in a quiet, submissive tone, 'it wasn't my intention. As you say, you're the boss. But I'd like you to give the situation some thought. The situation is very delicate, the mergers between oil companies are constantly accelerating. Word gets out about things, including Riabine turning down our offer.'

'So? I'm supposed to kill the man for refusing to sell me his oilfield?'

The Chechen did not answer.

'So that's it? You think I should have killed him?'

'No, probably not. But you could have let us handle things. You had two men with you. All you had to do was ask. They can be very persuasive.'

'Very persuasive? I'm sure they are. But it's not my style. I won't have anything to do with such methods.'

The man picked up his hat.

'If I might suggest, Councillor, give the matter some thought. Another week and Liekom will get Riabine to sign, whether he likes it or not. It would be better for us – and for him too – if he were to accept our offer.'

The door closed. Lev's head ached and he felt tired. Lying, cheating, threatening, bribing, he had done all these things. He could not quite understand how, but he had been that man, he took no pleasure in it, but he was ruthless. But torturing a man for his signature, that was something he could not do. He knew exactly how such things worked: the men would simply walk in with a briefcase full of money in one hand and a gun in the other. They'd open the briefcase, point the gun at the man's head and the negotiations would proceed at a fantastic pace. But Riabine would refuse, Lev was sure of that. So then they would start hitting him. Until he gave in, or died from the blows.

And he did not want to give the order. Litvinov would decide whatever he decided, but he could not do it. No, such methods were not for him. Not murder. If he gave the order, he was lost. Everything he had believed in, however faintly, however tempered by his cynicism, would be lost. He would never again be able to think of himself as an ordinary businessman forced to make difficult decisions by prevailing circumstances in Russia, just as one must weather a storm, whatever the cost. He would become a criminal, nothing more. As surely as if he himself had beaten Riabine.

Lev walked across his office, picked up his coat and went down to the street. He needed to walk. When he walked, he thought more clearly. Time was, at the Institute of Economics, ideas would come to him too.

The thunder of jackhammers assailed him. He walked faster. The two Chechens behind him were almost running. They were probably cursing him. He was convinced they despised him. They would be only too happy to put a bullet in his head. They were just waiting for the word. All it would take was for him to fall out with the wrestler. Not just some fit of pique, obviously. This he had to admit, the wrestler did not easily get worked up. Business was business. He was a professional. But if they were to have a serious disagreement on their strategy for dealing with Liekom and the Brotherhood . . .

What would Litvinov do about Riabine?

The answer was obvious. And if he, Lev, did not make a decision, in a matter of days Litvinov would be the winner. Whatever happened, Riabine was lost.

And besides, why was he so concerned about some *muzhik*? Did Stalin think twice? Millions of peasant farmers died during the *forced collectivisation*. Not to mention the war. No leader in history, even those whose benign names are celebrated, had hesitated to kill.

It was a fact: they had to get rid of Riabine. After all, if he was reasonable, everything would be fine. He would take the money. He'd understand immediately. The men would march into his house. How many? Three or four maybe? Heavy-set men. Maybe the wrestler himself. He would have no qualms about getting his hands dirty for something like this.

Lev looked up. He no longer recognised the district he was in. Next to him loomed a huge building, a tower under construction. Huge cranes swayed, drunken birds, black against the grey sky.

Though the country had changed radically in a few short years, the shockwaves from the original blast petered out as they moved away from the cities, meaning that the remote backwoods were still as they had always been, the crash of the present collapsing on the ancient empire of the steppes. But Moscow had been at the epicentre of the upheaval. This dreary, petrified city suffocated by torpor had exploded, for better and for worse. A luminous, modern city now thrummed, sometimes repossessed by the silence and the stillness of the vast monumental avenues with a sort of icy coldness reminiscent of Soviet greyness. Huge property fortunes had been amassed thanks to deals struck with the state and the city council, the result of which was this modern metropolis, both disturbing, since it shook up the lives and the memories of the inhabitants of old Moscow, and exciting because it was a city of money and pleasure.

He hailed a taxi. Without even looking at the driver, he gave his address. He needed to talk to Elena. But fresh arguments now presented themselves.

Yes, Riabine was lost. But what sort of justification was that? Litvinov could do as he saw fit. Why did he have to show himself to be just as brutal? If Litvinov was corrupt and violent to the point of adopting the most savage methods of the Brotherhood, Lev had no truck with such corruption. He would do better to *save his soul*. The expression sounded almost comical to his ear. *Save his soul*.

When he got home, Elena was in the library. She was reading.

She was surprised to see him home.

'I wasn't expecting you so early,' she said.

'I was bored at the office.'

He sat in an armchair, studied the books that lined the four walls of the room. He always found this room calmed him. He had been born surrounded by books, given that in the tiny apartment his parents lived in the family's vast collection of books took up every nook and cranny. As a child, his bed had been surrounded by books. Though he did not read as much now as he used to, at heart this room was still his favourite place, all the more so since Elena had bought all the writers banned under the Soviets, which added quite a few titles to those he knew by heart.

'I should have been a professor,' he said, settling back into the armchair.

Elena considered him curiously. She didn't for an instant believe this myth, which Lev came out with at regular intervals. If he had wanted to be a professor, he would be one, end of story. Lev needed money and power, and he was a man of action. Perhaps he had something of the intellectual in him, like many of the first-generation oligarchs. But this phrase invariably presaged an explanation. She waited.

'We've found this field.'

'An oilfield?'

'Yes.'

'Where?'

'In Siberia, near Garsk.'

She said nothing.

'The field belongs to a farmer,' Lev went on, 'a man called

Riabine. A pig-headed peasant. His family has been working the land for generations and he wants to keep working it till he dies. We've made various offers to him, but he's turned them down.'

He was hoping for a question, a comment. Nothing. He had to carry on, but the words were heavy.

'He really should accept our offer,' he repeated forcefully. 'Because if he doesn't, Litvinov will end up with his land.'

'What if he doesn't want to sell?' Elena protested. 'If he's not prepared to sell to you, he's not likely to sell to Litvinov.'

'You don't refuse an offer from Litvinov.'

'You mean . . .'

Elena was reluctant to draw the conclusion.

'Of course,' Lev muttered, 'Litvinov will decide for him, by force if necessary.'

Elena set her book down on the coffee table.

'To think we've had him here in our house . . . and *this* is what he's become,' her face contorted in disgust.

'This is what everyone has become! They've lost all sense of morality. The slow day-to-day drip of corruption. All it takes is a single action, you know, the first time you turn away from morality, that first step is the most difficult. Then there's a second and a third . . . each more serious than the last.'

Elena was staring at him.

'Who are you talking about? What do you mean, *everyone*? Who are you talking about, Lev?'

Lev, embarrassed, ran his hands over his face.

'Everyone, yes, more or less. Because business is tough. Because the country has gone through a revolution that destroyed the old corrupt order, and replaced it with a new form of corruption. Because we have no choice.'

Elena was silent for a moment.

'*We* have no choice?' she asked.

'That's right,' Lev's tone was firm. 'We have no choice.'

Elena got to her feet.

'So you've made your decision. This Riabine, you're going to make him a . . . final offer.'

'I shouldn't have mentioned it to you.'

'On the contrary,' said Elena, 'you were right to talk to me about it.'

'I haven't made a decision, Elena,' said Lev, alarmed by the expression on his wife's face. 'That's why I wanted to talk to you. In fact, I decided to leave Riabine to Litvinov. Let other people do whatever they like, I won't be like them.'

Elena stared hard at him, as though trying to discover the truth in him. 'But you're tempted, aren't you, Lev? Tempted to take that oilfield by force, because that's what Litvinov would do, because you're afraid that Liekom will get it and the name Lev Kravchenko will be synonymous with failure? Because you're afraid everyone will walk all over you?'

Lev didn't answer.

'You're scared, Lev. I know you are. That's why you're hesitating, that's why you talked to me. You're afraid to be brave. You were never scared of anything, now you're terrified. You're tempted by violence, but it's fear that's eating away at you.'

'What fear?' Lev said scornfully. 'I've never in my life felt fear.'

'Not physically, maybe, though even that has changed. It's

true that once even in a street brawl you wouldn't have been scared. But you've got older and fatter, and most of all from a moral point of view you've completely changed. But none of that matters. The fear I'm talking about is more deep-seated. You're afraid people will snatch your whole life from you. Your company, your wealth, your reputation. You're afraid of becoming so weak in people's eyes that they'll crush you. But I'm asking you to be brave, Lev. I'm asking you to overcome your fear and act according to your conscience. Think about it, Lev, please. There's never been a more important moment in our whole life. I swear, this is the most important moment, the moment of choice.'

And suddenly, tears were streaming down her face.

'Be brave, Lev. For us, I'm asking you, I'm begging you.'

She buried her face in her hands and sobbed. Lev went to her, took her in his arms, hugged her tears, her pain. He hugged this woman who, from their very first conversation, he had admired for her dazzling intelligence. For that dagger of terrifying lucidity that was her mind. It was even possible that this was why he had married her, this feeling of intellectual inferiority he felt when he was with her. He kissed her.

'I'll be brave, Elena.'

Lev trudged out of the room. He sought refuge in his office. For some time he sat motionless, his face a blank. Then he got up, looked at himself in the full-length mirror, a tarnished mirror, and through the black spots of tarnish, the marks left by time, in this same mirror where once the prince must have looked at himself, Lev saw a man with a fleshy face, bloated with fatigue, with food, with alcohol. His thoughts sharpened by what his wife had said, he could discern the corruption and the fear.

He contemplated this man with a sort of detached contempt.

The corruption and the fear.

He grabbed the phone. Called the Chechen.

'Go and find Riabine. Make up his mind for him.'

# 16

Things were now clear: money was their master. It had taken Simon some time to realise it but the uneasiness he felt when he was with the traders had eventually clarified the situation. No one took any notice of him  because he earned nothing – or nothing much – even if he thought he earned a lot.

The question was this: how much did you have to earn a year to exist? Five hundred thousand dollars, a million, five million, ten million? At first Simon didn't really understand the indifference of his colleagues towards him, but though he hid away behind his computer, assimilating, sorting and exploiting statistics for every asset, option and option of an option in this world, the knowledge of his social status inevitably reached him through looks, tones of voice, a thousand little signs. And he quickly realised that his position in the Kelmann hierarchy was not high. He was a quantitative analyst – a quant – meaning nothing very important. He was, as he put it, a 'cost centre' rather than a 'profit centre'. A necessary, indeed an essential cog, but poorly paid compared to the traders because he took no risks. He calculated risks, he didn't take them. He didn't take positions worth tens or hundreds of millions, making a fortune for the bank – if the market moved in his favour – part of which would come back to him as a bonus. A good trader took risks, a good quant *eased* them. Traders were men, they were manly, the way they talked was hyper-masculine, with frequent use of the word 'balls': 'I've got balls, I'll cut off his balls and make him eat them, I've got him by the balls,' and so on.

How much did you have to earn a year to exist? Simon remembered a conversation he had had with a Paris taxi driver who told him twenty thousand was what you needed to live decently. In ordinary life, most people would have agreed on that figure. As soon as someone was earning thirty or forty thousand, he was rich and you envied or despised him for it. When you were working in finance, the same salary was evidence of failure. And the more you climbed the greasy money pole, the higher the price of failure: a hundred thousand, two hundred thousand, three hundred thousand. You had to start counting in dollars, otherwise the sums took too long to say. And you had to leave the bank and move into investment funds where managers, who randomly kept 20 per cent of the profits they made, earned sums that were beyond comprehension: fifty, a hundred, two hundred million dollars a year! Even a billion! A billion dollars for buying stocks with other people's money in a bull market.

The taxi driver calmly went on driving, the teacher passing on his knowledge, the doctor healing and the researcher ... actually, the maths researcher was beginning to hesitate. Young graduates with PhDs in games theory realised they could earn ten, a hundred, a thousand times more on the stock markets. And though they loved pure mathematics, boasted about the absolute freedom of research, still the great, dark energy emanating from London or New York exerted a terrible magnetism.

First and foremost, the money, but also its more reputable cor-
ollaries: a game played in real conditions with all the thrills of
the biggest casino in the world, the competition, the insistence
on results, the action, the stress . . . it was like a gauntlet thrown
down to their youth. And as the tide began to swell and as they
heard that other engineers, researchers, friends were banging
on the doors of the banks, so gradually, deep underground, the
thought began to spill out like a wave, carrying off more of
them. Money swept them up, each in unconscious imitation of
the others, and they cut their ties with their home countries and
headed for London or Tokyo, or more rarely the US, where
they lived as expats in a bubble of money, utterly oblivious to the
Paris taxi driver. This was exactly what Simon had been told:
the banks were draining the brains of the entire planet. But in
doing so, the banks transformed them, forced them to evolve
in a bubble the like of which had never existed, one entirely
divorced from the life of the country, in which everyone spoke
English, moved with astounding speed, almost as fast as funds
closely followed a particular geographic area only to desert it at
the first sign of trouble. They were drunk on this life of stress,
targets, bonuses, and the rest of the time, they partied. Simon
could see this. He and Matt went out all the time: once you
reached a certain level, London restaurants were very good,
much better than they'd been in the 1980s, because they'd been
forced to adapt to the demands of these young tycoons, in particular to the refined palates of the French, more than 300,000
of whom lived in the city working at various different professions. The elegant parts of town had also become very expensive as property prices exploded – bankers' salaries triggered an

inflation that relegated English people in other professions to the distant suburbs, to gruelling journeys on overpriced trains that were invariably late. Simon and Matt routinely booked tables for eight or ten, all bankers, all under thirty, and they would spend as much money as they could. They showed up in Ferraris, in Porsches, in Mercedes which they casually handed over to valet parking, they were like lords, they threw money around then went on to nightclubs where they drank to excess and beyond. Stressed by their work, full of themselves, obsessed with an image fuelled by money and results, an image that was shattered when the money and results failed to materialise, something was happening all too often in 1998 as crises in Asia and Russia caused the markets to plummet, they needed to live large, physically and financially. They needed to express this intoxication.

This was how the whole world turned. Vast capital was needed for all the developing countries, and as for developed countries, they were caught up in an excess of conspicuous consumption fuelled by debt. Salaries were low, what was on offer was vast: everyone bought on credit. The whole world was on a drip-feed of credit, no one had the money to pay for it, but that didn't change anything, the wheel had to turn and go on turning until everything exploded. And the people at the centre of this credit quivered with the movement of the wheel, caught up in a whirl all the more frenzied since in this universe of short-termism and vast fortunes everything could collapse overnight.

How much? How much did you have to earn a year to feel indestructible? How long before the pride of excess took hold?

Now, when he went back to France, Simon was a Polytechnique student who had got himself a job at Kelmann. He was a success. People looked at him with respect, and maybe they were wondering how this idiot had pulled it off, but there was none of the condescension, the humiliating contempt he had endured his whole life. At work, he was just another young quant, which was considerably less glamorous. But even so, when he and Matt went out to dinner, he no longer felt like an outsider. Enjoying the slightly more relaxed sense of hierarchy that prevailed on nights out, he had the impression of being part of this world, although in a way that was more diaphanous, more fragile than the others, a ghostly double of their appetite for living and for money. The gestures, the conversations, the clothes were familiar to him. He was one of them. True he came by tube or took a taxi, he didn't own a Ferrari, but he was one of them. He had crossed over.

He would probably not have gone out as much as he did if it were not for Matt. Matt made a fantastic trader – the dazzling smile, the aggression, the macho posturing. He knew everyone in London. He had friends at Merrill Lynch, Kelmann, Lehman Brothers, SocGen, Deutsche Bank, at some of the hedge fund companies too, a party was not a party without Matt. He had clearly found his niche. He had inexhaustible reserves of energy. He could last all night, intimidating even the toughest party animals. His track record with girls was almost as impressive as in Paris: young, smiling, anonymous, identical blondes threw themselves at him. *Almost* as impressive? That was only because London was a city devoid of women. Bankers for the most part were men, and the tough, clever women in the business terrified Matt so much he didn't dare try to seduce them. But waitresses, interns, other bankers' girlfriends, foreign students studying English at the London School of Economics, all were perfect prey for a trader with his tongue hanging out. All he was missing was the Ferrari.

Why didn't he buy one? One simple reason. Matt didn't earn a penny. He was a trader who didn't trade. He knew everyone, fitted in perfectly with this world, he spoke the language, understood the gestures, wore the clothes, but he did nothing. Hence his boundless reserves of energy. He told people he worked for a small hedge fund, dealing with Russian investors, Saniak, a murky company whose managers no one knew which made it an ideal cover for Matt. He had no problem lying, a lie came to him as easily as the truth. What difference was there between them? At most an effect of language. In fact Matt probably did not feel as though he was lying: he slipped on his job as he might a new jumper. He needed this hedge fund so he could exist in the eyes of others, therefore the hedge fund employed him. Besides, he could only get a job if he had a job already. People only lend to the rich. Matt was gifted with the magnificent fluidity of the compulsive liar, criss-crossing the porous borders of truth and fiction. When he was clubbing, he told people he worked hard and earned a fortune in a frank, easygoing manner that convinced everyone. He wasn't pretentious, just sure of himself. Simon barely noticed any more, though he was the one who paid the rent, his friend's additional expenses being covered by his savings from Paris and handouts from his parents.

This inactivity remained mysterious. It was true that Matt

had not been to university and had no experience, both of which might have proved awkward. But in England, where things were rather more relaxed than in France, the banking world was more open to highly motivated people from different backgrounds, and lots of arts students worked in the City. You'd often find examples of secretaries or waiters who'd ended up with high-profile jobs, and as everyone kept reminding him, originally traders had been nothing more than the barrow boys of the stock exchange. And it was true that before the 1980s, stewards, out-of-work actors and posh boys with no university education had dabbled on the stock exchange and made money back in the days before deregulation, when finance had been a boring business. Those days were gone now, but there was still a slender opening. But Matt was unable to take advantage of it. His slickness, his lies, the friends he hung out with in the clubs made it easy to get interviews, but he never got called back. He always said he was good in the interviews but that something about him didn't click, something he couldn't explain, something that was starting to eat away at him, some deep-seated, fundamental difference he didn't understand which meant that he was never hired, while people he considered dreary, dull and stupid got hired instead. Over time he arrived to interviews more stressed and consequently more arrogant. Bracing himself for the humiliation to come, he puffed out his chest, became stiff and brusque and lost his greatest asset: his charm. But in any case, even in his early interviews his smile and his drive hadn't helped. He did not please. A terrible discovery for a charmer.

Why did he fail? Because his career profile was atypical,

because he had only a limited knowledge of the financial sector, even if he could chat about it casually, but mostly because of this *something*. This nameless factor.

'I don't understand,' he said one day to Simon. 'I'm good, I'm a born trader. I've got a feel for the market and the cold-bloodedness of a killer. I'm capable of giving them results like they've never seen. I know it, I'm sure of it. But they won't hire me. They're cretins. Complete fucking cretins. Just because there's something about me they don't like.'

'But what?'

'I don't know what. That's the problem. And obviously they don't tell me. Hypocrites, the lot of them. Otherwise it would be easy. So I end up lugging this problem, this thing from one interview to the next without being able to do anything about it. I should go and talk to them, look them in the face and hiss "What is it? Why won't you hire me, arsehole? What's wrong with me?"'

'Probably better not. Banking is a small world. You'd only get yourself blacklisted.'

'It's pathetic,' said Matt, getting to his feet and taking his head in his hands. 'Here I am desperate for the opinions of these losers who won't hire me because I'm not a loser like them.'

One weekend Simon went back to Paris for Nicholas's birthday, his former colleague at the laboratory. Since the party on the terraces, they'd become firm friends. His birthday was an opportunity to meet up again. Arriving by Eurostar, Simon took a taxi to Nicholas's place, a one-bedroom apartment in the 19th arrondissement. The narrow, run-down stairwell made him feel uncomfortable. He thought of the soft, shimmering whiteness of his London flat. He rang the doorbell and found himself staring at . . . Julie, the girl who had a fleeting encounter with Matthieu on the terrace of their old apartment. She gave him a smile; he stood there speechless.

'Surprised?' she said. 'Yep, I live here, with Nicholas.'

Embarrassed at this reminder of an amorous escapade, she stood shaking her head nervously. Then Nicholas appeared, all smiles, wearing jeans and trainers.

'Oh la la . . . still wearing the broker's outfit then,' he said checking out Simon's suit. 'I'm afraid it doesn't go with the dress code in this place,' he smiled. 'You'll have to lose the jacket.'

'No problem,' said Simon, taking it off.

'You know Julie, yeah?' Nicholas said smugly, squeezing his lover's shoulder. 'She's moved in with me. She's my angel.'

Simon found this last comment stupid. He stepped into a room with a sloping ceiling, utterly devoid of charm. There were already five or six people in there, two of whom Simon recognised from the maths laboratory. Nicholas introduced everyone. Everyone noticed his designer suit.

'Don't worry,' was what Simon wanted to say to them, pleadingly, awkwardly, 'I'm just like you, actually I'm worse than you, I don't hunger for money, I don't lust after power, I don't even strive for recognition as much as you and I'll never fight for a research post or a university chair. For years I lived holed up in my bedroom, terrified of life like a sick kid, and I'll always be that kid. Don't look at me like that. It's just a twist of fate that pitched me into the world of money, and anyway in that world I'm like a sort of ghost so you're wrong to look at me like that. It's unworthy of you, all it does is make you seem mean and petty. All I want is for us all to get along, for the sake of the birthday. Please.'

'Sorry, I've just got in from London,' was what he actually said. 'I didn't have a chance to change.'

'London?' asked one of them. 'And does Monsieur work in finance?'

'And was Monsieur lured by the golden calf?' joked another in a curious tone, at once jokey and venomous.

'No, it's just that I love mint sauce and warm beer,' Simon joked feebly.

They all laughed politely and, now reconciled by this barb at the expense of the English, they passed round the champagne. Julie poured and Simon couldn't help feeling a twinge of bitterness in the pit of his stomach as he stared at her pale, slender hand with its elegant nails which, from the moment he first saw it, had seemed to him the supreme epitome of beauty. So, she had chosen Nicholas . . . A night with Matthieu, a lifetime with Nicholas. They seemed to get along well. Simon thought sadly – and all the more sincerely since he barely knew her – that Julie was his dream woman. Beautiful, charming, rather funny.

'So, did you finally get your degree in maths?' he asked.

'You remember about that? I feel honoured. Yeah, I got it, I even passed my teaching diploma, I work in a secondary school now in Aulnay-sous-Bois.'

Simon felt he had to ask a question, but didn't know what it was. At random, he ventured: 'You don't find it too hard?'

She smiled. 'Let's just say it's not exactly easy. But it's so rewarding, working with kids.'

If they stayed on the subject of teaching, the conversation would become difficult. By some miracle, Julie already seemed bored with the subject and suggested everyone sit down to eat. The tablecloth covered the large wooden top of what was probably Nicholas's desk. Two of the chairs were wobbly.

The guests included colleagues of Nicholas and Julie and two friends, an actor and a businessman. The actor talked a lot and managed to keep up the party mood which Julie's two colleagues rather spoiled, as both were clearly exhausted after a long week at school.

'So what do you do?' Simon asked the businessman.

'I sell software,' he answered chewing on a piece of lemon chicken dripping with sauce.

'What kind of software?'

'It's for banks. Financial markets.'

'Really? I know the territory, that's what I work in.'

'So I figured,' said the man, still chewing. 'Me and my partner, we've been approaching banks directly. We've had a couple of interesting propositions, but not interesting enough.'

'To buy your software packages?'

'Actually, there's just one software package, very high-performance. Really high-performance. It was developed at Stanford University, in a lab my partner used to work at. It's the best piece of financial software ever developed.'

'How much are you selling it for?'

'Ten million dollars.'

'Ten million dollars for a piece of software?' Simon choked and was about to go on when he noticed an awkward look flash between Julie and Nicholas.

'It's a fair price,' the man went on. 'The banks will earn billions with it. Traders won't be able to live without it.'

'There's a lot of software like that out there. In fact in my own job, I develop statistical models for traders . . .'

'Oh, really?' said the man, giving Simon a broad smile, though his eyes were expressionless. 'So we're in competition.'

Since people were now staring at them, looking increasingly embarrassed, Simon did not reply. But the businessman was on a roll. He began extolling the merits of his software and the longer he went on the more Simon realised that he knew almost nothing about finance, that under a veneer of technical terms and English words, what he was saying was preposterous. There were thousands of software packages out there whose sole purpose was to help traders make decisions. Setting a ten-million-dollar price tag was insane. He turned to Nicholas, who was listening politely as though to a child. He made an apologetic gesture. Everyone else looked at the smooth talker warily. Julie blushed and stared down at her plate.

'We've been friends since high school,' she said suddenly, looking up at the businessman. 'Matthieu has a great imagination,' she stressed the word, 'and I hope this project gets off the ground.'

'I hope so too,' said Simon, noticing for the first time that the man bore the same name as his friend.

A liar or a lunatic. Probably not a fraud since he would have been incapable of fooling anyone. Just someone lost in words and dreams. '. . . I'm telling you, it's the perfect tool for a trader. No risk manager will be able to work without it, they'll be recommending it to all their teams . . .' The most astonishing thing was that Simon's presence did not faze the man at all. Given that he was sitting opposite a quantitative analyst, he should have shut up, but the prospect of making a fool of himself did not stop him. He ploughed on, eyes utterly blank, speaking easily and fluently like a gifted but superficial actor, caught up in his daydream, an illusionist. 'A complex collection of algorithms analysing correlations . . . In fact, our software can even calculate volatility . . .'

He suddenly saw the man in all his miserable condition, a mediocre student who had never really grown up, living in a dream world, utterly destroyed by his unconditional, pitiful need to exist even if it meant lying, a pathetic version of the demons of greed that had taken hold of his contemporaries, twisting and sobbing in their need to exist, like a loud wail launched at the icy blue of the heavens.

'It sounds very interesting,' Simon interrupted him suddenly. 'Actually, you should ask for fifteen million.'

The fabulist's face lit up.

Finally, someone understood him.

# 17

Lev was worried. The crisis was more serious than expected and his little oil empire was faltering. In fact, it was a surprise that Russia had held out as long as it had after the transition, what with a government incapable of governing, a clapped-out economy and a people that had lost its way. The country had survived for a time owing to the shock tactics of Gaidar's government, in spite of shortages even more devastating than those of the Soviet period, and slowly basic commodities had found their way back to the shops. But the government had problems paying civil servants and some of them now earned nothing at all. Elena had not been paid in over a year. The logical result of a bankrupt tax system, given that businesses and individuals alike paid taxes only under extreme duress. Uncollected tax revenues were estimated at 50 per cent. Across large areas of the country, barter had replaced money and a number of businesses paid their employees in kind, the onus being on them to then sell the products.

ELK was caught in a pincer movement between plummeting oil prices and the credit crisis affecting the banks. A number of banks had been wound up and some oligarchs had been completely ruined. Lev was not in this position, since, although his reserves of roubles were worthless, his dollar investments, some with a London hedge fund called Saniak, the rest dispersed in various tax havens, were flourishing. That said, there was no possible comparison between his personal fortune, large though it was, and the value of ELK, and if the business went bankrupt, he would be nothing.  An oil empire was not built in a day, nor without major investment. Lev's debts were colossal.  But now the drying-up of credit following the banking collapses meant he was boxed into a corner. He could afford to pay salaries for the next two months, but after that . . .

Yeltsin could have helped him. With his influence, he could have found money. But what was the President now? A sick old man given to fits of authoritarianism,  preoccupied with his own interests and blinded by the oligarchs in his entourage, seven of them, known as 'the boyars', like the Seven Boyars of the Time of Troubles in the seventeenth century. They had bankrolled his re-election campaign in 1996, when all was lost, when all the polls predicted the Communists would win, something which obviously no oligarch was prepared to accept. At this point the seven oligarchs – Berezovsky declared they were 'half the Russian economy' – did a deal with 'The Family', as Yeltsin's inner circle was known. They controlled the raw materials, the banks, the media. All the powers in the country, in fact. They poured money back into the economy, spewed propaganda through the media, they were lavish with 'gifts' and rumours of electoral fraud were rife. All the incredible, unscrupulous energy upon which they had built their empires, they placed in the service of a lost man.

And their man won. They used him like a puppet, dangling his heavy-set frame, at once unpopular and charismatic, in front of the crowds, and the hero of 1991, standing on his tank, had been re-elected, ensuring the power of the seven puppeteers laughing behind the screen. Litvinov was one of the Seven. And Lev was not among them.

In a sense, his absence was unsurprising. He had neither the money nor the power of the Seven. And he had no influence with the media. But in the race between the oligarchs which began with the transition, his absence signalled his defeat. Wealth feeds on wealth. Retreat and delay were costly. Now that he was in trouble, where could Lev find an ally? The Seven were in a position of strength and if banks were rescued, it was their banks. And their businesses were afforded every advantage.

It was a dangerous moment. Fate was hesitating, something of which Lev was well aware. A game had begun on which his whole future was to depend. And he did not hold all the cards, since his fate was tied to that of the country. As usual, since the period of transition, he was an attendant to History, an economic and social cog in the great machine, exploiting the flaws and the pitfalls of the half-blind mechanism to try his luck, to elevate his status as a man, vulnerable to the slightest reversal of fortune. For the moment, he wasn't broke. Though he had no illusions about the role he had played, Lev still felt that he had been at the right place at the right time, had known how to make the most of it, with a little intelligence and a lot of effort. Though he sometimes doubted how much scope he had in his decision-making, he was still Lev Kravchenko, Russian billionaire, a paradigm of power and wealth, even if Lev knew better than anyone the flaws in the paradigm, in its fleeting and illusory nature.

That evening, he got home late. The lofty gates parted for his car, operated by the austerely deferential caretaker, heralding the tedious ritual of his evenings. Lev walked up the steps, briefcase in hand, with, he noticed, a heavier tread than usual.

But this evening, the ritual was different. Elena did not appear. The hall was empty. Vast, cold (these things were normal), but empty too.

'Is my wife not here?' he asked.

'She went out, sir. With the children.'

Where could she possibly have gone at this hour?

It was true their relationship had deteriorated since the Riabine affair. And yet, when he swore to her that he had rejected violence, she had believed him. Her whole body had seemed to crumple as though exhausted at having had to bear such a terrible weight.

'You're a brave man, Lev. You rejected fear. You're the man you used to be.'

He had closed his eyes and kissed her. He felt no guilt about lying to her, because he wanted to save their marriage, but also because for a long time now words had not meant the same thing to him as they did to her. Elena's words described the realities she believed in, however misguidedly, whereas for Lev, words were weapons designed to persuade, to seduce, to attain. His aim was to appease her; he had succeeded. They had made love with somewhat exaggerated passion. It was a game he found not unpleasant, although deep down he no longer had the innocence for these displays of affection, the caresses, the devoted looks. It was not that he no longer loved his wife, not at all, it was simply – tragically – that he was too shut away inside himself to express his feelings or to show them. It is impossible to become a statue without harmful consequences; Lev's tragedy was that he had lost all contact with the world and if he had won a reputation, what he had lost as a man was irreparable.

The following morning, when he woke up, the conversation had continued, blithe and cheerful. Then came the question: 'But what's going to happen to this Riabine? Are Liekom going to take him over?'

Lev could lie, but Elena would easily be able to check later. And he was almost sure that she would do so.

'Absolutely not. We'll make him a better offer.'

'You said yourself, he's very attached to his land.'

'And he is,' Lev said in a soothing tone. 'But he's not stupid. I'll make him a very advantageous offer. It'll bankrupt me,' he added, laughing, 'but I'll get his land.'

Perhaps Elena thought his laugh sounded false. In any case, she slipped out of bed, put on her slippers and left the room without a word. And later, each time he tried to recapture the harmony of the previous evening, he failed, because his wife, her eyes like those of an inquisitor, could see right through him. A translucent glass partition came between them, distorting what was seen, muffling every sound. Doubt. Their conversations became stilted and monotonous, all vitality sapped. Nothing but words that underscored the tension. Elena wondered what Lev had done to Riabine, and in doing so, what he had done to himself, because she thought his soul hung in the balance. His soul! What a thought! Yes, of course Riabine had given up, and from what the wrestler said, they didn't even have to shake him up too hard. He'd signed and moved out.

Within the hour. Taking his cheque with him. He was probably in the Bahamas by now, gratefully lying on the sand by the sea, his pale, silent family sunning themselves and eating in the sunshine, far from icy Siberia. Why cling to that muddy patch of ground when he could be rich? And if they'd shaken him up, it was for his own good. And ELK had acquired a promising deposit of something which, in these difficult times, was not to be sneezed at.

Why was the palace so deserted?

Lev opened the wardrobe. Missing coats and dresses left a gaping void. He checked the children's wardrobes: half the clothes were gone.

He searched for a note, a message. Nothing. She had left nothing. Explained nothing. But what need was there to explain? She had discovered the truth about Riabine. How? Because she knew everyone in the city and because through the leaky cracks of a lie, the truth finally comes out.

Lev sat in the living room. The vastness of it was comical. Over the years he had grown accustomed to these surroundings, but now that he was alone the cavernous rooms with their anachronistic proportions resumed the ridiculous appearance they had had at first, that farcical air that had prompted Lev to buy this palace of fallen princes.

Lev could understand his wife's reaction. He felt no anger, nor did he feel sorrow. This was how things were, that was all. He had gambled, he had lost. He had tried to resolve the situation as he thought best, to come up with a credible lie, and eventually he had been found out. But he had had no choice. Riabine's oilfield was crucial. The crisis only confirmed that.

He could not show any sign of weakness.

Lev was alone now, and though he could use every reason on earth to try to justify his position, he could not change the fact that the only woman he had ever loved had just left him, because he was a coward, because he was corrupt. And in a world of predators, Lev could survive only by fighting and winning. The departure of his wife and children left him weaker. At a moment as dangerous as this, this first desertion was inconvenient. He would fight, as he always did. He would try to win back his wife, but his chances were slim. He would try to save his business. Always the struggle.

But in this moment beyond time and battle, on a white sofa in a deserted palace, Lev was not thinking about fighting. Everything in him that had not been hardened, all that is weak and frail in man, yielded. And the eternal question posed itself: 'What was it all for?'

He stayed there for hours until late into the night. He could think of no answer. Suddenly he got to his feet, took a couple of paces, went and fetched his briefcase from the next room and took out his address book. He picked up the phone and dialled a number. Someone answered. He said a few words.

He heard a warm, sleepy voice: 'Councillor Kravchenko? It's very late for you to be calling . . .'

He apologised.

'It's the weariness, isn't it? I told you long ago at that wonderful party. It comes to every fighter in time.'

'I'd like to be rid of it,' said Lev.

The woman laughed. He remembered how sensual her face was when she laughed.

'I've been waiting, Councillor. I've often thought of you, I was sorry you never came.'

'I'm here now,' said Lev.

'Not entirely. Come over, Councillor, I'm waiting for you. The night is still young.'

# 18

One evening, after an interview, Matt came home particularly disheartened.

'It didn't go well?' Simon asked.

Matt shook his head and slumped onto the sofa and lay there for an hour.

In the kitchen, Simon was making pasta – which, with salads, formed their basic diet – when he heard something in the living room.

'It's not the job that's the problem,' Matt said in a monotone, staring into space, addressing some unspecified audience. 'I don't give a fuck about the job. I've no desire to work for someone else, I hate being an employee, I loathe hierarchies and I couldn't give a toss about banks. All they're good for is inflating cash, they're parasites. No, what I want is money. And I swear, it's not that I love money in itself, I feel no admiration for people who earn it and I despise people who worship it. That's not the way I am. But I want money, I need it. Because I can't go on sponging off you.'

Simon went over to his friend, making a vague gesture of protest which Matt did not even notice.

'I can't spend the next fifteen years claiming to work for a hedge fund I've never set foot in,' Matt went on. 'And I'm convinced that in a few years, in ten or maybe twenty years, it'll be every man for himself. I'm sure this whole thing is going to explode. These societies, these social systems. Only money can protect us. Life in the West is based on myths. Social security, retirement, unemployment benefits . . . That stuff is never going to last. The coffers are empty. Governments are kidding us when they say we're in a period of economic growth. Look at the financial crisis in Asia, look at Russia, everything's falling apart. And we'll end up going the same way. What we've got is a slight upturn, all funded by deficits. It's nothing but debt, the whole thing. Everyone's living on credit, Americans are constantly borrowing while Europeans are digging themselves into a hole to fund social security and programmes for the feckless. The whole thing's going to implode, take my word for it. Governments around the world are going to fall apart because there'll be no more money, because the businesses and the mafia will be more powerful than them, because the movements of money they can't control are increasing by the day. Thousands of billions are sloshing around the stock markets and who knows where it comes from? Who can differentiate between speculation, money-laundering and industry profits? When money is invested in the Emirates, how can anyone prove it's come from trafficking in prostitutes, drugs, arms sales, not just delivering Ferraris? The whole world is a gigantic laundromat. Money flows freely for the benefit of the few and everything's organised to make sure it stays that way. I'm telling you, the scale of the disaster is growing. All the conditions are in place, it's bound to happen. There'll be minor crises, major crises, then suddenly the whole thing will explode and the tower will crumble. Just like Babel, but this will be the Last Judgement. Ghosts will wander the streets prophesying the end of the world. All the walls will crumble, the apocalypse will rain down with a fist of steel. I know you think I'm a madman but that's because I'm telling the truth. It'll all collapse. Bankrupt states will provide a skeleton service, they'll be a smokescreen of big words and grand gestures with nothing to back them up. Until the time comes when they can no longer front it out. They'll stop paying civil servants, everything will fall apart, first the utilities, then the schools, then the courts, the army, finally the police. And at that point the streets will be ruled by gangs. I can see it. It's not a theory, I can see it happening. Borders will collapse and immigrants will flood in by the millions to enjoy wealth that no longer exists. And at that point, cash will reign supreme. All we've experienced so far is a little overheating. What's coming will be in a completely different league. Why do the Russians seem so obsessed with buying gold? Because they have no choice. Because without gold, they'll die. Money is what will save us when it happens, Simon. We'll have private militias, we'll live in ghettos for the rich with armies manning the gates. The way the world works is that the rich get richer, the poor get poorer and the middle classes explode. And it's the middle classes that make for peaceful, liberal democracies. The rich and the poor make for war.'

Matt babbled on, increasingly agitated.

'They reject me. They all reject me. Because I didn't get a degree, because I act like a waster, because I fuck all the hot girls while they have to screw the slags. Because there's always something about me that's wrong, something they don't like the look of. But I'll tell you something, Simon, the real reason they reject me is because I *know*. I was the one who said we needed to be where the money was, and in your case at least I was right. And what I'm telling you now will happen too. It's just a matter of observation and logic. Being on the lookout for the thousand little signs all over the world that signal the beginning of the crash. The tower will collapse. They brush me aside, they make like they're so aloof and superior but I'm telling you they won't be laughing so hard when the banks collapse, when they're digging their graves. The distinctive feature of these cretins is that they're just technicians, little men who've seized power in an unpredictable era. I may be nothing, but I *know*. It's not a matter of intelligence, or not the way they think, it's a matter of *vision*. Make money, Simon, make as much as you can, don't hang around in that underpaid job you've got, get yourself promoted, get out there, start earning big bucks. And I'll do whatever I can to earn money. To protect myself, to protect us. Because we're brothers. Blood brothers since the first time we met. We've pooled our blood, we'll pool our money. I'll have an estate built that will be like a Tower to protect us, with a private army, with high walls. We'll be our own State, our own protection, our own private utopia. But to do that we need to earn money, lots and lots of money. By any means possible. We'll build a tower of marble and steel which will be the witchcraft of the new world, impervious to crime, to violence, to misfortune. A tower raised against the apocalypse, impregnable, so powerful that the waves of destruction will break against it. Yes, they'll break against the walls and we'll be inside, brothers, twins, with all the women and all the servants we could ever need. United against everyone. This is what we need, by any means possible.'

And as abruptly as he had begun, he fell silent, like a drunkard collapsing suddenly. But Matt wasn't drunk, he was simply desperate – and his despair had the power of the greatest revelations, like some prophet struck dumb by a vision that overwhelms and engulfs him. He had seen; he had spoken. Ridiculous and prophetic all at once. He might be mad, eaten away by his lust for power, but weren't his friend's crazy flaws why Simon loved him?

Simon went off to set the table. He reheated the cold pasta, made a little sauce to which he added *herbes de Provence,* got out a bottle of red wine which he decided they needed to drown his friend's sorrows and set out the best plates and the best glasses. It was a festive dinner, celebrating failure and the predicted apocalypse while trying to come to terms with it. They had to boost Matt's spirits and get back to real life, away from the visions, the dreams and the madness.

The horsemen of the apocalypse ate their pasta in silence. Not because they had nothing to say, but simply because they were comfortable that way. Mute friendship. It was one of the best dinners, not as good as the one at Lemerre's restaurant, perhaps, but without the distractions of thugs like Ruffle and waiters with broken noses.

Simon's concern was all the more remarkable because at the time he had a lot of worries at the bank. The white carpet in the communal hallways was still beautiful, and when he stepped out into the calm, tree-lined square, wearing one of his designer suits, he was still a gangster, but just now being a gangster wasn't easy, and he would rather be a researcher as he had once been.

To date, he had proved a diligent quant, stringing together his equations, conscientious in his work. Zadie was satisfied, which was more than enough for Simon, who was still in awe of the head of the trading desk. But he had taken a dangerous initiative: he had taken a risk. The magic word, this word used to justify imbalances, was now a part of his world, which was specifically intended to model risks and thereby tame them. He had become interested in the concept of the ideal price, a concept similar to the pot of gold at the end of the rainbow. *The ideal price*: the thought horizon of every quant, indeed the very reason for his labours. In fact one of Simon's chief tasks was to create models which helped traders forecast commodity prices. But with the complex commodities he was dealing with, pricing was anything but straightforward.

So far, he had failed to come up with anything groundbreaking in this area. His models were much like those of his counterparts at other banks and he had never managed to give the traders at his desk a particular advantage. Then came POL, an oil-based derivative devised by a couple of structurers at Kelmann, had been something of a success. It was a structured product designed to protect oil producers against unanticipated fluctuations in barrel prices which, in 1998, were in freefall. Simon had been carefully considering the product for some time. But however much he studied, he did not come to the same conclusions as the other quants: he felt the price was overvalued, everyone else thought the price was undervalued. And even if the product was a success, all the banks would sell it and profits were slim since they had to be spread out.

'Zadie,' he approached his boss timidly one day, 'I've got a suggestion to make about POL.'

'Oh?' she said distractedly.

'I think we should drop the price.'

'Drop the price? You're kidding.'

'No, I really think we should. In my opinion we can sell it cheaper, the maturity price will be lower than we've calculated.'

'The traders have calculated the maturity price based on models provided by the quants,' Zadie said curtly, 'we were following you.'

'I wasn't involved in those models. But I drew up a new model: I think the risks were overestimated. I really think we can lower the price.'

'You realise what that means? If we're wrong about the model and the price ends up being higher, we'll lose millions.'

'Yes, but I also know that if we set a lower price, we'll corner the whole market. And in oil, even for a single derivative like POL, that's big.'

'And you're absolutely sure of your model?'

'We can never be absolutely sure, you know that. But I did something new,' said Simon with a hint of pride, 'something I think no one's ever done. I didn't just estimate the volatility, I estimated the volatility of the volatility.'

'What are you talking about?'

A flicker of interest appeared in Zadie's eyes. Her inner mathematician was stirring.

'I read a research paper about it,' explained Simon. 'It's never been applied to markets before, but I'm convinced it's sound.

We make do with factoring in volatility, meaning the standard deviation of the asset return. But that volatility in turn can be modelled; it's possible to measure the volatility of the volatility.'

Zadie nodded. 'Standard Brownian motion?'

'Exactly. Simple as that,' said Simon.

Zadie called a meeting. Structurers, quants and traders all gathered around the table. She explained Simon's suggestion. All the quants were indignant. They were confident of their models. In fact everyone in the market was agreed on the price.

'That's not the issue,' said Simon in a barely audible voice. 'I think everyone has overvalued the risks. I realise this might sound conceited but . . .'

'It is conceited. What, you think you're cleverer than everyone else?'

'Not at all. But on that point . . .'

'It's not a point, it's a financial model we all worked on here. You didn't lift a finger to help and now you start pissing all over it. I'm sure you're wrong about this and this bullshit of yours is going to lose the team a shitload of money.'

'I don't think so,' said Simon, his eyelids fluttering desperately. 'I estimated the volatility of the volatility and I can tell you that . . .'

'The volatility of the volatility? What sort of bullshit is that?'

'Not at all, not at all,' said Simon feebly, 'it's stochastic calculus, a Brownian model. It can be done, I assure you, there are papers on the subject going back to 1993 and even if no one has ever applied it to markets, I'm convinced . . .'

'Look, we're doing serious work here, if you want to do experiments, go back to your lab.'

'I tested it,' cried Simon, 'I've run simulations using figures for the past two years. It works, I'm telling you.'

There was a deafening silence. Simon could feel the hate-filled stares of everyone. It was at this point that Samuel joined the conversation, smiling and relaxed.

'The volatility of the volatility . . . It has a nice ring to it, doesn't it? I'm not against the concept. If you're right, we'll corner the whole market.'

Samuel was the best trader on the team and one of the best in the room. What he said carried decisive weight.

'We're all aware of that,' interrupted Zadie, 'that's why I called this meeting. What we need to do is put personal egos aside and make the best decision.'

This comment was redundant. If Simon was right, it would be a complete humiliation for the other quants. They had been too vehement in their opposition.

'I calculate the optimum price to be forty-five,' Simon said in the utter silence, 'rather than forty-nine, which is what we're currently selling at. If we drop the price to forty-seven, we'll corner the market and make a healthy profit.'

One of the quants got to his feet. He was a giant, a rugby prop from Oxford who considered himself king of the world.

'Bullshit! I've always thought this guy was a fuckwit. You go with him and I'm out of here.'

Zadie's expression was electric. She remembered her interview with Simon. He had been good, really good. His English was terrible and he had absolutely no charisma, he had a weak, even fragile personality, but he was an outstanding mathematician . . . The volatility of volatility . . . It was a brilliant idea. Pushing back the boundaries of risk. She glanced over at Simon. The tall quant's outburst had completely crushed him. His shoulders had slumped, everything about him seemed shrivelled, diminished, drained. It was obvious all he wanted to do was go home and hide away in his bed; in all probability he was sorry he had ever had the idea.

'We're going with him,' she said, articulating each syllable. 'The meeting is over.'

Simon lived in dread for the following months. The traders had offered the product at the price he had set; they had cornered the market and the model seemed to be working out. But it might still go pear-shaped.

After the rugby player had departed, slamming every door along the way, not a single quant had spoken to him except on urgent professional matters and then only to try and catch him out. Try as he might to speculate philosophically as to why working environments pushed people towards hatred and confrontation, the practical experience of being knifed in the back was so distressing that he found he no longer slept. His face became gaunt.

Through the brokers it became clear that other banks were in a panic. They no longer knew how to deal with their clients. New data models were being generated all over the place, quants worked through the night, but none of them could reproduce Simon's model. In the jargon of the trade, they weren't asking the right questions. There were widespread rumours of some new method of calculation based on the volatility of the volatility but no one knew how to use it.

Then, within a week, the market converged on Simon's

price. The shift on this single product was universal. The banks admitted defeat. They cut their risks and fell into line with Kelmann.

At 9.55 am on 29 July, Zadie came up behind Simon and said coolly: 'The market's ours, Simon, all the other banks are following us. I think you'll be pleasantly surprised by your end-of-year bonus.'

At that moment he didn't give a damn about his bonus. As these words were uttered evenly, Simon felt his heart leap in his chest. He felt *justified*. His life had meaning. He had been so afraid, here in the closed circle of the bank where criteria unrelated to money no longer existed, that the ideal price seemed like a personal achievement, in fact, in that moment of euphoria, his crowning achievement: he had been the first quant to exploit the volatility of volatility.

'Champagne tonight, Simon. I'm having a little get-together at my place. You will join us?'

It was common knowledge that Zadie never invited colleagues to her home. Occasionally she might invite Samuel to a restaurant, invariably with a group of old friends she'd known since Cambridge and who, for the most part, had nothing to do with banking. According to Samuel, they were terrifying (Samuel liked to play the hillbilly from Minnesota while underscoring this façade with a broad sardonic smile) because they were 'horribly cultured and refined'. They were professors of philosophy or literature, artists or writers with that ghastly elegance particular to rich families of good birth. Their conversations were dreadful, they talked only about literature, art and politics and, worse still, what they said probably made sense.

'Steel yourself, Simon! This is going to be tougher than anything you've ever been through,' said Samuel sympathetically, putting a hand on his shoulder.

In fact it was a signal honour, something Samuel was well aware of. That the famous Zadie, destined for a managerial position at Kelmann, should invite Simon Jude to her home, to her apartment where no one at the bank had ever set foot, was both incredible and humiliating for everyone. Samuel could joke about it because he did not feel threatened. He knew he would be a success, and his success did not depend on Zadie. In two or three years he would leave Kelmann and set up a venture capital fund. For everyone else, particularly for the quants who had laughed at Simon, the invitation was a snub. When they saw this shambling idiot, as drunk on alleviated tension as if he'd been drinking wine, leaving the trading room ahead of everyone else to prepare for the exceptional Zadie Zale's dinner party, their defeat was totally and utterly sealed.

'Tonight, you fuck her,' Matt announced simply. 'If she's invited you to her place, that's why. What other reason?'

What other reason? For his brilliance, for his dynamism, for his success, for the pure, precise definition, like a perfectly realised demonstration, of the ideal price. Surely there was a poetry of mathematics that meant he deserved to rub shoulders with artists? Banking, after all, was not a mortal sin. But Matt, gloomy as ever, was not persuaded by these arguments.

Simon carefully got ready. Far from the cold arena that had seen him tremble, the gangster artist descended the white staircase. A new life was waiting for him.

# 19

The image of the man with his hand raised haunted Shoshana. Not the man himself, but the image. In fact a double image. That of the man sprawled on the floor, fingers streaked with blood, and that of the man making the sign of peace. It seemed to her that the one was assimilated into the other and that by her actions she had cancelled out the calamity of the first. In apologising to this man, she had brought peace to discord.

That same evening, as they had dinner together, she watched Mark and Christopher reunited under her protection, saved, perhaps, by her intervention. They were eating, Mark talking about his day, Christopher saying nothing – but at least they'd managed to drag him away from the TV – and she kept the conversation going, all the while thrilled by this marvellous normality. She felt relieved, as though still buoyed up by the black waiter's gesture. The man at her table now was not a gargoyle but her husband, Mark Ruffle, a man who could be quick-tempered but who was endearing, full of vitality, the man she'd been with since her childhood. And setting aside the weariness and the outbursts, wasn't he the love of her life?

Mark was wearing a T-shirt that hugged his pecs. At regular intervals, in a tic he had had since adolescence, he'd flick his wrist to flex his biceps. This little quirk, which normally irritated her, Shoshana now found charming. The block of childhood from which the adult was emerging, she found poignant. And Ruffle himself, sensing Shoshana's gentleness, was happier and more talkative than usual. He ruffled his son's hair and the boy looked up, astonished, then stared down at his plate. He recounted a story one of his brokers had told him about going into an apartment so disgustingly filthy that he'd thought twice about getting the tenant to sign a contract, so pained was he at the thought that the beautiful house purchased with a loan from Ruffle Universal Building would be sullied by such a revolting creature. And Shoshana, who had often met her husband's brokers and was under no illusions about their moral standards, burst out laughing. Chris, not understanding what was going on, laughed with her.

The miracle of a raised hand.

They lived for a time in the wake of an image.

RUB's figures were impressive. The brokers, motivated by their bonuses, scoured the area and no one was able to resist their glib sales pitch. It was not simply their conjuring skills, it was the fact that all of America believed in mortgages. Ruffle made the most of the expanding property bubble in which prices rose steadily year on year. He had been among the first to market, had set up shop and now trees could grow to the sky: the property boom had begun. In Miami, it hadn't yet exploded, but there was a definite trend. Poor people moved into beautiful houses whose values constantly rose and suddenly the same poor people discovered they were rich: their houses were worth two and even three hundred thousand dollars. Ruffle Universal Building, now believing they had this money, hounded them to

213

take out supplementary loans. Ruffle had finally found what he needed to say and being a man of action, a man who relied on facts, he gave an example. He would say: 'I am the architect of the American dream. Through me, cleaning ladies can own their own homes.' And he would cite the example of Dolores, a forty-year-old cleaning woman from Mexico living in straitened circumstances who, thanks to RUB, had bought a little house and later took a second mortgage on a big house which she rented out. In passing, RUB had given her a loan to buy a car. Suddenly this cleaning woman with nothing now had everything: she and her three children lived in the little house, earned money renting out the big house and drove around in a Mercedes; her lifelong dreams had come true. When she went back to Mexico, to her squalid little village, children flocked around the car, looking at their reflections in the tinted windows and the gleaming polished bodywork of the Mercedes. And Ruffle never tired of saying: 'Before, she had nothing; now she has everything.'

People fell silent when he said this. In their eyes, he saw the awe and admiration of Sundays. He had become what he always wanted. This thing he had felt as a teenager once a week he now felt every day in spite of the staffing, administrative and financial difficulties inherent in running a business. His life was *justified*. He was an entrepreneur, which was the pinnacle of achievement in the hierarchy of his country, his family were together, he was rich and he did good around him. He was the architect of the American dream.

His satisfaction was flawless. All his life Ruffle had been searching for himself and, curiously, this man who seemed little more than a moron had found himself. His narrow mind constricted by prejudice had nonetheless allowed him to find the path to become what he had always wanted to be. He was rich, popular and respectable. In short, he had become a part of the image bequeathed him by his family. Doubt was therefore forbidden.

Shoshana had watched his act of self-realisation, by which a man who constantly doubted his abilities had managed to shore up the cracks, and build a statue of self-satisfaction that was solid as a rock. She had been vaguely surprised, particularly since she herself was plagued by self-doubt. She considered herself a woman of limited intellect, a mother tyrannised by an all-powerful, all-televisual son, a woman with no professional life. As such, her husband's energy left her paralysed and plunged her back into the depths of self-doubt. Essentially, she was simply a pleasing image, a snapshot brought to life by Mark in his living room, in his bedroom. She much preferred this self-satisfied husband to the bitter gargoyle who asserted himself through violence, though she knew the lies that propped up all his charming stories about cleaning women; the fractured man had found a purpose. At least he had found his role, which was more than she had. Shoshana had no role and this was what she truly lacked. With no identity to assume, she wandered through a maze of questions, constantly crashing into distorting mirrors that reflected hideous images of her.

In the end, the only image that still made her happy was her physical appearance. And though she was ambivalent even about this precisely because she felt it was the only thing Mark valued about her, at least it was a positive point. At the gym, there were mirrors everywhere. The women sweating and contorting, working on the all-important bums and tums, or some more minor aesthetic exercise, stared, wincing, at their bouncing reflections. When the pain barrier hit, when abdominal exercises became spasms, when thigh muscles cramped, the mirror became the Grail, the almighty, reassuring god of appearances to whom they offered up their panting and their pain. Shoshana was aware that the way other women looked at her had changed little since she was a teenager. In some sense, she was still the Clarimont cheerleader, envied and admired for her legs, her breasts. The tight buns squeezed into tight shorts, she did the exercises gracefully and skilfully. She knew that if the instructor was a man, he looked at her more than at the others. And when the exercises became more difficult, her effortlessness, since she had been an athlete, brought a discreet smile of pleasure to her lips, a sense of pride she still retained, a paltry but pleasant sense of pride.

After one such session, and without quite knowing what she intended to do, she headed for Sila's restaurant. As she had the first time, she stood staring through the window. Then, realising it was still early, that she still had time, she went inside.

He was there. She saw him immediately. He was talking to a waiter, asking him to do something. He turned. He stopped. Then slowly, very slowly, he walked towards her. She did not move, stood frozen in the doorway, breathing hard.

'Hello,' he said.

'Hello.'

'You left very suddenly last time.'

It was a statement, not a criticism, with a sort of acceptance she took for complicity. She nodded.

'Would you like to have lunch?'

'Well, a drink anyway. Is that okay?'

'Of course. I'll show you to a table.'

'Could I have the same table please?'

The restaurant was almost empty. Several waiters were standing around doing nothing. She felt out of place. What was she doing here? Why had she come? For the peace, obviously. To experience again the magic that, for a time, had brought peace to her house but was fading now, leaving her anxious, like an emptiness inside her. Yes, to relive the magic of the man with the outstretched hand.

He reappeared with a Coke. She couldn't remember ordering one, but he would know better than her.

'Take a seat,' she said.

'I have to work.'

'Please,' she insisted. 'I'd like to talk to you. I was stupid, running away like that last time . . .'

Sila sat down opposite her.

'You didn't run away . . .' he said calmly, 'you apologised, though you had no need to since the offence was entirely your husband's, and then you left because you felt you had done your duty. Thank you for your gesture.'

'I'm the one who should be thanking you,' she stammered. 'When you got up, I mean when you put up your hand in a sign of peace, I thought that it was wonderful, you know, I thought, oh, I'm sorry, maybe this isn't what you meant at all, but I thought that you were prepared to forgive me, to give me inner peace.'

'Inner peace?' Sila asked, astonished.

'Yes, really, inner peace. I felt like I'd been in torment ever since that terrible moment, that nothing was right with my life, with my marriage. I was so angry with my husband, I couldn't bring myself to touch him. You'll laugh, but he reminded me of those grotesque animals carved in stone at Notre-Dame.'

'The gargoyles?'

'Exactly,' she said, 'a gargoyle, brutish and dangerous, taking it out on the weak.'

'I am not weak, Madame Ruffle.'

It did not even occur to her that he shouldn't know her name.

'I didn't mean to offend you,' she said, 'I . . .'

'It's okay, I'm not offended, in fact I shouldn't have reacted like that. But I'm not weak,' he said, still completely composed.

She looked at him. His calmness impressed her.

'Of course, you're right. It's obvious. It's just that my husband was so stupid, so brutal, so . . . grotesquely violent. I couldn't bear it, what he did. I felt so guilty, so upset. And it was a wonderful stroke of luck running into you like this.'

'It wasn't luck. I came to Miami because I knew your husband lived in Florida. Not because I wanted revenge, I assure you, not for any particular reason. I just wanted to be closer to this man. I don't know why. I just did. Because, like you, I was stunned. I couldn't understand. That night, I was just doing my job, waiting on tables, and a man got up and punched me. Because he thinks he's entitled to do what he likes. Because he's paying a lot of money for his meal. Or some other blindly stupid reason. So I came here. I took my time. Since your last visit, I did a little research. I know where you live, I know what your husband does for a living. I've seen how he exploits the gullibility, the poverty of the people in this city. I can't say I'm surprised. He's still hitting people. He's just less obvious about it.'

'You know who we are?' Shoshana said, her voice faint.

Sila smiled.

'Yes, Madame Ruffle. I've even been past your house. On a bicycle. Just a little Sunday bike ride. I didn't see you, the house is too big, too well protected. It's very beautiful, actually. So white . . .'

'What did you want?'

'Nothing. Absolutely nothing. Just a little unhealthy curiosity. I'm here, that's all,' Sila said, his voice more determined.

'You're here,' Shoshana said solemnly. 'Are you going to hurt us?'

Sila looked into the fearful, trusting face leaning towards him. He realised she believed in him, for good and for ill.

'That was never my intention. I'm just an observer. I wanted to understand.'

'My God!' Shoshana burst out, burying her head in her hands. 'I'm so ashamed.'

The man facing her with the impassive face of a judge said nothing. She stared at his hands as they lay on the table, young powerful hands. If only he would make the sign again.

He got to his feet, placed a hand on her shoulder.

'You have nothing to be ashamed about. There's no reason for you to take the blame for this. And don't be afraid. I haven't come her to sow fear and discord. You can go back home and have no fear. I won't bother you.'

In his eyes, she could see only peace, but this time she did not feel comforted. Quite the reverse, she felt more fragile and more guilty.

'I'll go now,' she said. 'Thank you for listening.'

Shoshana slowly took her leave. Discord and shame weighed on her more heavily than ever. It was time to say something. It was up to Mark to make things right. She had to tell him the waiter was here in Miami.

## 20

In the voluptuous sob of destruction, Lev stood firm. He knew everything could collapse, but for the first time in a long time, the dangerous instability of his life offered some amusement. Building was interesting, managing was boring but struggling on the edge of the void was entertaining. ELK was close to bankruptcy. Salary payments were suspended, as were payments to businesses and subcontractors, but there was no choice but to keep paying interest to the banks, which would otherwise cut off their credit line. Only the great god money could save him.

Every evening, he would go home to a gorgeous prostitute to whom he was paying a small fortune. Oksana asked for nothing, demanded nothing.

'Councillor Kravchenko . . .' she would say in her warm, sardonic voice.

And the world would melt into fragile, fleeting pleasure. Only Lev's money interested Oksana, but she wanted to win it in this elegant game played by two. For as long as he paid, she entertained him. Lev remembered once seeing a young French boy, in the south of France, trying to chat up a Russian girl, an oligarch's daughter who was lying on a sun lounger on a private beach. He'd tried to talk to her; she'd looked through him as if he was invisible.

The young man had probably never in his life seen an expression of such utter disdain – one that had not a whit of hostility or anger, merely the conviction that he was nothing. This celebration of power and money that precluded the existence of almost the entire population of the planet was something Oksana possessed on a more playful level which made it worth the price. She probably knew all about his troubles, which thrilled her like a mayfly's sting, the enduring and suspended force of things destined to die. But what did it matter, since they were playing a game.

Elena had demanded a divorce and half of Lev's fortune.

Back to the wall, he had to fight while his waning strength encouraged new enemies. Decidedly, it was all simultaneously appalling and comical.

It was at this point that he received Litvinov's invitation. A plain card delivered by a man in a dark suit.

'Dear Lev, we find ourselves back in the old, blessed times when everything could be born or die. Let's talk about this next week, you pick the date.'

The tone of the message was somewhat surprising coming as it did from an enemy, but it was also somewhat expected. Liekom had their eye on ELK.

When he stepped into Litvinov's office the following week, he was not alone. Viktor Lianov, the head of the Brotherhood, was standing next to him. What little hair Litvinov still had was white. His complexion was flushed and unhealthy. Too much food and alcohol.

'Lev! Wonderful to see you!'

Lev thought he was sincere. They had not spoken in a long time. Of course they had always been rivals, and the encounters between them had simply served to measure the progress of the battle on an ever-increasing scale of power and money while changing nothing, fundamentally, in their relationship. They stared at each other, sized each other up. One had the advantage of position, the other of relative youth. They measured their progress, surveying each other like animals. And yet, secretly, something they shared brought them imperceptibly closer together: they shared a time. They had awoken to power as part of Yeltsin's team and since that time they had hurled themselves into a primal struggle: a fight for survival in an economy that had returned to the roots of industrial capitalism.

They sat. Lianov stood off to one side, leaning against the wall, as though he had no part in the discussion.

Litvinov made a little vague pleasant small talk. Then his heavy-set body stiffened and he drew a stark picture of the situation.

'We're back at the beginning, Lev. We're Yeltsin's team, we've got power now but just as we were in those early days, we're confronted by the same alternatives: fight or die. These are interesting times, Lev. We're coming to the end of the Yeltsin era. The man who made us is on his way out. He can't hang on much longer. He hasn't got the strength or the skills. The oligarchs are keeping him at arm's length, but we need a new man. Russia has only got a couple of weeks, the crash is coming any day now.'

'You're sure?'

'Positive,' said Litvinov. 'The coffers are empty. The tax system is dead, there's not a rouble coming in, it's total collapse. The Russian state is bankrupt.'

'How long?'

'Like I said, a few weeks, a couple of months at most.'

'What are you going to do?'

'First, try to save us, then restore order.'

'With who?'

'We don't know yet. Yeltsin is still acting on a whim: he's just fired Chernomyrdin and the guy replacing him just isn't up to it. Kiriyenko isn't going to go far, we need someone else.'

'But not someone too powerful, right?' Lev said. 'Someone strong enough to run the country and shrewd enough to maintain our beautiful triangle: an economic oligarchy indestructibly linked to the Kremlin and the central and regional administrations, in our best interests, obviously.'

The head of the Brotherhood burst out laughing.

'You're quite right,' he said, 'a magnificent triangle. But don't forget us, the oligarchs need us. Without us, you become very vulnerable. Terribly human. The triangle becomes a square.'

'Of course he's right, Lev is always right,' said Litvinov. 'Everyone on Yeltsin's council admired you. Such intelligence!'

Lev knew that he was despised even for this. He waited for Litvinov to get to the point.

'When the crash comes,' Litvinov went on, 'the rouble will plummet, banks will collapse. It's going to be hard to shore up the triangle. What are our options? The IMF and restructuring.'

Lev said nothing.

'The IMF is a no-brainer. A bankrupt Russia is too much of a threat. They can't let us go under and they know it. The whole bloc would collapse. In a couple of months, they'll be pumping in billions, and I'm telling you, Liekom is well placed to make the most of it. Trust me, not everything will be going into Yeltsin's pockets. I've already set out a couple of nets, we'll make a healthy catch.'

'What about the restructuring?' asked Lev, his mouth a little dry.

Litvinov hesitated. He too seemed a little nervous. He chose his words carefully.

'Liekom needs ELK. And ELK needs Liekom.'

There was silence. Of course. It had to be that. Why else organise this meeting?

'ELK is not for sale.'

'I'm sorry Lev, but you're broke, you can't afford to pay anyone.'

'The banks are behind me.'

Litvinov's eyes froze. Lev understood: he was going to shut down the banks. The Seven controlled everything. If Litvinov made their minds up for them, Lev's credit would be completely cut off.

'We'll make you a very generous offer. And obviously, you'll stay on as the head of ELK. You're the man for the job. You've got a first-rate company. But the financial crisis is too severe. We have to pool our resources. Several of the smaller oil companies need to merge, it's inevitable. The future belongs to the multinationals. Divided, we're weak. United, we're invincible.'

Lev knew this argument by heart, and the hackneyed sentence made him smile. That smile, a fleeting suggestion of a detachment he did not feel, surprised Litvinov.

'We've been fighting a long time, my friend,' Litvinov said, putting his hand on Lev's arm. 'Ten years. More than most men have to in ten lifetimes. Now it's time to enjoy life. To spend time with our families. These are our most precious assets.'

Litvinov clearly knew what had happened in his personal life. In fact, all of Moscow probably knew that Elena had left him. Yet Lev thought he sensed a surprising melancholy in Litvinov's tone.

'We have braved a difficult period in Russian history. And we have come through it with honour, defending freedom and free enterprise, just as we promised when we were Yeltsin's team. I won't mince words: I wanted power, I have power. And my interests merged neatly with those of the country. We built up vast companies, we are the face of modern capitalism. And we did it ourselves. Us, the oligarchs. Through our energy, our skill. But that era is coming to an end now, it's time to retire. This is an opportunity for you, Lev! You'll be richer than ever. Free to go on running your company or to go and soak up the sun in the most beautiful palaces in the world.'

Lev knew what he was going to say. He had to say the words slowly, almost regretfully, because these words, which signalled his defeat, his reversal of fortune, were not his own. It was not he who was speaking but a peasant farmer bound to his land by all the ancestral power of ownership.

'I want to be independent.'

He had said it as he should have, in the silence of last words. Slowly, forcefully, as one might repeat the noble words of a great writer. Riabine had been a great writer. Riabine was the perfect writer of a Russian scene.

Litvinov turned to the man leaning against the wall. The man remained impassive.

'I was hoping for a different answer, Lev.'

'I'm not surprised, my friend.'

Lev had never referred to him like this.

'What do you want to make you change your mind?'

'Nothing. My mind is made up.'

Litvinov turned again, shrugged helplessly, and again the man remained deadpan.

Lev got to his feet. He looked at Lianov, who held his gaze. Litvinov also stood up.

'Stay well, my friend. A terrible time lies ahead for us. I hope that we survive.'

The warning was clear. Curiously, it was with a certain cordiality that they shook hands. They shared the times. The victories, the defeats, the shifting eras. It would all be different. The transition was coming to an end and from the ruins a new world would doubtless rise, one whose features were not yet defined.

Lianov opened the door.

Lev moved away down the corridor. Destruction carried on. Communism was dead. Transition was dead. The times ahead would know the brutality of power stripped of the tatters of democracy. The Brotherhood had asserted itself and it was Lianov now who ran Liekom. There could be no doubt. The former lords could begin to stray through the melancholy ruins of power. Power was passing to others, in the terrifying nakedness of violence.

# 21

Elegance is chilling. Elegance, culture and ease are chilling for those who do not possess them. Particularly so for a shy, narrow-shouldered quantitative analyst. It was not as bad as Samuel had warned. It was worse.

The nightmare began with a Chelsea flat that was perfect, terrifyingly perfect. Why couldn't it at least be a nouveau-riche apartment? Why, from the moment he walked in the door, this supposedly aristocratic English taste, the immaculate perfection of art and literature? Why did the library shelves have to soar all the way to the ceiling? Why did the paintings have to seem so brilliant, so quintessentially *modern*? Why did this woman have to be both a banker and a sophisticate, nourished by centuries of wealth and education?

The nightmare was Zadie's friends greeting him with a politeness so perfect, so *chilling*, with a hint of pensive aloofness corresponding exactly to the time they needed to weigh him up and, inevitably, find him wanting. They were beautiful, well dressed and doubtless devastatingly intelligent. Their accent was high-flown, so English that a student as poor with languages as Simon was inevitably ridiculous.

The nightmare was also, was especially, the rapid-fire conversation, filled with rapid-fire allusions and in-jokes based on their long friendship, references that completely eluded him and denoted an intimacy from which he felt excluded.

Simon stood there, glass in hand, in the grip of his crippling shyness, quite simply crushed by this elegant gathering. How could he escape? How could he avoid these well-meaning glances, somewhat bemused by his utter silence. How could he get out of here?

Perhaps he should have avoided knocking over the vase on the hall table as he arrived. It was an outdated movie gag. But then it was crystal clear that Simon was an outdated gag. A man pierced with the paralysing arrows of shyness is always an outdated gag. He feels so clumsy, so ugly.

'Simon is our most brilliant quant,' said Zadie, to help her guest out.

'Bravo,' a young man named Peter commented ironically.

'It was completely by accident,' muttered Simon.

Everyone laughed. My God, this feeling of being ridiculous . . .

'And I can recite Rimbaud,' he added.

His statement was so absurd that they took it for English humour. They laughed again.

'What exactly is a brilliant quant?' Peter asked him.

'I have no idea. Zadie is brilliant, I solve equations.'

'But solving equations is brilliant,' interrupted a young woman, 'at least I think so, I was never able to, even at school.'

Simon turned to her gratefully. She was pale and had a long nose and light green eyes.

'Really?' said Simon, his tone too shrill and strange.

He thought it incredible that someone would not be able to solve equations at school. It was a gesture of friendship.

'Really,' said the young woman.

'Neither could I,' a number of others said in concert.

'You haven't answered my question,' protested Peter, who was having fun. 'What is a brilliant quant?'

'A brilliant quant is an analyst whose equations make money for the bank,' said Zadie simply.

'In that case, a brilliant banker is a banker who makes money for the bank,' said Peter.

'Exactly.'

'Then let me rephrase the question. What are the qualities of a brilliant banker?'

Zadie thought.

'Greed?'

Everyone turned. It was Simon who had spoken. His mouth was dry, he didn't know how he could have made such an outrageous remark. Zadie looked at him, a twinkle in her eye.

'Yes, greed. That's the primary quality of a banker.'

The young woman with the pale eyes smiled.

'A taste for gambling?' Simon ventured.

'A taste for gambling. Taken to the extreme. The urge to take maximum risks.'

'The ability to lie?'

Zadie hesitated.

'Sometimes,' she said at length. 'Yes, it is sometimes necessary.'

'Blindness?'

Everyone stared at Simon in astonishment. But no one is more foolhardy than a shy person on a roll.

'No. Little bankers blind themselves. People of no real worth. Blindness is the mark of a trader who's on a losing streak. He buries his head in the sand. Keeps playing even when he's losing, even when he's losing the bank's money.'

'The headlong rush? said the woman with the green eyes, decidedly friendly.

Zadie nodded.

'It's a feature of the system. It's not about the bankers themselves. Credit, and hence the essence of our system, is inevitably threatened by the headlong rush since it's based on futures. The future is our only maturity date. By definition, we're constantly moving forward, and if things move faster we have to move faster. The financial world is a race circuit where the cars have no brakes. When things are going well, all the cars race round. If one of them has an accident . . . anything can happen.'

Everyone fell silent. The young woman with green eyes glanced at Simon. Then suddenly, there was a thaw in the atmosphere. The narrow-shouldered quantitative analyst felt he had been adopted.

A caterer had prepared a buffet. Simon was hungry. The young woman complimented him on his appetite. He asked her name. She was Jane Hilland.

'My mother's French,' she explained.

'And I suppose your father's a British banker?' joked Simon, referring to the Hilland Bank.

'He is. I didn't realise you knew him,' said Jane with a big smile.

The young woman was an art history professor at Cambridge. All this was overwhelming; clearly Simon's first impression had been right: he should never have come.

'What I love about Vermeer,' he said suddenly, 'is the silence that radiates from his paintings.'

It was something he had read in a class many years ago. He still remembered it. Jane looked at him warily.

'Yes . . . I'm sure,' she said.

'It's all the more surprising given he was conceived during a thunderstorm.'

There was a flicker of doubt in Jane's eyes as though she suspected he was making fun of her. Simon panicked.

'Maybe I'm wrong,' he said.

'I have to confess, I don't know one way or the other,' said Jane magnanimously, 'I don't think so, but never mind . . .'

'I love art.'

'And Rimbaud, don't forget Rimbaud!' Jane reminded him, smiling.

In two minutes flat Simon had managed to blow any impression of intelligence out of the water. But though he did not realise it, his innocence was more touching than the cleverest speeches. Jane liked unusual people. In Simon she had found a perfect specimen.

She asked about his parents. He told her they were dead. His face tensed at the word. Again she found him touching.

'You enjoy working in banking?' she asked.

'Yes. It makes me feel like I'm a gangster. I used to be a maths geek, now I'm a gangster in a foreign city.'

'A gangster?'

'Just an expression. A tough guy.'

Jane thought of her father. No – this was not how she had ever pictured a banker.

Simon, who still had a glimmer of common sense, started laughing.

'I'm joking. Let's just say I find the image makeover interesting.'

This spark of lucidity in an otherwise absurd conversation had the benefit of stopping Jane on the fatal path towards maternal feeling.

'I'm afraid I have to leave. I've got somewhere I have to be. But I'd like to see you again, you are a remarkable person.'

Simon shuddered.

'I'd love to.'

'A remarkable person,' he thought to himself. '*Remarkable* is very positive. A lot better than *banal* for example.'

That evening, he ate a lot, drank a lot, talked a lot, more often than not coming out with gibberish so off the point that he kept everyone in stitches. Without realising, he was the clown prince of the evening and everyone complimented Zadie on finding a Frenchman with such a deadpan sense of humour. Blessed are the simple-minded.

When he got home, Matt was waiting for him.

'So, did you fuck her?'

At this late hour, the question was exhausting. Simon answered that he had met a wonderful woman who taught art history. His friend stared at him with the barely disguised scorn he reserved for matters of women, as though he alone was capable of making a judgement in this domain.

'Art history, eh?'

'Yes. She seems very clever,' added Simon though he had no idea.

'Good-looking?'

'You could say that.'

'So, you mean she's ugly?'

Matt sighed. Then he stretched and yawned, clearly bored. Simon felt humiliated. He had managed to charm and now he was being denied his victory. Now his conquest was ugly when actually she had been wonderful, so icy at first and then so warm.

'You going to bang her?'

This was how Matt always talked. Always in the crudest terms. Naive though he was, Simon sensed a maliciousness in Matt, a desire to put him down though he could not understand why.

'I'd happily see her again.'

Matt nodded disdainfully.

'So how was the party?'

Simon gave a detailed account of his every gesture, his every fear, his encounter with Jane, his conversations.

'You really said that a good banker was a greedy, blind liar?'

'Yeah.'

'Are you crazy? You've worked your last day at Kelmann.'

Simon felt his heart hammer. Unfortunately his best, his only friend had a knack for coming out with a cruel truth, a bitter prophecy.

'I don't think so.'

Matt sniggered and explained why what he had said went against the fundamental rule of business, which was hypocrisy. The cake must be all gold and diamonds, even if it was nothing more than a thin film concealing all the treachery in the world. Words must cloak things with a dazzling layer designed to reflect the majesty of desires, otherwise, if the truth was told, it would all explode. Developing his argument, in one of the lyrical flights he so favoured, especially late at night, he went on to state that in fact the rule applied to the whole of society, which lived on myths and put all its hopes in ideological constructs, pure egalitarian populist images, feeding the social Moloch with necessary illusions.

Simon only vaguely listened.

'Maybe,' he said. 'It's possible. But not only was Zadie not angry, she's asked me to join her team. She's been appointed head of derivatives and I'm going with her.'

Matt's smile froze into a rictus.

## 22

The fire bellowed in the night like some great monster. Flames climbed the rigs, licking at the oil rising from the bowels of the earth with the speed of a conflagration. The fire was sticky, liquid, heavy and devastating, cloaking everything in sweltering suffocation. Dark clouds of gas rose into the heavens, drawing the fire upwards where it spread across the blazing sky. The initial explosion had sent up an incandescent geyser in front of the security guards and then the barrels began to explode, belching torrents of flame. The ground, the air were thick with this blistering blindness and everyone had dashed from the surrounding sheds and fled.

Lev was called and he came by helicopter to survey the disaster.

Stock still, he uttered not a word. The high explosives needed to snuff the wellhead were on their way; meanwhile the bulldozers, black ants in the flickering flames, were digging trenches to check the progress of the fire.

Over his head the sky was burning. Nothing in his face betrayed the least flicker of emotion. The workers were impressed by his calm. Lev Kravchenko, on the brink of the abyss, seemed unmoved. No anger, no determination, no despair. Apathy perhaps, mingled with shock. They'd been quick to act ... They'd made an offer; he had refused and immediately the punishment. Naked violence, he had thought last time. The time had come.

*I want to be independent.*

Lev had talked like Riabine; he had been treated like Riabine. But he was not like the farmer. He was not an animal holed up in his lair. Standing on an embankment before the fire-ravaged landscape, he had nothing in common with the *muzhik*. He felt none of the primeval terror the man must have felt when threatened. Obviously, his complete indifference was simply a facade. No one can remain completely indifferent when his property is being destroyed. This bubbling oil slick creeping across the ground, stippled with flame and smoke, was eating away his money, his only protection in these troubled times. He himself was being diminished there, but the real danger would come at the critical moment when he would stand alone, naked in the face of danger, protected only by the fragile rectitude of his body. The moment when he would simply be himself, Lev Kravchenko, the man he had once been, with no support, no money, no men.

Already, though he did not realise it, his figure standing on the hillock, a dark twig silhouetted against the wall of fire, displayed his tragic weakness in the face of the elements. Even as he stood thinking that his empire was beginning to shrink, it was his body that seemed to have been weakened by the attack. And in the thunderous roar of the fire, Lev was no more than an inconsequential silence.

It took three days and nights to extinguish the blaze. The well was not capped. Soon the mechanical insects would be able to resume their ballet, though a considerable number of them had been amputated. And Lev did not have the money for the repairs.

Back in Moscow, Lev spent the better part of his days with bankers. They were not unresponsive to his overtures, proof that the Seven had not yet reached an agreement. The reason for this was clear. They feared Lianov and were reluctant to put him at the head of the vast multinational that would result from the merger of Liekom and ELK. Nor had they united against the head of the Brotherhood, for several reasons: because Litvinov was still head of the company, officially at least, and Lianov did not yet have complete control. Because their interests were linked inasmuch as the Brotherhood's activities, especially in the field of investments, were becoming more legitimate. Lastly, because they had their own disaster to deal with. Russia was bankrupt. As expected, the IMF provided money. Traces of it could be found the very next day in the offshore accounts: part of the manna had been misappropriated by the oligarchs. In Russia, however, the same oligarchs were still in a difficult position and the political future remained uncertain. Who would replace Yeltsin?

In all the chaos, the confusion of insolvency and embezzlement, in the midst of all the trafficking in power, money and influence, Kravchenko's problems were of little consequence. So the banks had not closed their doors to him. Instead cold-faced men simply informed Lev that their own positions were too tenuous and that, with the bank liable to collapse at any moment, they were in no position to lend such large sums.

In August 1998, the Saniak hedge fund declared bankruptcy.

No one had had an inkling they were in trouble. The management of the fund had always been obscure, focused primarily on the founder and CEO, a Ukrainian of dubious background who had suddenly become rich, and the fund had been too exposed to Russian debt. While the monthly newsletter gushingly boasted unprecedented earnings, increasingly risky investments, intended to shore up losses, had finally led to its collapse. By the time the investors realised what was happening, they'd already lost everything. And the Ukrainian vanished as swiftly as he had appeared.

It was a serious body-blow. The company's losses amounted to almost a billion dollars besides which Lev had lost a third of his personal fortune. Everything else was salted away in tax havens and seemed to be safe. But even tax havens could be dangerous. Nauru, an island grown rich from mineral deposits and money laundering, had also gone bust. Its inhabitants now lived in rusty Mercedes, with no wheels, no petrol, trying to live off the remnants of an island devastated by strip mining.

Lev's divorce seemed likely to hasten his bankruptcy. When they met with the judge, Elena was thinner and more beautiful than ever. She gazed at her Hun with a last flicker of tenderness and a lot of hostility.

'You were to blame for Riabine,' she whispered to him.

She didn't know how right she was.

'And I hear you've been seeing a lot of some prostitute. Congratulations.'

Lev did not react. But in private, when the audience was over, he quickly explained the situation to her. He was in desperate straits. Elena listened in silence. As always, she was quick to understand and he wondered whether she already knew all about his problems. But she did not waver.

'I already told you, I want half your fortune – or what's left of it. It's not for me, it's for the children. They have to be protected. And I want them to be schooled abroad. They need to get out of this country. Just look at what you've become.'

She was a different woman. Or perhaps she was revealing a part of herself which had been masked by her love for him. The force of her intelligence made her stiff and cold and if, now and then, Lev thought he caught a glimpse of the woman she had once been, a sudden reversal revealed to him the icy face of his enemy.

Dreams of fire haunted the oligarch's nights. Sheets of flame that had him waking up in a sweat. In the depths of sleep, towards 3 am, in that perilous moment of weakness and fear, Lev would tear himself from his nightmares as though ripped from sleep by sheer terror. He gazed at the room, the bed, the windows, probing the depths of his solitude.

During one such wakening, he remembered something Elena had said: 'You were lost the day you did nothing to help that black waiter in the restaurant in Paris. That day was your downfall. And it was mine too.'

The accusation had seemed totally unjust to Lev. He remembered nothing about what had happened. How was he responsible for this waiter?

So, he would also have to fight his wife. Unless she was prepared to accept half of his debts. This was a fortune he was more than happy to give to her.

As he struggled, back to the wall, the curious pleasure of

defeat carried him forward. Life was no longer that strange boundlessness of time made up of a thousand exertions and hazy with uncertainty and patience; now it was a swift jolt where everything was at stake: his fortune, his reputation, his life. For a man tormented by the absurd, hounded by self-doubt, danger was the promise of action. It was now or never.

ELK needed two hundred million dollars if the business was to ride out the crisis. The world was desperate for oil. The world economy, beset by local crises, was guzzling energy, plundering the earth to fuel development. From everywhere, money flowed. Vast loans. The crises in Asia, in South America, in Russia, the famines and the massacres in Africa, nothing could curb the enormous energy of the planet, awash with money, with consumption, with unquenchable desire. The great body needed oil, gas, it needed energy, even wars and massacres required energy, death drawing on deep wells of greed. Burning up with money fever, inflamed by each new revenue stream, the world economy was going through one of its greatest periods of prosperity. All these furnaces crammed to bursting point were bound to explode, but while it lasted, Lev was convinced he could get the money.

He left for London. Bored one day long ago he had – for an absurd sum – bought a huge house there that he never stayed in, one Elena occasionally used when she went clothes shopping. She was fascinated by the change in Britain's capital, irrigated by money and a constant influx of people, where wealth and opulence were now so common that a city which had always been a rather eccentric old maid was now hiking up her petticoats to get down and dirty in sports cars and five-star restaurants.

Lev was happy to leave the stifling atmosphere of his empty palace. He took Oksana with him. His private jet was waiting and he noted with amusement that bankrupt men are still rich.

The London house, some 1,000 square metres, seemed to him an ideal size since he did not get lost in it. Oksana liked it.

'You need to forget about business, Lev. By all means go to your meetings, but the rest of the time we're spending in restaurants and nightclubs.'

This they did. Lev spent staggering sums which, given he was bankrupt, meant nothing. Bouncers queued up to escort them and get a tip. He ordered the most expensive vintages and his extravagance was so talked about, no one could have imagined the true nature of his financial situation. Oksana herself succeeded in making some saleswoman's year, buying all the dresses she had tried on in an hour. The Russian billionaire and his girlfriend were mobbed by the paparazzi. Lev knew that this would do him no harm. True, the British wrote in clichés and the handful of articles he read were pathetically trite, rehashing platitudes about 'the oligarch's fabulous wealth', 'the madness of Russia', 'the oil prince'. But at least he was being talked about, and he acquired a celebrity status he had not previously had in Britain, where other oligarchs were considerably more famous. Once or twice, the alcohol, the darkness and the throb of the music brought him peace in the tangle of crowds, of lights, of dancing. He watched the moving figures, revelled in the youthful faces, the emptiness of pleasure. He was no longer thinking about anything and the mindless state that came over him, disturbing in its serenity, was a wonderful drug.

At a meeting at Kelmann, he noticed a brilliant young

English woman. She reminded him of Elena. The same intelligence, the same distinguished features. She was much less pretty, but it was Elena just the same. He felt a tightness in the pit of his stomach. Everyone else at the meeting seemed to disappear. There was only this woman. In the terrible slow motion where negotiations seemed to hang motionless, the figures melded and as a vague bitterness welled inside him, Lev felt the crushing wave of time: his life closed in on him, his youth disappeared in a flash. Suddenly, nothing had meaning.

He froze. Words died away. If he could, he would have grabbed this woman on the other side of the table, this ghost of his youth, but he simply sat staring as he experienced, like a whirlpool, the terrifying swiftness of loss, not of his fast-disappearing fortune, but simply, ineluctably, of his life.

# 23

Zadie had never felt remotely attracted to a client. She dealt with portfolios, not people. But during the meeting with this Russian client, she felt herself quiver. This despite the fact that she was surrounded by her team and the catastrophic situation of the business they were discussing should have precluded all other considerations. The man was not handsome. He was short and she did not find his somewhat Asian features attractive. He needed two hundred million dollars. And suddenly, she sensed he was no longer listening to them. She glanced at him; he was staring at her. It was not an intimidating stare, he was not trying to impress her, nor was it a look of curiosity or attentiveness. Nor was it desire, or if it was it was a desire so particular that the man seemed almost desperate, teetering over an abyss.

And it was at this point that she began to tremble. From the depths of her harshness, her biting sharpness, welled a stifling feeling, an overpowering emotion. And suddenly this short man in the black suit, this man she had never met before, became closer, more important to her, than all the members of her team.

Simon Jude had placed a hand on her forearm. She felt the pressure, realised she had to come back to reality, that several people around the table had noticed she was no longer paying attention. This was an important business deal, she could not afford to make a mistake; she had just been promoted, given greater responsibility, there could be no question of easing up.

She closed her eyes for a second. When she opened them again, she was no longer trembling. She was once again steady, confident, despite the combination of fear and longing lodged deep inside her.

They arranged a second meeting in New York at head office.

The man took his leave. His handshake lingered a fraction too long. Zadie was taller than he was, yet once again she had a feeling of weakness simply from being near him.

'It would be a pleasure to see you again,' said the man. 'You're a brilliant woman and I like working with brilliant people.'

There was no trace of despair in him now. He had composed himself, he was as he had been at the start of the meeting. She nodded, unable to say a word. She knew she should say something, if only 'thanks' or 'see you again'.

'Impressive guy,' said Simon after Lev had gone. 'I got the impression I've seen him somewhere before.'

'It's possible,' said Zadie. 'It's a small world, and the financial world is tiny. I mean, you're dating Hilland's daughter.'

Jane Hilland had wanted to see him again. They had met up in a pub and, once again, Simon had been inordinately awkward, but the young woman seemed to like him all the more. She laughed a lot at his unwitting jokes.

'What I find striking about you is your naivety,' she teased him.

She did not know how right she was. No one in the London financial world had ever been as innocent as Simon, so much so that his survival in the City was a purest miracle, owing perhaps to the subtle magic that innocence sometimes gives rise to. Far from being crushed, he floated like a bubble, protected as always, admittedly, by the chainmail of mathematics that was his armour. But what was most surprising was that any woman should ever be fascinated by his survival mechanism, this curious solution, a combination of blindness and innocence which he adopted in the face of a hostile world. But Jane Hilland herself was an extraordinary woman. Her father's vast fortune meant she had absolute freedom. And since the money was wedded to a keen intelligence and a certain personal eccentricity, she was little influenced by prejudice. So this goldfish no woman had ever found interesting had managed to pique her curiosity. They went to the cinema to see one of those English films that defy common sense. In fact, the goldfish was part of this world. He wasn't French, he was English, funny English.

Jane wanted to discover his world. Simon invited her home, taking care to ensure Matt cleared out. They had a very pleasant evening. They drank, they talked, had a quick bite.

Late in the evening, Simon gave a start. He could hear the key turn in the lock. Why was he worried about his friend coming home? Because Matt enjoyed making him uncomfortable, because Matt would love to look down on Jane, but most of all because Matt could seduce any woman.

But Jane surprised him. Everything about her father's wealth that might translate into a sense of superiority, a glacial indifference, she demonstrated now. Hardly had Matt said hello, with a casual wave and that aura of booze and contentment he had, than this charming woman became haughty. Her eyes grew cold, her smile vanished, her whole body seemed to be armoured with steel and detachment.

Matt started boasting about the restaurant he'd just been to.

'I find it rather pretentious,' she said.

She asked him what he did for a living.

'I used to work for a Russian hedge fund that's just gone belly up. But it won't take me long to find something else.'

'A trader?' she asked condescendingly.

'Yeah.'

'That's strange. I know a lot of traders, I've been around them my whole life. My father's a banker. I don't see you as a trader.'

'And where do you see me?' asked Matt.

'In the dole queue.'

The quip was fired off without a trace of a smile. Then Jane got to her feet and said: 'I'm sorry, I have to go.'

She kissed Simon on both cheeks and left with a wave, without even saying goodbye to Matt.

He blushed. The door slammed.

'Friendly, your girlfriend,' he commented.

'She's not usually like that. I don't know what got into her. She was being so charming.'

'It doesn't surprise me. The Hillands – all silver spoons and self-importance. Apparently her father fucks every whore in London. Well, the expensive ones at least.'

Matt was so humiliated he forgot to say that she was ugly. Never had he felt such contempt. This woman had tapped into all his insecurities and his fears. He felt as though he had just come out of a job interview where instead of smiles, he'd been spat on.

'I've never met such a complete bitch.'

Slowly the spite machine ground into gear again.

'I don't know what you're doing with her,' he went on, 'London's full of charming girls but, oh no, you have to pick the worst of the lot. A complete bitch.'

Matt fell silent. He ran his tongue over his lips. He was still flushed with humiliation.

'And ugly as fuck to boot.'

Finally. He'd said it.

Two days later, Simon saw Jane at her place.

'I was a bit offhand with your friend.'

'A bit, maybe.'

'I hope I didn't embarrass you. I have to say I didn't like him. That smugness . . . That second-rate Casanova look he's got going . . . You're nothing like each other. He hates you, doesn't he?'

'Hates me?' Simon repeated, flabbergasted. 'No, he's my friend, my best friend.'

'That doesn't preclude hate. Quite the contrary.'

'I don't think he hates me, no, I don't think so,' Simon stammered.

Late in the evening, as they were sitting on the sofa, a terrifying thing happened: Jane kissed him. Not urgently, passionately, but a fleeting playful kiss. In spite of his terror – what was he supposed to do, how could he be sure not to do it wrong, not to seem ridiculous? – Simon kissed her for a longer time.

'You kiss like a cat,' said Jane.

Meaning a vague wet nuzzle, he supposed. He tried harder, she tried harder. The kiss continued, melted, lingered, Simon forgot to be afraid. Jane pulled away and smiled at him, a red mark on the corner of her lips.

'You've never kissed a girl before?'

'Of course I have.'

She stared at him like a clinical case.

'Really very special,' she murmured.

She didn't seem to dislike it. She went to get a glass of water, her high heels clacking across the floor. Her hips were narrow, her body slender. Every detail was etched on Simon's memory. The sound of the fridge being opened. The clack of heels again. The mounting terror: what was he supposed to do now? What did she expect of him?

Jane came back with two glasses of water. As soon as she sat down, he lunged at her, not feeling the least desire, almost out of a sense of duty. She looked shocked, but leaned towards him nonetheless. They kissed again, somewhat laboriously. Then she looked at him, stroked his hair. It felt like he was still a child. She opened the top button of his shirt. He felt a pain in his stomach. He took it as a sign. He placed a hand on her breast, as though opening a door. She looked at him in astonishment then took his hand. He stayed like this, motionless. Simon was wondering: what should I do? What would Matt do? Thinking of his friend troubled him even more. Matt would be in bed by now. But how did you get from sofa to bed? By what impossible journey? This was all so terrifying. He felt no desire, nothing but fear and a flicker of humiliation, sensing impending failure that would make another date impossible. She seemed so experienced to him. She had probably already had several serious relationships with handsome, intelligent young men like her friends. After all, she was a Hilland. His eyes widened in fear. Jane watched all this, guessed the agonies he was going through. Shaking her head sympathetically, she set Simon's hand down again on the sofa and kissed him slowly, tenderly. This gentle pressure, this confusion of tongues, and of bodies since she was pressing herself against him, began to blind Simon. This dispelled the images, the fears, there was nothing now but the warm, pleasant contact which drew down an intimate darkness. Eyes closed, he gave himself up to the warmth. He wished it would last for ever.

And then suddenly, Jane got to her feet, as though she had made a decision. She led him into a dark room and pulled him onto the bed and the kissing began again. Jane took off his shirt. He fumbled with buttons and by some miracle managed to take off her blouse and, fingers shaking, tackled her bra, failed. But with a patient smile, a faint outline in the darkness, her hands moved behind her back, unhooked the fractious clasp, releasing her breasts that he kissed and sucked, taking no pleasure in doing so but realising what he had to do. Jane's breathing came faster now. She unhooked her skirt. He slipped it off her, aware of the rustle of her tights, of the warmth radiating from the centre of her body. Then he peeled off her panties, though it took several attempts to get them past her cold feet. She was naked. He did not feel close to this woman who worried him so much, who was nothing but a task he had to accomplish, who called into question everything in his life. He could barely see her in the darkness. This reassured him somewhat: she seemed less human, less conscious. He no longer wanted to escape, he wanted it to be over. So he entered her, feeling no pleasure, and was surprised to discover that it seemed to work. The young woman beneath him was moaning, he didn't know whether she was doing it simply out of kindness but it was reassuring nonetheless, he felt better, in fact he felt more brave. Jane's breath came faster now, this was a good sign, things were going well. Then her body tensed.

How to describe the pride at having overcome a terrifying ordeal and to have done so with flying colours? The goldfish had been given everything: he was a gangster, he was part of Zadie Zale's shock troops at Kelmann, he was dating a wonderful woman called Jane Hilland and living in a flat in Chelsea many people would have envied. It was no longer maths that saved him, but life itself, which he finally filled with his presence. He did what other people did. Everything he was supposed to do, all the things dimly understood from television programmes, from the things his schoolmates and even his teachers had talked about, he had done it all: getting into a prestigious university, finding a good job, earning money, and – finally – having a girl on his arm. He had ticked all the boxes.

When he went to a meeting with a Russian client looking for two hundred million dollars and everyone at the meeting panicked when the famous Zadie Zale began to tremble with an intensity his whole body rejected and desired; when he went to a restaurant with a group of intellectuals, artists and bankers he never in his life imagined he might meet; as he hugged to him a woman that every gold-digging man in London coveted, Simon was well aware that his previous identity was exploding. Sometimes, he would look at Jane in astonishment. Intelligent as she was, it was a look she did not understand, she did not know from where this timid, evanescent being was coming, from what darkness he was emerging. He couldn't believe that, a creature of flesh and blood liked him. She might not be in love with him, he didn't know – she was not one for declarations, perhaps she was too well brought up for such things – but at least she called him, she saw him, she spoke to him, she slept with him. This was the most incredible part, this contact between two bodies, for someone who had always found it difficult to touch others, who flinched at the slightest brush. His desire was astonishing. Desire was astonishing. She wanted him, he wanted her. Bodies existed, entwined, penetrated each other.

Though in his shock he did not realise it, Simon Jude was completely happy.

Matt's path had taken the opposite course. He spent more and more time in his room. There were no more interviews, he had been made redundant by Saniak – there is a coherence to lies – and he went out less often because he found it difficult to shore up his fictions. A crack had opened up, a chink through which words leaked. He could no longer talk and, without words, he was reduced to nothing. His ability to seduce evaporated. He talked about going back to Paris, something that sounded like an admission of defeat, but Simon thought that finance was not really his world and that he could easily find a position in his previous work. In the meantime, Simon paid for everything. He didn't even think about it. Matt was his friend, his only friend, and besides, he was the person who had transformed him. Matt had offered him a new life. In return, money was nothing.

Of the former profusion of words, there remained only the spite machine. Matt loved Simon and hated his success, since

Simon had achieved what he himself had wished for. Matt had wanted to mould him, to turn him into a copy of himself – inferior, of course – and the strength of their friendship rested on the power he had over him. But the statue had come to life, had outstripped him, had come to embody his dreams – dreams of money and success. Matt was not a base individual, but he was maddened by frustration, he needed to desire, he needed life to be gilded with a veneer of money and he could not bear the fact that Simon was living that life. Simon was the thorn in his side that reminded him of his failure, and he lived with him. He watched him go to work at the bank; watched him go out with his friends, friends he refused to have anything to do with, fearful his hatred, his jealousy would explode; he watched him go out on dates with the heir to the Hilland fortune.

'Why don't you ever come out with us?' Simon asked one night.

'I can't stand those guys, loaded with money. And frankly, I can't see what you see in that girl. She's ugly and stuck-up.'

'You're wrong. I swear, you're wrong. The two of you just got off on the wrong foot.'

'Anyway, I've got a date with a Greek goddess.'

This wasn't true. There was no date, there were no more Greek goddesses. As in a children's fairytale, from his mouth came bitter toads. Princesses were not attracted to croaking, muddy creatures. He no longer promised sunshine, love, pleasure. His persona was fractured, he no longer attracted women – neither princess, marchioness or baroness, neither commoner nor slattern.

He was left only with toads.

# 24

'I've had cameras following me round since I was in high school!'

As in a made-for-TV movie, everyone burst out laughing. Ruffle, the journalist, the two studio engineers and Dolores, the cleaning woman whose destiny he bragged about having changed, plus her three children. The weather was perfect, the light radiant as a spotlight. Against the sparkling backdrop of the day, the city gleamed like the silver screen and smiling people prepared to glide across the froth of the everyday.

Ruffle was dressed in white like a Southern plantation owner. He had hesitated a long time over what colour to wear, initially favouring a dark financier suit. But then he decided that the dream would give him the upper hand. He wasn't a financier, he was the architect of the American dream. He didn't talk about money, he didn't talk about investments, he talked about dreams. And dreams are immaculate.

On this special day which was to make his reputation, everything about him was American. His suit was American, his shades were American and – though he favoured fast European cars – he had borrowed a cream coloured Cadillac. There could be no false notes. The name Mark Ruffle would be trumpeted throughout the state and he would become to Florida what Dario Fesali was to the United States.

The TV crew had called him two weeks earlier. Ruffle had immediately felt himself almost bursting with joy. *A documentary about him!* On the biggest local station. He had long since prepared his speech and repeated it to anyone who would listen. But not until now had he had the opportunity to broadcast it on such a scale. Mark Ruffle, his life and work. Publicly, he gave the impression that he attached little importance to the programme. Privately, he talked about nothing else.

The big Cadillac glided through the streets of Miami, through Brickell financial district, its skyscrapers glittering in the sun, this hub of power and money that thrilled Ruffle and in which, he felt, he was an important player. He was one of these creators of the new world, the peninsula, the headland of affluence welcoming poor Latinos, Cubans, Haitians. The gateway to America. Builders, men like him, had built these skyscrapers which brought new wealth to this city. Their entrepreneurial spirit had built the Four Seasons Hotel Miami, the Wachovia Financial Center, this towering grandeur full of arrogance and defiance. All this was the advantage property tycoons like him had over others, this ability to incarnate their work in stone, in steel, in concrete, protected against the winds of fortune. Gazing up at the city, his heavy hand over his mouth, Ruffle had felt himself glorified by this district, these towers.

And then abruptly, without anyone understanding why, the glittering façade disappeared. The driver turned the corner and another city suddenly appeared, squat yellow-brick houses like a Mexican village. This was where Dolores had once lived. A dozen men sprawling on the ground watched the car as it passed. One of them spat.

'Fucking ghetto,' grumbled Ruffle.

These people were tarnishing his day. He needed them, it would make Dolores's rise from rags to riches all the more magnificent. But he had forgotten they were so poor. It put all the brokers off. You couldn't get a contract signed here. Everything was paid for in crack and cocaine. The Cadillac jolted, there were potholes everywhere. Weeds grew through cracks on the sidewalk and as the car drove on, neglected sandlots stretched away into wasteland. On an abandoned lot lay the rusting hulk of a car. The place was desolate, the leprous face of poverty. On the corner of the street, a pair of bare legs stuck out of a foam mattress.

'He's found his home,' Ruffle commented. 'The pigs round here are happy to live in shit. There's another contract we'll never get.'

The driver bared carnivorous teeth.

The car had pulled up next to the TV crew at 10.02 am. Ruffle had been expecting more people. He climbed out of the car. The reporter proffered his hand. He was a short, unshaven man with stooped shoulders. The technical team could also have made more of an effort. But the camera glittered in the sun and that was all that mattered. Standing a little further off were Dolores, looking intimidated, and her three children. She had arrived in a Mercedes, a small maroon Mercedes now parked on the opposite kerb which she kept an anxious eye on, like a devoted mother. Ruffle rushed over to her, his face a mask of joy, and threw his arms around her – something he had never done. She looked like a panic-stricken bird.

He turned back to the camera. It wasn't rolling; he felt terribly disappointed, though he didn't let it show.

It was at this point that he said, in a plaintive, ironic tone: 'I've had cameras following me round since I was in high school!'

And everyone burst out laughing. Suddenly, Ruffle felt better. The day was dazzling. And this was only the beginning. He told them that once upon a time he'd been a promising quarterback and that he often watched films of his old matches. When this was greeted by an embarrassed silence, he remembered he had to be modest.

'I mean my old man had a Super 8, you know with the shaky picture and all.'

They nodded.

'So this is where it was,' said the reporter, looking down the desolate street.

Ruffle adopted a serious tone.

'Right here. In this gódforsaken hole. This crime-ridden wasteland. Yes, this is where the family lived when they first arrived from Mexico.'

Dolores nodded. The children watched the scene, vaguely bewildered. The reporter walked over to the trailer.

'Can we go inside?' he asked Dolores.

'My cousins, they live here,' she said with a thick accent.

The reporter looked quizzical.

'Her cousins took over the trailer when she moved out,' Ruffle explained. 'More people chasing the American dream. I'll help them sort themselves out. Give it a bit of time and they'll be moving into a beautiful house too. I mean, hey, this is America, right?'

The reporter turned to the cameraman.

'Get some shots of all this, the surroundings and the interiors.'

They all squeezed into the trailer. Ruffle wondered how the four of them could ever have lived in such a hovel. The cousins had washed and scoured the whole place but the meagreness, the yellowish taint of poverty could not be erased.

'Jesus,' thought Ruffle, 'and I get people accusing me of exploiting the poor. Anything's got to be better than living here.'

'Señor Ruffle is our benefactor,' said Dolores suddenly.

And, in chorus, like a poorly learned recitation piece, the three children chimed in: 'Yes, señor Ruffle is our benefactor.'

'If he no help, we still live in this trailer,' she went on. 'The beautiful house, thanks to him.'

It occurred to Ruffle that he should have sent her for English lessons. But it didn't matter . . . this way, she was all the more convincing. How did she manage to keep such a terrible accent?

The reporter did not seem particularly gripped by this protestation of gratitude. He glanced at the Mexican family. The cameraman was finishing up the interior shots. They all trooped out and some shots were taken in front of the trailer. Dolores repeated her line and this time the declaration was captured on film. Ruffle adopted the unassuming air he thought would suit the occasion. Once again he hugged the panic-stricken bird in his arms and once again the cameraman regarded this touching scene without the slightest interest. It didn't matter. All this asshole had to do was film Dolores's new house. The comparison between the two would glorify Mark Ruffle and if there was a single solvent family left in the area, they'd be rushing to the RUB offices the minute this thing was broadcast.

Ruffle suggested riding along with the reporter, who rudely

declined his offer and, with the rest of the crew, clambered into a small clapped-out black van that looked like it might not start. Dolores, of course, with a care that demonstrated her love for the car, got behind the wheel of her Mercedes.

It took barely fifteen minutes for them to reach a suburb with a dozen houses all bought thanks to RUB financing. And Dolores quivered with pleasure standing in the driveway of a little house which, compared to the trailer, looked like something out of the Arabian nights. This was something even the reporter – probably a lefty like most intellectuals – would understand. And if he didn't, the image would speak for itself. Sometimes cameras understand things better than moronic minds.

A magnificent shot framed the Echeveria family in front of their new home, standing next to the entrepreneur who had made it possible for them to achieve their dream. It was all good. The camera moved inside, put the finishing touches to the positive comparison before Mark Ruffle himself explained his project: 'What I wanted was to make it possible for anyone to achieve the American dream.'

Hearing the phrase for the fifteenth time, the reporter gave an exasperated scowl which Mark did not like.

'Dolores Echeveria had nothing,' the businessman continued, 'now she has everything. She had some tough times when she came here, fleeing the poverty of Mexico. But she worked hard, she had faith in herself, in the future. At RUB, we helped her get financing for this house. Now, she and her family have a roof over their heads, she's got a beautiful car to drive to work. She's integrated into the community. Her kids go to school, they'll go on to college and become citizens she can be proud of. I'm happy I was able to help her, but obviously I am not important here,' he went on, 'it's all down to her.'

Big smile, thumbs up.

'Señor Ruffle is our benefactor,' chorused the kids.

'Her achievement is all the more impressive when you consider that Dolores here owns another house that she rents out and makes an income from.'

The reporter was surprised.

'A cleaning woman with a second house? When she's already got a mortgage on this house and a loan on her car? You don't think that's a bit over the top?'

'No sir,' said Mark patronisingly, 'it's the miracle of the modern economy. There's no risk here. Worst case scenario, she just sells off the house and makes a fat profit. But she won't need to do that. This is just the beginning for her happiness,  take my word for it.'

'But what about her monthly payments? They must be astronomical.'

'Nope. Not a cent,' said Ruffle. 'It's an interest-free loan. At RUB we lend because we want to make people happy. The repayments don't start until later and by then Dolores won't be a cleaning woman any more, she'll have more money, she'll have no problem meeting the repayments. This is the new economy, my friend, the infinite growth economy.'

The reporter stared at him intently. Ruffle had the unpleasant feeling he used to have back in high school when he'd come out with a particularly dumb answer. But he wasn't in high school any more, and he was the one who was rich. So he simply patted the reporter's shoulder and went back to join Dolores's family.

'Señor Ruffle is our benefactor.'

This time, he'd made it. All he had to do now was ride the wave. The pictures would put up the statue. It was all over. In the shimmering light of day, a man in a white suit had triumphed over his contemporaries. The end zone was just in front of him and no linebacker now could stop him making this winning touchdown. Mark Ruffle, his life, his work.

In the Cadillac driving him back to his house, to which he had invited the TV crew for lunch in order to win them over, since he was suspicious about their political sympathies, the founder and Chief Executive of RUB savoured his perfect performance. Within this thick layer of complacency, no pothole could bother him, no detours or delays, and so the journey back seemed very short.

He got out of the car. The crew had not yet arrived. They should have come in his car. He looked at the house. For a fleeting instant, after the trailer and the suburban house, he thought about his wealth, then he pushed open the door.

Inside there was a man waiting for him. He was sitting on the sofa with Ruffles' wife bolt upright next to him. Shoshana looked so rigid that at first he wondered if someone had died, if there were some terrible news.

'Hi Mark.'

He didn't answer.

'I wanted you to meet Sila,' she went on, a lump in her throat.

'Good to meet you,' said Ruffle curtly. 'What's going on?'

'Nothing. It's just . . .' Shoshana seemed a little breathless. 'I really think you should talk to him.'

Ruffle studied the man on the sofa more carefully. He was a young black guy, twenty, twenty-five, elegantly dressed, he seemed serene and not in the least aggressive.

He walked over. The man got to his feet. He was taller than Ruffle and much slimmer.

'Sila works in a French restaurant on Lincoln Road.'

What was this about? Why bring a waiter back to their house? If he was looking for a job with RUB, let him send in his CV.

'That's nice. But what's that got to do with me? Look, I don't have much time and . . .'

'I really need you to talk to him,' Shoshana interrupted, almost trembling. 'It's important, for you and for me. Please.'

'I think I know you,' said the black guy.

Unconvinced, Ruffle stood rooted to the spot.

'We met at a restaurant in Paris.'

Then suddenly Ruffle remembered.

'You're the waiter! The waiter who yelled at my son!'

'I didn't yell,' Sila said quietly. 'I never shout, certainly not at a child. But you hit me. You broke my nose. Because I asked your son to go back to his seat.'

Ruffle stared at him in silence, then mumbled: 'I guess.'

He sniffed.

'Okay. I've got a lot on,' he said, 'there's a TV crew turning up here any minute. This isn't really the time to rehash old memories.'

Shoshana hesitated. 'Oh? I thought you'd finished with the TV people.'

'I asked them over for lunch.'

He took a step.

'Why did you hit me?' asked Sila.

'You shouted at my son. I flipped out. Any father would have done the same.'

'I didn't shout,' Sila said again gently.

Ruffle shrugged.

'Why did you hit me?'

'My guests are going to turn up any minute,' said Ruffle, his tone more menacing now. 'I'd like you to leave.'

'You need to answer my question,' said Sila, moving closer to him.

'I don't need to do anything. And you can push off.'

Ruffle brutally shoved the man backwards. A moment later, his face contorted with pain, he was bent double. Drawing himself up to his full height, Sila had grabbed Ruffle's fist and was twisting it with considerable force.

'Why did you hit me?'

Ruffle whimpered from humiliation and pain. Gradually, without realising he was doing it, he brought his knee to the floor. Sila's muscles tensed. He wanted to remain calm, he wanted to go on asking his question, to compel this man to answer him, to settle once and for all this question that had been nagging at him since that episode in the restaurant, but the problem, the real problem was that he was beginning to forget the question, his whole being was focused on the pressure he was inflicting on this man and the tension necessary to maintain his vice-like grip. He should have seen Shoshana, heard her begging him to stop, should have taken pity on her tear-streaked face, but he saw nothing, heard nothing. He felt nothing but this rage inside him which, far from being appeased by the man's suffering, became incandescent and uncontrollable. He stood straight, jaws clenched, his large hand gripping the man's fist, wrenching it to the left, twisting his wrist which was now at a worrying angle. A small voice inside him whispered, but he was not listening because he could feel nothing but this rage, muted, menacing, rippling like a storm that swells and does not break. And he stared at the man's mouth, gaping on a terrifying silence even as his hand twisted at the wrist. Suddenly there was a cracking sound and the man on the ground began to howl.

Sila dropped his hand as though burned, backed away, then fled.

Out in the driveway, he ran into three people getting out of a car.

The day was dazzling.

# 25

October 12, 1998 was a holiday for the city of New York. No
one realised this, they all went about their business, walking
quickly or slowly, wearing suits or jeans or tracksuits, tall or
short, rich or poor, shopping or strolling, happy or unhappy,
clever or stupid, loving or indifferent. And yet they should
have noticed it was a holiday by the very fact that nothing
was happening. October 12, 1998 was a day on which nothing
happened. An unimportant day, which means a day doubtless
filled with the blaze of millions of destinies but shielded from
the blows of history which leave people in peace, only to beat
them senseless later.

And it was on this holiday that three men met, brought
together in a fractured world by power and money. Their
paths had crossed during dinner at a Paris restaurant; now
they crossed again, though their lives had completely changed.
Their fleeting reunion – fragments of time coinciding – took
place in Manhattan in the lobby of Kelmann Tower and the
neighbouring streets.

At 10 am, from the window of his hotel suite, Lev
Kravchenko stared out on Central Park, his eyes expressionless. In another hotel two blocks from there, Simon and Jane
were taking a shower. They were making the most of a business

trip to roam the streets of the city Jane loved above all others. One floor down, Zadie was putting the finishing touches to her make up. Her face inscrutable, she was determined to be ready to confront the source of her inner turmoil, the Russian with whom she was scheduled to discuss contractual terms at the Kelmann building. In a small hotel several blocks further south, Matt was simply sleeping. He had been clubbing until the early hours and, despite his aversion to Jane Hilland, was glad he had accompanied the couple on their trip.

Lev, Elena, Simon, Matt, Ruffle, Shoshana, Zadie, Jane, Oksana, Sila, all gathered in the labyrinth, doomed to bump into one another again and again in the interlacing metal branches of modernity. A soaring trunk of glass and steel topped with boughs and branches sprouting leaves ocellated in gold and silver, winking gently. A towering tree whose branches, stretching out infinitely, invariably cross in a knot of destinies.

Lev left his room. His bodyguard stepped into the elevator before him. The two men rode down to the ground floor. Their figures were reflected in the mirrors. The bodyguard was heavy-set and inexpressive, as was his wont. Lev himself, deep in thought, gave nothing away. In the hotel lobby, ELK's chief financial officer and an American attorney were waiting for them. Lev was wary about the forthcoming meeting. He greeted the two men briefly. A car was parked outside the hotel; they climbed inside and drove off.

En route, it passed Simon, his arm through Jane's, chatting cheerfully but walking quickly so as not to be late for the meeting. He had insisted on walking. The weather was too beautiful to be shut inside a car.

Half an hour later, dressed in a tracksuit, hair dishevelled, Matt stepped into a branch of Starbucks to get some coffee and cookies, just as, at the top of Kelmann Tower, a short man with slightly Asian features sparked a timorous uneasiness in a young English woman anxiously watched by her assistant who stood directly over the void, next to the window of this immense glass skyscraper that towered above the city.

Lev sat down. A long-legged young woman in a short skirt asked if she could get him something to drink.

'Coffee, please.'

Everyone was pleasant, indeed friendly. Lev feared the worst.

Around the board table five attorneys sat ready. For a business on the brink of bankruptcy. It promised to be a difficult battle.

'We're here to discuss the proposed loan of two hundred million dollars to the company ELK, owned by Mr Lev Kravchenko.'

The associate who spoke first was a lean, thin-faced man of about forty-five. His name was Frank Shane. Almost bald, he was famous for constantly suing people, mostly recently a masseur who had injured his shoulder, a lawsuit he had won. His greatest joy was eating away at the lives of others. He was one of the most feared associates at the most feared bank in the business.

'Mr Kravchenko . . .' Zadie began.

Lev looked at her curiously. He recognised her as a strong-minded intelligent woman. He remembered how much she had disconcerted him at their previous meeting, or rather how much, through her, Elena had disconcerted him, their faces merging in the rubble of his ruined life. But now, he could think only of saving his company.

Zadie, on the other hand, felt the same awkwardness she had felt that first time. This little man, with his intense energy, his dispassionate intelligence, fascinated her. She had studied the ELK dossier carefully, she knew what desperate straits they were in and she knew what she should do. But just as battle was beginning, this feeling of unease unsettled her.

'We've considered your application for a loan of two hundred million dollars,' she went on. 'Given your company's extremely difficult circumstances, and the parlous economic situation in Russia, I have to say your request seems problematic.'

Her voice was quavering slightly. Probably the strange sensation of damning a man you find attractive and knowing that in doing so you damn yourself.

'The economic situation is indeed difficult,' said Lev, 'but ELK is sound because our oil reserves are extensive and easy to extract and global demand is constantly rising.'

Discussing the matter in English did not suit him. Only Russian suited him. In a foreign language he lost something of his intelligence, his perceptiveness, his subtlety. He was the same yet less sharp, as though using his left hand rather than his right. Besides, he realised that Zadie's opening remark was just a teaser.

Frank Shane was staring at Lev. As in every negotiation, he felt hostile. He despised this man who sat in front of him, demanding money he did not deserve since none of the oligarchs deserved the fortunes they had amassed, because Russia was completely controlled by the mafia. The man's Hunnish face exasperated him, as did the bankrupt billionaire's self-confidence. The situation was clear: this man was in his power.

'We're bankers, Mr Kravchenko, not philanthropists. Our objective is to make money.'

'I couldn't agree more,' said Lev, somewhat surprised by the banker's aggressive tone.

He realised that battle had commenced.

The young woman set a coffee in front of him. He didn't drink it.

'Let me be frank, Mr Kravchenko: we don't want to take risks. We would require your existing assets as collateral.'

A jaded expression tinged with scorn flashed across Lev's face. It was then that Simon recognised him: the Russian at Lemerre's restaurant. It was him. That same expression of indifference. Years later and several thousand kilometres away, here they were again.

'What collateral?' said Lev. 'ELK sells oil to Russia, to Europe, to the USA. Sales in every market are rising.'

Shane found Lev's scorn intolerable. Those soliciting loans had no right to be anything but meek, indeed humble, when they found themselves in such straitened circumstances.

'Output from your principal oilfield,' he said, 'has dropped significantly following an attack on the site, and there may be others. You have enemies, Mr Kravchenko, and you are well aware that they may attack again.'

'There was no attack, it was an accident. And the purpose of this loan is precisely to return to previous extraction rates.'

Lev's expression did not change. It bore that same indifference as though he were arguing with obstinate farmers grumbling about paying their rent. In fact, he was worried that he had not yet heard the word 'loan' pass Shane's lips.

'The company is sound,' interrupted the chief financial officer. 'The accounts are healthy; the current situation is the result of a temporary slowdown in the Russian economy.'

Shane did not even deign to look at the man. Leaning on the table, arms folded, he addressed only Lev.

'We need guarantees. We need your assets as collateral. ELK is virtually bankrupt, but you are still a rich man, Mr Kravchenko.'

Lev did not react. Shane fell silent for a moment. He considered the man sitting opposite him. Having constantly striven for success, sacrificed his life for his career, eliminated his opponents one by one, Shane despised this Russian, the wealth he had amassed, the pleasure he had experienced, the women he had known. Zadie had talked to him about the oligarch's London parties and the attorney had been appalled as though by some crime. He didn't know Lev, he imagined him. And even if what he imagined was nothing like the real Lev, only ruin seemed a fitting reward for his actions.

'We want a claim on ELK.'

Lev did not react.

'We want mortgages totalling thirty million dollars on your London house, ten million on your chalet in Gstaad, fifty million on your palace in Moscow. On your summer house on the Black Sea, a total of seven million. On your villa in Cannes, twenty million.'

He reeled off the amounts in a peremptory tone.

'And why do you need two thirty-five-million-dollar jets?'

he added. 'Or your twenty-million-dollar yacht? You don't need these things. No one needs such luxuries.'

Zadie glanced at Shane. This was nothing. The real announcement was to come. At this moment, she admired Lev's calm. He did not react. She had seen so many men in this situation lose it, seen them stammer, sweat, blush, sometimes even break down in tears, that the Russian's perfect composure seemed exceptional.

In fact, Lev was filled with a cold anger. Brimming with such rage that he wanted to hurl himself at the attorney and crush him. But he controlled himself, because his whole life was at stake here today, because he needed this money, because he had no choice. Bolt upright, vaguely contemptuous, he looked like a man listening to someone talking nonsense. He had expected a negotiation; all that was being offered was an ultimatum.

'Without going into considerations of the utility of luxuries,' said Zadie with a smile intended to calm things down, 'I would like to point out that lending is not part of Kelmann's core business. Consequently, though such guarantees are necessary, they are not in themselves sufficient.'

Lev blanched with rage.

'You want to take the bread out of my mouth, is that it? I don't have much else, you know.'

'On the contrary, on the contrary, Mr Kravchenko. We are thinking only of the best interests of ELK.'

'And your own, I assume,' said Lev.

'Our interests are your interests. The best solution for ELK is not a loan, which would probably be insufficient and which is extremely risky, since you could lose all your assets.'

Zadie left a dramatic pause, then went on: 'An IPO – a stock market flotation – is the only way to increase your assets and attract investors.'

There was no answer. The chief financial officer stifled a sigh and flushed scarlet. Lev gave him a disdainful look, then stared at Zadie, who held his gaze for a moment, then lowered her eyes.

'There are other banks, you know,' he said.

'Feel free,' Shane interrupted with a triumphant smile. 'No one will lend you a red cent. The merchant banks would propose the same solution; as for the others, they're not going to get involved in such a risky venture. And our team is the only one with the influence to successfully float ELK on the stock market. An independent expert will evaluate your assets, oilfields, drilling rights. He could also put a price on the portfolio of commodity derivatives we sold you.'

Lev remembered that his chief financial officer, probably to get into Kelmann's good books, had indeed bought structured products he didn't understand. For hedging purposes, allegedly . . . More likely it was speculation.

'Assuming the parameters are favourable,' Shane went on, 'the portfolio could represent as much as a third of the total value of your company. The expert evaluating your assets will be the best in the business. And we can guarantee both the quality of his evaluation and his favourable consideration of your case. Once the issue price has been fixed, I can assure you, ELK will be the talk of the markets. Money will come flooding in.'

Lev weighed up the situation. Shane was right. No bank would lend him the money. The offer to discuss a loan had simply been a lure. As always, Kelmann would make its money on the IPO. Teams of financial experts and corporate lawyers would get to work racking up billable hours.

He got to his feet.

'I'll leave you to sort out the details with my lawyer.'

He left without saying goodbye.

'He held up pretty well,' said Zadie.

The attorney looked at her without a word. He had won, his victory had been total, yet his prey had got away; the man hadn't so much as quavered.

'I hope he chokes on his money! He'll be back to us begging, I'm telling you, and he'll wind up in the gutter. What we're giving him is just a band-aid.'

Shane moved away to talk to the lawyers.

'For a man on his knees,' Simon said admiringly, 'he stood up to us pretty well.'

Alone in the corridor, Lev was shaking. But he composed himself. The money from a stock market flotation meant he would be able to save ELK and afterwards he'd be stronger than ever. As always, the crisis would be a bloodletting, only the strongest would survive and they would have a stranglehold over the market. All the smaller companies would die and he would profit, he would make back his lost billions and come back to this same boardroom to meet with this man and give him a piece of his mind. But in the next couple of months, he needed to save his skin.

On the forecourt outside the Kelmann building, his bodyguard posted behind him, Lev took a deep breath. He closed his eyes.

When he opened them again, he saw a woman looking at him as she walked past. It was Jane Hilland, who, having spent an hour window-shopping on Fifth Avenue, was heading for the restaurant where she was to meet up with Matt and Simon. Knowing he had been in a meeting with the oligarch, she assumed Simon was already waiting for her. From the state of the Russian man, the meeting had clearly been tough.

And yet as she walked into the pleasant, understated restaurant she did not see Simon. She wandered through the dining room but he had not arrived yet. She found a seat, ordered a drink and read a newspaper. After some minutes, she heard a voice say: 'I believe we've met before.'

Matt was standing in front of her. Since they had been on the same flight, she assumed his comment was intended as a joke and gave him a polite smile.

'Oh, hi. You're here.' Her voice was flat.

'Yep. Almost on time,' said Matt.

'Please, have a seat.' Her tone belied the words.

'Simon not here yet?'

'Well spotted,' said Jane.

Matt did not reply. He was in his element. Sitting at a table with a girl, everything seemed possible.

'Good choice, this restaurant.'

'Sorry, I'm just finishing this article.'

Matt looked her up and down. He found her ugly and sophisticated. He loathed her and that excited him.

'Is it earth-shattering, this article?'

'No, it's stupid. But stupidity has its attractions.'

Matt felt awkward with Jane because everything about her

seemed settled and established. Nothing unnerved her; the way she looked, from her clothes to her make-up, was flawless and meticulous; her reactions were perfectly controlled and the way she spoke – the imperious, loathsome way she spoke – typified all the elements of her control: efficient, precise, peremptory.

But Matt knew his own strengths, and he knew too that Jane had been too rude with him at their first meeting to be completely indifferent. So he set to work.

He told her about his evening. She looked bored. He was funny. She condescended to make a comment or two. He mocked himself. A spark of interest flared.

She found him affected, pathetic, infantile. The designer stubble, the playboy posturing, the veneer of confidence concealing a chasm of self-doubt seemed to her ridiculous. She was astonished: how could Simon be friends with this man? But she had to admit he was quite funny.

'What hotel are you staying at again?' she interrupted.

'Hotel? That's an overstatement. I can't afford a hotel. No, it's more a hovel. My job is to hunt down the cockroaches. It is a task to which I apply myself with my innate sense of duty.'

He gave her an obsequious look, his shoulders sagging, palms turned upwards. Jane smiled – a genuine smile this time. Matt knew he was on the right track. Don't try to be clever, successful, dazzling: she wouldn't buy that for a minute. The poor self-mocking schmuck, that was the role he needed to play. It was just one more mask, and one all the easier for him to wear given his actual circumstances.

His face was transformed. The hint of brutality, of arrogance that sometimes hardened his features disappeared. He was just a nice guy.

He asked her about herself, about where she grew up. He led her further and further back into the innermost recesses of childhood, of pleasure, of nostalgia. Matt knew his subject. Exploit flaws, this was his role, his talent. Nosing into places where he would not be rejected, where there were no defences. Jane was a little surprised to find herself telling him about a horse she had loved when she was ten years old. She would groom and curry-comb it, and was the only one to ride the horse. Sometimes, without her father knowing, she liked to sleep next to it in the straw, in the warmth.

He asked her about her father. He was coming close to the heart of the matter, to the complex mix of admiration and resentment she felt for this man who had never really taken an interest in her, who spent all his time at work or with his mistresses. And now she could not help but lose her perfect control, could not help but be taken like all the others, so completely did Matt seem to understand her heart, the mixture of love, of fear, of bitterness, dark feelings that he himself had been plagued by all his life. To his surprise, he realised that beneath her cold exterior Jane was weaker than most women, that deep down she yearned to surrender. Her expression changed too. Behind the self-control, behind the make-up, behind the adult, the traits of childhood and adolescence began to appear. He rolled back the years. Working brilliantly and effortlessly, a skilled manipulator.

A voice called them back from this childhood, an unpleasant croak. It was Simon. He took off his coat and sat down.

'Sorry, the meeting went on longer than expected.'

Jane and Matt fell silent. What was he talking about? They had to give up the landscapes of the past. With some difficulty, Jane came back to the present.

'I ran into Kravchenko. He looked upset.'

'He's got good reason. We insisted he put all his assets up as collateral. And float ELK on the stock market. We took everything down to his underpants. So his balls are hanging out.'

Simon was ineptly trying to play the hard-nosed banker.

'Why did you have to stay behind? Kravchenko had left.'

'He was the only one to leave. Everyone else stayed. Including his CFO and his attorney. There were a lot of details to sort out. I'll be working with a specialist on the structured products we sold ELK to prepare everything for the IPO. It's a huge task . . . and a serious sign of confidence. Sorry to keep you waiting.'

'Kravchenko's lost everything?' Jane asked.

'Why are you so interested?' Simon teased.

'I find ruin is always interesting.'

Simon shrugged.

'I don't know if he's lost everything. To be honest, I think he'll survive. He'll find investors. He's tough, he impressed us all, even Shane, one of the partners, who hates his guts. You know how hard it is to impress Zadie, well, she was completely shaken up. Kravchenko didn't turn a hair. We told him we were taking his fortune and his assets and he just treated us like servants. Then again, his debts are colossal and he has powerful enemies in Russia.'

'Well, it just means one less Russian, which can't be bad,' said Matt.

'You remember that dinner we had at Lemerre's place where the waiter was punched?'

'What's the connection?'

'The Russian guy that night, it was Kravchenko.'

'Really? In that case, I'm even happier he's bankrupt. The pampered oligarch is having to beg for his survival now. I remember the woman who was with him. She had class.'

'Elena Kravchenko, she's a well-known academic. They're separated and she's suing him for half his fortune – though we've got every rouble earmarked as collateral. He's with some prostitute who demands extortionate amounts of money. Everyone's bleeding him dry.'

'How do you know all this stuff?' asked Matt.

'Bankers probe hearts and minds,' interjected Jane.

Matt felt a twinge of jealousy. Even this was slipping away from him. His insight into others. Into their secrets. The area where he felt most comfortable. And the person with the edge was the autistic Simon. The guy hiding behind his numbers and his hang-ups.

'But why do you want to destroy Kravchenko?' asked Matt.

Simon looked surprised.

'We don't want to destroy him. The bank just needs assurances, that's all.'

'If his company doesn't pull through, Kravchenko will end up frozen to death under a Moscow bridge.'

'They've got bridges in Moscow?'

'I've no idea, but if they have, that's where he'll wind up. Honestly, I have to say, the whole business seems bizarre.'

Jane looked at Matt. She realised he was not as stupid as she had thought. Not stupid at all.

A waiter came to take their orders.

A few hundred metres away, Lev Kravchenko had walked into Central Park, sat down on a bench and was staring into space.

A squirrel hopped across the grass in front of him and scampered up a tree, its paws rustling on the bark. In short, sudden bursts the rodent climbed to the topmost branches then, with a bound, leapt to the next tree. It gripped the branches and, with disconcerting ease, took off for the next treetop.

Lev had not noticed the squirrel. He was thinking about what had happened at Kelmann. He would have to start all over again. Though he had already made and lost his fortune, he would play again for the pleasure of winning or losing, just so that he might feel again the thrill of the game, feel the blood pound in his veins once more. The flash of rage he had felt for Shane had done him good. It was good to experience life directly unmediated by boredom or indifference. He had to gamble to survive, to try to recapture the distant feelings of a past that was so remote that perhaps he had never lived it.

Yet there was one episode. A carnival in Moscow with food stalls and fairground attractions. Out walking with Elena in the first months of their relationship, both bundled up in winter coats, they had happened on the fair in a square and Elena had insisted on looking at the attractions. They found themselves at the shooting gallery. Plastic ducks on revolving plaster pipes that you had to shoot with a rifle firing pellets. Lev had grabbed a rifle, fired . . . and missed. He tried again and again but the lead pellet missed its target. Under the slightly mocking gaze of the stallholder, he had tried again and failed. And then Elena began to laugh and laugh ... And he laughed too at his ineptness; he had always been clumsy and a poor shot.

He remembered this laugh like some great moment of recklessness. A dazzling fragment against a backdrop of merry-go-round horses prancing to the music of tinkling bells in the whirl of the carnival's multicoloured lights.

Now, sitting on this bench in this city at once familiar and strange, a city of meetings, of hotels he'd stayed in fifty times but barely knew, he thought of this scene, and he thought too about a phrase from Tolstoy which had struck him as a young man, a terse sentence that summed up the peaceful, humdrum life of the magistrate Ivan Ilyich as it faltered after a long howl lasting three days and nights at the age of forty-five: 'Ivan Ilyich's life had been most simple and most ordinary and most terrible.' And if this phrase had profoundly marked him, it was because he felt he understood its true meaning: 'Ivan Ilyich's life had been most simple and most ordinary and *therefore* most terrible.' It was because life was life that it was terrible. It was because Ivan Ilyich Golovin, realising his disease was terminal, recognised the absurdity of this life which had been respectable in every way, that he suddenly howled, and that this howl went on for three days and three nights, foundering in the darkness of his torment. And to Lev, the death of Ivan Ilyich had always remained the real issue. Would he too die howling for three days and nights, life's illusion suddenly exploding in his face? Or would he die remembering a laugh heard at a carnival? Lev knew that the answer to these questions was undoubtedly more important than losing his business or his fortune. Howling for three days and nights or remembering a laugh.

And it was partly because of these questions that he had to stay strong now, for he would not howl so loudly if he risked his life heroically, considering that the only true beauty in life was life itself. So he had to play the game to the end without dwelling on doubts.

Lev, Simon, Matt, Jane, Zadie brought together in the fragmentation of fate. But all these creatures had become tiny, as minuscule as the gleam in the eye of the squirrel. The little creature is bounding still in an endless, headlong rush from tree to tree, high above human lives. He leaps while around him New York looms, vast and vertical, on this public holiday. Around the lush green heart of the city, the skyscrapers soar, ochre, white or translucent, slender or squat, erecting impassible bodies to the ocean's undertow. Begotten of steel, concrete and cement, standing stones along the horizon, the mythology of power. And the squirrel disappears in the tremendous pulse of the city, swelling like some mythical monster, devouring destinies and melting them into a million others.

The doors open: the buildings disgorge their human cargo, subways empty. Buses screech to a halt, doors opening, passengers disembarking, then pull away again. People hurry through the streets. Countless unknown quantities merging into vast concordances, billions of possibilities, in a frenzied breathlessness.

A deafening racket winds through the streets. Traffic is at a standstill; horns blare. It is impossible to hear anything. The horizon is filled with sounds, people, lights, buildings, sparks. A glut.

At the base of the towers the ocean beats. As one gradually pulls away from Manhattan, from the financial district, the Twin Towers, the sound fades, the horizon clears and suddenly there is nothing but the stark immensity, the surface dark with waves flecked with foam.

Everything has disappeared.

# 26

The IPO was a success. Simon had done a good job, meaning he had obeyed orders. His risk assessment, picked up by the expert dealing with the portfolio, had been outrageously optimistic, the issue price extremely attractive and, as always, Kelmann's publicity machine had been so powerful that everyone had been able to sing the victory song. The oil company had attracted large and small investors. ELK had become a top-rated company, money flooded in and if Lev was no longer running the show on his own, at least he knew he would be able to save his company.

'It's a total success,' declared Simon one evening in Zadie Zale's office when it was all over.

She nodded.

'You don't seem very happy.'

Zadie studied Simon.

'He's not going to survive.'

'Who?'

'The Russian. He was never supposed to survive. ELK will cease to be an independent company. That's how it's going to pan out.'

'What are you talking about? He can make it. The company's completely sound.'

'It's completely sound and he won't survive. Now leave me alone, I need to finish dealing with this project.'

'I don't understand.'

'Of course you don't understand. You don't understand anything. That's why you were brought on board. To do the maths and not understand things.'

Flabbergasted, Simon said nothing. Zadie got up, took him by the arm and led him out of the office.

'I'm sorry Simon, I'm tired. Just leave me to it, it's been a bad day.'

Simon related the conversation to Jane.

'There's obviously something she's not saying. You need to worm the information out of her.'

'She'll be pissed off,' said Simon anxiously.

'That's exactly what she needs to be. Otherwise she won't tell you anything.'

The following evening, Simon went to Zadie's office. He had steeled himself to do this.

'What did you mean yesterday?'

'About what?'

'About Kravchenko – and about me, while we're at it.'

Zadie's tired eyes were ringed with dark circles.

'He's interesting, the Russian, isn't he?' she said. 'Well, I find him interesting. A lot more interesting than Shane or anyone in this bank. Obviously whether or not I find him interesting makes no difference, but it's something. Even if I'm forced to admit that Kravchenko doesn't exist.'

Once again Simon did not understand anything, though for very different reasons from the previous evening.

'Kravchenko doesn't exist any more than Simon Judal, renamed Jude, any more than Zadie Zale or even Shane. No one exists in this world. I really should have worked in finance before I studied philosophy. I'd have written much better essays. I finally understood the meaning of life when I came to work in the bank. We are nothing. It doesn't matter that we exist since we exist only to ourselves and a handful of close friends. Kravchenko will disappear and it will be of no consequence: just a ripple on the surface of things. And it's not some capitalist plot to reduce people to nothing, it's simply the irrefutable reality of our world: so many creatures that are so similar that they are nothing. And even if each one of them squawks like a duck loudly proclaiming their existence, it means nothing. Kravchenko is doomed, there's nothing I can do to help him, in fact I'll play a part in his downfall, as will you, and none of it will matter because we don't exist, because we'll be merely a handful of banking transactions.'

'I still don't understand.'

Zadie sighed. She got to her feet, took a few steps.

'It will be a simple process,' she said wearily, 'extremely simple. Now that the IPO's gone well, now that a little time has passed, Kravchenko will call us, in a couple of days maybe, a couple of weeks tops. It will be a pleasant conversation. We'll congratulate each other for the umpteenth time on our success. And then Kravchenko will ask for his money. Hardly surprising, he needs that money, he's fighting off his creditors. Everyone's cash poor. There'll be a silence on the phone. Then we'll tell him it's not possible. At that point he'll ask in that gruff Russian accent: "And why is it not possible?"

285

And we'll tell him the truth. We'll tell him that Liekom, having acquired a controlling share via an investment fund, has taken over ELK and that Lianov is now his boss. We'll tell him the whole deal is fraudulent, that it was based on falsified business valuations and if word of that spread, the share price would tank. We'll tell him that Lianov controls ELK but Kelmann controls the information. Incidentally I should tell you that we sold all the ELK shares at a healthy profit so we have nothing to lose. We'll tell him he no longer controls ELK and that his fate is in Lianov's hands. We'll tell him that, as far as he's concerned, it's all over.'

'That's completely immoral!'

Zadie stared at him in astonishment.

'Only you could come out with something like that in a place like this! Immoral! Am I hearing things? What exactly is immoral? Stripping an oligarch of a fortune he owes to the carve-up of the Soviet Union? A man who expanded his empire by taking over dozens of other oil companies using money or threats? Kravchenko's fate will be exactly the fate he forced on others, the same way that I'll be tossed aside for the very reasons I've been successful. It's possible some of the directors of Kelmann will end up in prison some day when the rules of the game are changed. Is that immoral? No, it's something much worse. It's a trap, we're all caught up in it. And I don't know how to get myself out.'

'But you liked Kravchenko! I saw you with him! He charmed you. I've never seen you like that with a man.'

'He charmed me and we are going to ruin him. That's the trap, Simon. It's just the trap. No one escapes. The moment you try to move, fate springs the trap. Make one movement to join the ranks of humankind and it's all over.'

'I don't want to be a part of that. Shane can do what he likes. In fact I think I'll tell Kravchenko what's going on.'

Zadie shook her head.

'Who did the valuations, Simon?'

He drew back.

'You're involved, Simon. The IPO dossier was based on your valuations and your risk assessment. I'm telling you this as a friend, Simon: if there's anyone who might suffer as a result of that dossier, it's you. If anyone's to blame, it's you.'

The colour drained from Simon's face.

'You were the one making the decisions, not me.'

Zadie gave a sad little smile.

'We'll see what the SEC have to say. There are malicious rumours that they're very soft on billionaires,' she added, 'but I can assure you, they won't be soft on you. And American jails don't exactly have a good rep.'

'But I obviously work for Kelmann, you're the ones who'll be held responsible. You're the ones who told me to overvalue the assets.'

Zadie's expression hardened.

'I personally gave you no such order. And anyway, I hardly know you. You're a junior quantitative analyst, as far as I know, one of my team in London. Like I said, Simon, no one gets out of the trap.'

Simon left the office. It was a cold night. He buttoned his coat, turned up his collar and plunged into winter. Zadie was right: the trap had sprung shut. He felt scared. He felt as though he was about to be crushed. But terrible as his fear was, the thought that he had been hired for his gullibility pained him most. He had thought he was competent; with his work on the POL product he had felt on top of the world. But his greatest talent was his stupidity: Zadie had kept him on her team in order to con him, to use him, to exploit his naivety. The goldfish was back in his bowl.

A thin drizzle started falling. He pulled his collar tighter. His personality leached away into the dark night. The gangster's suit, his recent illusions, everything was dissolving and slipping away. His terrible fragility was once again rolling out its baneful power – with its cortege of doubts, of misery, the black banner of failure. He was swept up by the rain, by murky drizzle, by dark thoughts. He felt so stupid, so powerless, with nothing to protect him. The streets were deserted, no flicker of life brightened the darkness of the city. Simon quickened his pace. He needed warmth. He needed Jane to reassure him. She would find the words.

# 27

The news came as no surprise to anyone in a capital pervaded by excess. Many such incidents had happened before. And every day there were comparable events that no one mentioned, since the victims were unknown.

Until now, Lev had invested all his energy in the struggle. He truly had started again: he had been prepared to risk his life. Sometimes, in the evening, as he thought about the frantic activity that had been required during the day to dole out what little money he had, in precise, targeted operations to areas of the business threatening to collapse, he smiled. He smiled because he was deferring the moment when he would howl, because he was tempering the scream, because life bubbled up inside him like a fountain of youth. Everyone was surprised by his cheerful mood. The workers and managers in the company felt a closeness to this man in his struggle that they had never felt before, despite the fact that Lev still could not afford to pay wages, doled out a little cash from time to time, simply repeating that the company flotation had gone well and money would soon come flooding in. Even the managers who trooped into his office and left frustrated having received some meagre handout, the promise of a week's or two weeks' salary, of a 10 per cent pay increase 'as soon as the money comes in', felt a sort of sympathy for him. And perhaps he was also less aloof, less calculating. He was fighting. He tried to get production figures up, to have the damaged oil wells repaired, to keep his creditors at bay. He had no family, no friends, no allies. Only enemies and those who did not care. The evidence of this fact delighted him. The situation had not changed, it was simply more straightforward, more clear-cut. But it thrilled him like a spark of life in an old man who is dying. He was alive. He worked like a maniac, played like a maniac, slept with Oksana and with other women. He hungered for women's bodies. There was in his pleasure a profound truth he had forgotten, one revealed to him in Oksana and other women as they offered themselves to him: the tremulous present. Lev was the great philosopher, the great sage because he lived in the present. And so time stood still, a tinkling of cymbals, a marvellous suspension before moving on to other pleasures that were fleeting and therefore eternal, since they were gilded by the magic of the moment.

Lev Kravchenko was a happy man. At some party, he ran into Elena on the arm of another man. Even though their divorce had not yet been settled. They chatted. And Elena's eyes were shining, with love or with sadness, because she rediscovered the man she had known long ago, because the ghost had been made flesh again.

The following night they slept together. There was nothing to hope for, a fact they both realised, Elena perhaps a little less clearly because she was still haunted by the ghost, whispering in her ear words of the past and of lost illusions of love. But there was also an exhilaration to spending the night together, to take the gifts offered by life because there could be no way back, no second chance – just the marvellous luck of being alive at least for a little longer.

'Do you remember the shooting gallery?'

'What shooting gallery?'

Lev didn't answer. The memories were his. His alone.

One day, he phoned Shane. They joked for a while with that menacing undertone of enemies. They congratulated each other again on the success of the IPO. Then he asked for his money. Shane told him it wasn't possible.

'And why is it not possible?'

And the other man, the enemy, told him everything. He explained that the business valuations had been false, that Liekom now owned the controlling share and therefore now controlled ELK. That he, Lev Kravchenko, had no further say in the matter. Shane added that Kelmann had hedged its bets and made a profit in betting against him, against Liekom, and in selling the shares. That it would take just one article in the *Financial Times* for the value of the company to plummet.

'Lianov might not be happy.'

'The time of the gangsters is over. Besides, Liekom needs us. I'm sure Lianov won't be happy, but he'll get over it. It's nothing personal. We're just doing our job. Making money.'

From the outset Lev had wondered how they would try to hoodwink him. He had tried to find out, had sent men to investigate, but his enemies had a talent for keeping out of sight and he had found nothing. This was why he had lost and Shane and Lianov had won.

And yet Lev could have won. In fact he had already won

since he *existed*, but he might also have triumphed in the battle against his enemies, something that would have been an added pleasure. He was convinced there was a solution. That he had only to think about it. He still had faith in his intelligence.

He would have marched into the board room in New York to meet Shane and Lianov and addressed them in the tone of a master.

Yes, he could have triumphed.

But just as his Mercedes, on its usual route, was overtaking a small red Fiat, the bomb exploded. Shards of glass and metal sliced the air like lethal weapons, decapitating the driver. Lev did not howl. His body suffered barely a scratch. When it was found, many people were surprised: he was smiling.

He had died smiling.

# 28

In American football, however uneven the game, there suddenly comes the moment of reckoning – the moment when a player breaks away from the scrimmage and runs hard and fast for the end zone, wreathed in glory.

Sila was running. Since his regrettable fit of anger, he had been running. He needed to run. He had made a naive connection between his violence and his lack of physical exercise. And this was why he now wore himself out on long runs, far from the city, through the Everglades where he could be alone. In the maze of waterways, along an often marshy course riddled with inlets, barred by expanses of water he had to skirt round, a primitive environment inhabited by prehistoric animals, a vast confusion of small mammals and huge reptiles surrounded him, giving him a sense of boundless freedom. He shook off the identity of the polite, methodical restaurateur and ran, ran endlessly, his pace faltering now and then, given the unforeseeable obstacles of the course.

On this particular day, Sila had been running for about an hour. The air was crisp, the sky grey, perfect weather for running. A four-by-four appeared suddenly about a hundred metres behind him. He was not surprised, since the narrow sandbar strip of land flanked on either side by sawgrass marshes was a popular thoroughfare. Several boats tied up along the bank stood waiting for alligator hunters. But when a second four-by-four appeared around a bend ahead of him, an unpleasant shudder ran through him.

The two vehicles stopped about fifty metres from him. Now Sila knew what was coming. He wondered only whether Ruffle was part of the pack. He stood stock-still, alert, catching his breath.

A car door opened. Sila ran, trying to get as far as possible from the two vehicles, though he knew that the trap had been carefully planned since the spit of land was only a couple of hundred metres wide. But no one had reckoned on just how fast Sila could be. Running as hard as he could towards the swampland, he tried to skirt round the cars to go back the way he had come. If he had enough time, if he could make it back to the washed-out dirt track about a kilometre back where the ground was so rutted, no car would be able to follow him. And he was sure that no man in the world could catch up with him when he was running, especially if he was running for his life. But how could he make it as far as there?

No one had tried to block his path, and the car door had slammed shut again. The two cars drove after him, their engines roaring, and suddenly all Sila could hear was this sound, this mounting threat. A viscous fear surged through him, but still he ran, his breathing regular, determined to get through.

And he made it past them. About twenty metres from the marsh, he took a sharp right and stared ahead at the barren ground, knowing he had a kilometre to run. The long dash for the end zone.

In a surge of desperation, he sped on. He knew he was running too fast, that no one could sprint for a whole kilometre, but the engines were roaring behind him and even if the cars could not reach their top speeds on these dirt tracks, their acceleration rate was second to none. He tried to focus on his breathing, to become nothing more than this breath, this pounding movement. He tried to become the race itself. His years of training, the magnificent machine that was his body hurtled forwards at extraordinary speed while behind him the cars spluttered over the potholed terrain. At this point one of them veered away from the swampland back to the solid road. Sila realised in panic that it would try to overtake him on the right and cut him off. He ran even faster. Ran as though the finishing line was in sight, as though there were only fifty metres between him and salvation while far away, too far away, the band of trees offered an illusory promise of deliverance. He had no choice. If the car overtook him, he was finished.

It overtook him; the men surrounded Sila, they stopped the car and climbed out. There were four of them, armed with baseball bats, and Ruffle was one of them. Sila was alone and his chest was burning. Tears of pain rolled down his cheeks. He tried to maintain his speed but without realising it, his pace had slackened. Ahead of him, unmoving, the pack fanned out to form a barrier.

In American football, however patchy the game has been, there suddenly comes the moment of reckoning, the moment when a player – to the roar of the crowd – stops a running play, brings his opponent down with a hard tackle. Ruffle could feel this moment coming. Suddenly, he forced himself out of his immobility and rushed towards Sila at a surprising speed given his size. He was carried forwards by his rage. Sila, exhausted, panting, lurched sideways trying to dodge the blow. But his body no longer responded as it should. The movement was neither fast enough nor clean enough. Even so, in a football game Sila would have managed to dodge his opponent. But Mark Ruffle's hand, his bandaged hand, the hand that had been broken was clutching a baseball bat. And it was this bat that broke Sila's run. A blow that sent him sprawling to the ground.

The four men surrounded him. Four more clambered out of the car behind to join them.

With a single blow, Ruffle broke his left knee. Then the right. Methodically, without uttering a word.

Beyond the line of trees, far beyond the end zone of salvation, Sila's scream was heard.

# 29

Shoshana did not hear the scream. But somehow or other, over the swampland and the forests, she sensed it. Perhaps through the fragile bond she had forged with the waiter or perhaps, more rationally because, knowing her husband, she had been expecting it. The nigger had to pay, he said over and over.

She had wanted to warn Sila. She had wanted to go to his restaurant and talk to him. But, without knowing why, she hadn't. Because she secretly hoped that her husband would not act on his threats, because she was afraid, because she felt betrayed, for all sorts of bad reasons which, in any case, would have changed nothing since Sila was not a man to be frightened by threats.

When Ruffle came home, he had that Sunday air about him. Shoshana quizzed him. He told her he'd been out in the swamps hunting alligator.

'Did you catch one?' she asked.

'Yeah, big one,' he said curtly.

She went out to the car. In the trunk she found the baseball bats. She came back into the house carrying one of them.

'You hunt gators with baseball bats?'

'It's to smash their heads in. It's just a game.'

She got her coat.

'I'm going to find your alligator.'

She wandered the swampland without finding Sila. Her eyes were misted by tears. Her body, shaken by sobs, slowly crumpling in the driver's seat. In the middle of the swamp, after miles and miles of driving round in the maze of her despair, she stopped the car. All around her were the grey skeletons of trees. She buried her head in her hands. What had happened to Sila? She wept for this man, she wept for herself and she wept for her husband. She could expect nothing more of life now, she who had never expected much, who had simply wished, like in a soap opera, that she could love her husband and her children in a big house with a garden out front. Just a gentle loving husband. Reality was mocking her. And Shoshana went on crying.

As the past and the future fell away, only one certainty remained: she had to leave. She could not go back to the house, she had to take her son and never see Ruffle again. She had to leave.

It was over. Never again would she live in limbo, waiting for a change that would never come, moving between fitness centres and televisions and cold white rooms.

She turned the key in the ignition.

# 30

Simon slipped the key back into his pocket and stepped into the apartment, sadly dark and deserted. He was sorry that Matt wasn't there. While his friend hated his successes, he could be a comfort when times were tough. He always came out with crude expressions to try and cheer him up, his favourite being: 'Sling your prick over your shoulder and walk.' That evening, it would have taken a lot of pep talk to cheer him up.

On the kitchen table, he found a note: 'My pet, I'm heading for the centre of the universe. London's not enough for me any more. I got the wrong place. The rain of gold is falling in New York, that's where the real fortunes are being made. I'll get in touch as soon as I've become a new man. A quick name change, and I'll call you. Matt?'

The question mark made Simon smile. A new transformation was beginning.

He called Jane. He had tried calling her several times on the way home, left a couple of messages, but she hadn't called back. She was probably asleep. Everyone was deserting him tonight. He turned on the television. The channels flashed past. He barely noticed what was on. All he could see was Zadie. And her words went round and round in his head: 'Of course you don't understand. You don't understand anything. That's why you were brought on board. To do the maths and not understand things.'

The following morning when he told her what had happened with Zadie, Jane reacted as though she could hardly believe it. But he had the strange impression that she already knew all about it, that she was only pretending to console him. And this painful, unnatural sense that she was playing a part simply heightened in the months that followed. Simon was haunted by one question: if Jane had fallen in love with the gangster, how could she live with the goldfish?

Jane had not fallen in love with the gangster; nonetheless, Simon's heavy-handed attempt to conform to a stereotype that was a complete fabrication was irritating. She warned him: 'I love your weaknesses.'

He was crippled by his weaknesses. Obviously he couldn't go on working with Zadie. On the basis of a minimal but lucrative settlement, he handed in his resignation. He didn't look for another job. He no longer had any confidence in himself and besides, the banking world disgusted him. The humiliation he had suffered made him feel sick and he couldn't imagine ever going back to working as a quant.

'You'll have to get a job some day,' Jane would say.

Simon didn't answer. He was sinking. No longer living in a world of images was destroying him, and it saddened him to think that he was no better than the traders whose image of themselves crumbled under the weight of professional failures.

A month later, the break-up with Jane Hilland completed his annihilation. Within five minutes, the young woman announced her decision and left. He would never see her again.

# Epilogue

One morning, Simon received an invitation card:

On the back it read:

*Hôtel Cane*

### DEMOLITION DAY

### 21.04.2009/20:30

Prior to renovation the Hotel Cane would like to offer its regular customers an exceptional opportunity: come and break, smash, destroy, obliterate the old world. A new hotel, more beautiful, more welcoming, will rise from the rubble.

NB. A sledgehammer will be given to you on your arrival.

This unsettling invitation was all the more surprising since he had never been a client of the Hotel Cane, except for having had an – admittedly memorable – dinner at the restaurant years before, in another life. And furthermore, the card had been posted in New York. He tossed it onto the table.

He remembered that night perfectly. He had made it the symbol of the illusory parenthesis of his life, lost in these roles and since a number of the erstwhile protagonists had since passed away, there was a whiff of mourning about the memory. Lev Kravchenko had died in a terrorist attack and, in his successive transformations, Matthieu Brunel had vanished. In spite of his efforts, Simon had been unable to track him down. He had been swept away by some new identity, taking with him a part of Simon's life, a curious detour that Simon did not regret since he had discovered new sensations, but ones that had proved to be a dead end.

After it was over, he had travelled. But though he could go to the ends of the earth, still he came face to face with himself, endlessly revisiting the dead ends of his soul, confronted by a world that looked increasingly the same as he grew older and some strange alchemy brought countries ever closer, never knowing whether it was his own gaze which wiped out the distinctions or whether it was some terrible spell of regularisation.

He had tried to discover the new face of the world, journeying across Asia and the factory of the future. But often he simply saw it as an overblown West, bloated by vast crowds of people in a breathtaking destruction of nature. When the great whirl of countries had cancelled itself out in a vast, blank tedium, he came home.

He had rented a large studio in the 15th arrondissement and furnished it tastelessly, without realising that he was using his aunt's dated, old-fashioned apartment as a model. Since he had spent all his money travelling, he set about looking for work. His somewhat erratic career path worked against him. He didn't inspire confidence in prospective employers and research laboratories enjoyed the heady pleasure of rejecting the traitor. He eventually got a lowly job as a financial engineer, hired by a car manufacturer in Guyancourt, just outside Paris. He resumed the humdrum life he had known before Matthieu, now tinged with disillusion.

On April 21 2009, he emerged from Javel métro station at 6.57 pm and headed home. He took a shower, slipped on his bathrobe and, as he was towelling his hair dry, bumped into the dining table. Cursing under his breath, he pulled away the towel that was blinding him. There in front of him on the treacherous corner of the table lay the invitation card, creamy white, calling him to order.

He decided to go to the Hotel Cane. The handsome suits of his former life were no use to him: the wide square-shouldered cut epitomised the late 1990s. But he had nothing else to wear, so he pulled on a pair of jeans, his best shirt and a dark jacket from the past. The reflection in the tiny bathroom mirror seemed acceptable to him. No one would laugh at him.

A large crowd had gathered outside the Cane. People seemed excited at the prospect of demolition. Simon recognised the faces and the appearances of bygone days. Not as individuals, but from a certain air of opulence. Tall, slender young women strutted among the young men, the supermodel figures looking like anaemic flowers, though they seemed animated, gripped like the others there by the thrill of destruction.

Simon handed over his invitation. The revolving door turned. He recognised the grand lobby, still intact: demolition was not yet allowed in here. A flash of memory told him that Lemerre's restaurant was to his right. The double doors were closed.

He handed his coat in at the cloakroom and in return the attendant gave him a steel sledgehammer with a big smile and the words: 'Enjoy yourself.'

Simon went on his way in silence. A couple of young men, sledgehammers in hand, rushed past him. He stepped into the reception rooms: a tornado had swept through here. Broken tables and chandeliers lay smashed over the floor like glass jellyfish. People had been offered what they most loved: the thrill of destruction sublimated as spectacle. Simon walked past theatrical scenes and dumb shows where actors played out crimes or orgies. Pyramids of glass came crashing down beneath the artistic blows of a robot; a pink car froze in the act of crashing through the French windows; a bath equipped with an outboard motor steamed feverishly and in the midst of these creations, the faithful customers, fashionably dressed, wandered around with their sledgehammers casually destroying the old world as they passed.

Then suddenly, he saw him.

Matthieu Brunel or Matt B. Lester or whatever his name was now was wearing a dinner jacket, dress suited to demolition and rubble. Next to him was a beautiful girl, one of those impossibly tall, impossibly thin creatures, probably from Eastern Europe.

'It's amazing how good it feels to smash things,' Matt said, coming over. 'My speciality is mirrors. What about you?'

Simon didn't answer. This encounter stirred up such emotions in him that he didn't know whether to laugh or cry.

Matthieu hadn't changed much. His face was simply more brutal, his expression a little harder, inured to his every urge. And his features were curiously smooth, as though botoxed.

'So the invitation, you sent it?' Simon asked, his voice hoarse.

'Of course, who else?'

'How did you track me down?'

'Easy. I never really lost sight of you. Once or twice while you were travelling – I have to say you got about a bit – but the minute you were back in Paris I found out. I suppose I should have got in touch sooner but . . . You know how time flies. And then this demolition day came up and I thought it was a perfect symbol.'

'I tried to find you.'

'Really? That would have been hard. I transformed myself completely this time. Name, surname. I'd had enough. And it worked out: I'm a different man. Married, settled, kids.'

'What about her?' Simon asked nodding towards the girl, who looked sulky and bored.

Matthieu gave a wolfish smile.

'A hobby. Everyone needs a hobby. Marriage is tough. I've only just met her. Ukrainian. Pretty hot, don't you think? Sixteen, seventeen maybe, you can never tell with these girls.'

'You haven't changed,' said Simon dully.

'Thanks for coming,' said Matthieu. 'I really wasn't sure you would. It was good of you, especially as it's been a long time now ... Years. And years that count double. And here we are together again, just like old times. Though everything's changed in your life. It's not the golden age any more – London, the money, the excitement . . .'

'It was never a golden age, it was all just lies. And anyway, they've been hit by the crisis too. We've learned a few things. About banks, about money, about financial set-ups. I don't regret anything.'

Matthieu shrugged.

'Maybe people did learn something, but it doesn't matter. They watched billions, thousands of billions flushed down the toilet, lots of them lost their jobs, but it doesn't matter. Because nothing will really change. Because it was all just talk, just people pretending to be shocked, it's not like they actually *did* anything – except bail us out, of course.'

'Bail us out? What do you mean, *us*?'

Matthieu stood to attention with a mixture of pride and mockery.

'Us. The people who asserted themselves. I've set myself up at the top of the tower and no one will ever throw me out now. I told you, Simon. I needed money, lots of money, because some day soon everything is going to come crashing down and only the richest will survive. I told you I'd give you a place in my tower, my marble and steel tower. Well, the tower is ready: my apartments are reinforced, the doors are armour-plated, the whole ground floor is patrolled like a military base. I'm ready for the apocalypse.'

A triumphant expression spread over his face and Simon realised that this was where the physical change was, in this crass contentment. Matthieu had achieved his aims. He was happy. He had money enough to fill his pockets and more. His wallet, his office, his apartment, his safes, his houses. The brutality of his features was that of the predator sated after slaughtering its prey. Fortunate are the mad and the megalomaniacs! He had *triumphed*!

Simon had followed the soap opera of the 2008 financial crash just as he had followed the Russian crash of 1998 from the inside and, more distractedly, the bursting of the dot-com bubble while he'd been travelling in India and Thailand. He felt that the current crisis could not be compared to the others, that it heralded the end of the world just as, despite appearances, the crash of 1929 had ushered in American hegemony and eclipsed the power of the UK. This was the end of the West's supreme power. As a detached observer, he thought that, as usual, financialisation had heralded the end of an economic supremacy, just as it had centuries ago in Genoa or Amsterdam, financial skills having supplanted those of industry and commerce. This, in general, was the point at which one economy passed the baton to another; it did not vanish, and in fact kept much of its wealth for some time, but never again would it dominate. He even expounded on this historical analysis with his co-workers, who knew nothing about his past and were astonished by the breadth of his knowledge. But his analytical stance masked something unwholesome, as though he wanted some kind of revenge, the complete collapse of a financial world that had duped and humiliated him and whose profound immorality he understood only too well. He had first heard of the so-called 'subprime' mortgage crisis in 2007 without truly understanding its possible impact. But when Lehmann Brothers, to everyone's astonishment, filed for bankruptcy because of the collapse of its mortgage-backed securities, he had gleefully imagined the shock wave felt by his little friends in the banking business and he knew they would be trembling with fear because every bank's accounts were riddled with toxic assets. But nothing happened: the ordinary taxpayer had bailed out the threatened billionaires and the losses had been mutualised. The American Federal Reserve had bought up the toxic assets. In a scandal more astonishing than anything perpetrated by the Russian oligarchs, since by a little financial sleight-of-hand, no one had any choice – the banks had to be saved or everyone would perish – as small investors were bankrupted to the economic crisis, businesses went to the wall and tens of millions of people joined the dole queues, the foundations of the banking system had been preserved at the expense of a few scapegoats and the sacking of a handful of traders of no importance. And what with the state of the money markets and the disappearance of rival banks, people could look forward to exceptional end-of-year bonuses.

Matthieu had been right: no one would oust him from his tower. He was lord and master, by virtue, not of blood, but of money, with a universal *droit de seigneur*. He had everything. Everything, at least, that money with its magic, its furious and fascinating magic, could buy. Its power to transform. Lives, feelings, faces.

A man came over to them. A thick-set man of average height with a neat beard that softened his bulldog features and an overdeveloped upper body.

'Mark!' Matthieu raised a hand to greet him.

The two men high-fived and Matthieu said in English: 'How've you been? Good flight?'

He turned back to Simon and explained: 'I insisted that Ruffle come. He hadn't even opened the invitation. We've been seeing quite a lot of each other in recent years. We've got business connections. But you two know each other, don't you?'

'I don't think so,' said Simon.

'Sure you do. In fact you saw each other right here, a long time ago. Surely you can't have forgotten, Simon? I mean, you're the one who's so fond of victims. Ruffle gave some insolent waiter a hiding.'

The other man looked uncomfortable. This seemed to bring back memories.

'Shoshana's not with you?' asked Matthieu.

'No. You know how she is. Doesn't like to stray too far from home and with three kids, it's not easy I can tell you. What about you? How's the wife?' said Ruffle, eyeing up the bored young girl standing next to Matthieu.

'Fine, fine. With a husband like me, what do you expect?' he joked.

Ruffle brandished his sledgehammer.

'Well, I've got work to do. Catch you later, Hilland.'

At the name, Simon froze. For a moment, Matthieu looked a little embarrassed, then he regained his composure.

'That's my new name. Hilland. John Hilland. Not bad, eh?'

Simon didn't respond. He needed to know.

'She brought me everything, you know. Money, respectability, luxury. This is what I was born for: to satisfy my every

FABRICE HUMBERT

desire. I can't change now, you know that, we are what we are and my temperament was tried in the fire. No one in this world has been tried in the fire like I have, in the hell fire of desire, of energy and ambition. Desire is the only thing I believe in. My hand was made to grasp things. Material things, expensive things, objects. That is all that exists: things, and my hand to grasp them. And I grasped them. Not through intelligence, not through violence or crime. No, by sheer force of will. I went out into the world and carved out a place for myself.'

He shrugged and went on, 'Thanks to you, thanks to Jane.'

Simon felt overwhelmed with disgust. True to form, Matthieu had betrayed him. But here he was flaunting his betrayal, inviting him to this hotel where it all started, so he could scream in his best friend's face that he had stolen his woman to take advantage of her money, to finally achieve his terrifying desire to exist. Looking back over the years Simon realised that this man's friendship could only be fulfilled through cruelty because the bottomless emptiness of his soul condemned him to destroy those closest to him. John Hilland despised those he loved and at this very moment as he confessed his betrayal, he probably loved his friend unconditionally. From Matthieu Brunel to John Hilland, the bastard had found himself and if Simon had loved Matthieu like a brother, like a curious, capricious double, an inverted twin, he loathed John Hilland with a contempt that was reassuringly simple. This man was not Matthieu. He might well be the true Matthieu, finally revealed by his incessant metamorphoses, his every contradiction merged into a repellent coherence, but the bond of brotherhood was broken.

His voice quavering slightly, Simon changed the subject: 'I

hope at least some of your friends went bankrupt, if only to spice up your conversations.'

'A couple, yes, but nothing serious,' Matthieu joked. 'The most shocking thing was that there were no suicides. It's a clear sign of the lack of decorum in modern society. I mean, look at Ruffle, king of the subprime mortgage. He made his fortune at the expense of poor people who are homeless now, his debts were colossal, he even had to appear before the Senate Finance Committee. And what happened? A bank that had itself been bailed out by the US government bought out his company for a tidy little sum, probably not the billions it was notionally worth in the good old days, but enough to live on for several generations to come. All is for the best in the best of all possible worlds. He can go on happily living with his wife and kids – by which I mean his mistresses and his kids, because his wife Shoshana is a depressive and she can't stand him, even if she can't bring herself to leave him. But, well, that's America for you: family is sacred. And I think that if Ruffle got divorced, his father would drown him in the swimming pool.'

'I remember him very well,' Simon said with disgust. 'What a pig! He punched that waiter for no reason at all.'

'Yes. For no reason. But you didn't do anything, did you? You just carried on eating like everyone else. You accepted that man's humiliation. Or am I wrong?'

Simon raised his hand. A childlike gesture calling for peace. He didn't want to hear any more. He stammered an apology and walked away. He disappeared quickly into a long corridor and, suddenly stumbling across a sofa in a corner, slumped onto it. Images from his whole life whirled before his eyes: the faces of Jane Hilland, Zadie Zale and others; the image of Matthieu, his erstwhile friend, raising a glass at the party they had jointly organised, just below the heavens in the golden age of the three terraces when nothing had mattered, when it had been enough to be friends and to live. How wonderful everything had been then, suspended in time and space, between earth and heaven, in the dazzling glare of youth. It was an ordinary story of betrayal, like so many others, and yet it was also his whole life, revised and corrected, distorted by bitterness and by the insistent, guilty and ultimately unendurable feeling that he had not done as he should have, that he had not been equal to the situation. The girl he had failed to seduce at the party, the young maths student that Matthieu had taken to his lair on the rooftops, and who had later found a partner, a husband, a man like him rather than like Matthieu, that girl was his life! It was life that he had failed to seduce, because he had been afraid of it, because he had shown himself incapable of being its partner, because he had stayed in his goldfish bowl. Just as he had allowed the waiter to be beaten in an incident of breathtaking social revelation, the rich man hitting the poor. The other man had simply sat down again looking affronted, when in fact he was revelling in having established his power, having demonstrated his apelike strength to his son, to his wife, to everyone present. Secretly satisfied. If he had really been a strong man – and he was all too aware that this belated remorse was pathetically weak, terribly pusillanimous, like children who in retrospect see themselves as gallant knights – Simon would have got up, gone over and broken the guy's nose. A punch, a single blow to break the bone. But he hadn't done so. He had simply hesitated, glanced around him and then gone back to his meal, leaving the waiter to clamber to his feet amid the smashed crockery.

The strangest thing was that, of all his regrets, Jane's face was no more important than that of the young girl he had met only twice. She had probably cheated on him and he now understood why Matthieu had moved out of the apartment so suddenly. But Jane had at least given him a feeling for living, a fleeting completeness which deep down, he realised, was the only truth. Feeling and experiencing as intensely as possible. He chuckled: was this what he was turning into, a mystic?

Simon got to his feet and, stumbling awkwardly, looked for the exit. He pushed at the wrong doors, turned down several dead-end corridors before finding the grand lobby. And there, he stood open-mouthed.

They were destroying everything.

The party was over. The initial cheerfulness and jollity had turned, fuelled by alcohol, into a disturbing frenzy. Jaws clenched, muscles contracted round their sledgehammers, they pounded. They were breaking everything, mirrors, chandeliers, panelling, furniture. All these people had come from far-off countries to slake their thirst for carnage. They were drunk on their destruction. They hammered. They smashed. They shattered in a roar of annihilation. A barbaric pleasure came over them as they destroyed the old world.

Simon surveyed the scene, horrified and appalled. He walked across the lobby, invisible among these brutes, fleeing this orgy that sickened him. He stepped back into the street, whose darkness closed around him. And in the muffled echo of the carnage, he walked along the pavement like a disoriented puppet, his footsteps making a dull thud. Abandoning all struggles, he hoped for nothing now but darkness and silence.

He was happy: he was vanquished.

## ACKNOWLEDGEMENTS

I would like to thank my father, who has once again become one of my first readers, and my family for their support.

I would also like to thank the team at Le Passage, ever helpful and efficient, and my friends Julien Carmona and Emmanuel Valette for their precious information about the very precise world of finance – though this novel, of course, is entirely my responsibility.

Lastly, thank you to Caroline. For everything.